To Kathey

From The
Savino Sisters
Mystery Series

Regrets To
Die For

Enjoy!

Loretta Giacoletto

Loretta Giacoletto

Copyright © 2015 Loretta Giacoletto

All rights reserved.

ISBN: 1532960964
ISBN-13: 978-1532960963
Library of Congress Control Number: 2016906967

Cover Design: Elizabeth Mackey
Graphic Design

Regrets To Die For: From The Savino Sisters Mystery Series is a work of fiction. Names, characters, places, and incidents are either products of the author's imagination or used fictitiously. Any resemblance to actual events, locales, or persons, living or dead, is entirely coincidental. All rights reserved. No part of this publication can be reproduced or transmitted in any form or by any means, electronic or mechanical, without permission in writing from Loretta Giacoletto.

By Loretta Giacoletto

Historical Sagas
Family Deceptions
Chicago's Headmistress
The Family Angel

Mysteries
Lethal Play
From the Savino Sisters Mystery Series:
Italy To Die For
And
Regrets To Die For

Coming of Age
Free Danner

Short Fiction
A Collection of Givers and Takers

ACKNOWLEDGMENTS

My thanks to Elio Gaudi, Andrea Gaudi, Giovanni Imocrante, Marina Imocrante, Heather Giacoletto, Judy Hendricks, Lauren Baratz-Logsted, Diane Giacoletto Lambert; and Dominic Giacoletto.

Characters in Regrets To Die For

Savino Family
Margo, a paralegal
Ellen, school librarian
Margo & Ellen's mother:
Antonia (Toni) Riva Savino
Margo & Ellen's Grandmother:
Clarita Fantino Riva

Fantino Family
Clarita Fantino Riva
Clarita's parents:
Vito Fantino
Bruna Fantino

Rosina Family
Stefano Rosina
Stefano's son:
Franco Rosina

Abba Family
Donata Abba Bartolini
Donata's parents:
Silvio & Olga Abba
Donata's grandson:
Pio Gavello

Arnetti Family
Tommaso (Tommi) Arnetti
Tommaso's parents:
Cosmo & Aida Arnetti

Sasso Family
Lucca Sasso
Lucca's son:
Filippo Sasso
Lucca's grandson:
Amadeo Sasso
Cousin
Bernardo Sasso

Riva Family
John Riva:
Clarita's husband
Anna Riva:
John's sister

Ukrainian Sisters
Ivanna
Sasha

And
Jonathan Ballister from Iowa

From *Family Deceptions*
Isabella Rocca
Pietro Rocca/Pete Montagna

From *The Family Angel*
Tony Roselli
Mary Ann Roselli

1
1944
NORTHWEST ITALY

One night in late spring, after the snows had melted from hills surrounding Pont Canavese, a storm like none other hammered the village and countryside with unrelenting rain and damaging hale, some lumps half the size of a *bocce pallino*. The storm extinguished the village lights as thunder rumbled and bolts of lightning shot across the sky, ever so briefly illuminating an otherwise eerie landscape that included the rivers Orco and Soana. One such bolt provided a quick glimpse of a vehicle without headlights approaching the Soana, only to have the vehicle swallowed up by the night when the bolt disappeared.

A close up of the bridge spanning the Soana would have revealed that same vehicle making its way across, only to stop on reaching the middle. The driver stepped out of the vehicle but left the motor running. By the time he reached the passenger side, a second male had exited from the rear door. Together they pulled a third man from the back seat. The third man struggled until he broke loose from their grip and tried to escape on legs too wobbly to carry him far. In a matter of seconds the driver jumped the wobbly man, bringing him down on an already bloodied face. Not a soul was around to hear the wobbly man yelling and crying as the other two dragged him to the bridge railing. He begged for his life and threatened to get even when they bent him over the railing. He begged louder when they lifted his feet into the air and sent him into the rushing current of white caps. The man with wobbly legs screamed on his way down but after splashing into the Soana, he did not utter another sound.

The two who remained leaned over the railing. The driver extended his right arm and made a sign of the cross. Choking back a sob, he stepped back and crossed himself. The other man blew a fingertip kiss to the Soana. He slung one arm across the driver's back and patted his shoulder while escorting him back to the vehicle. This time the driver sat in the front passenger seat and the other man positioned himself behind the wheel. Instead of going forward, he shifted into reverse and backed across the bridge. As soon as all four tires rolled onto land, he made a one-hundred-eighty-degree turn and drove into the Canavese foothills.

On any given day when the sun cast its spell on Pont Canavese, the village presented a picturesque scene of clay-tiled roofs against a backdrop of lush, green foothills leading to the majestic Italian Alps. But a closer perspective of the village told a different story with its convoluted mix of loyalty, mistrust, pride, and defiance. Although the Allied Army had liberated much of Southern Italy, Germany still occupied the Piemonte Region and its war-torn capital of Torino where the Italian Resistance had been gaining momentum. And away from the city in those lush foothills and snow-capped Alps, the local *partigiani* did their part in gathering intelligence for The Allies and carrying out covert operations, whatever it took to secure their positions and eventually to liberate all of Italy.

When evening turned into night, the villagers of Pont crawled into their beds after turning out lights powered by the nearby hydroelectric plants. In the event the occasional alpine storms threatened to invade their sleep, the villagers made sure their shutters were latched and their animals secured before returning to thoughts of what tomorrow would bring. Not much since the German soldiers had confiscated more than their fair share of the local wines, mouth-watering cheeses and high-quality meats such as veal, beef, pork, and lamb. Such was the time of war. Open resistance invited reprisals, often deadly. The veiled cloak of secrecy produced better results with less shedding of blood.

2
2013
PORTOFINO, ITALY

Depending on her mood and the prevailing circumstances, Margo has on occasion referred to herself as the slutty sister, a somewhat narcissistic claim I neither confirm nor do I challenge. After all, she works as a paralegal for a personal injury lawyer who never lo

ses, a position that pays considerably more than mine as a librarian. Margo's usual predictable unpredictability has baffled me this past month or so while we've been vacationing in Italy. Or as the Europeans would say, *on holiday*.

After several encounters lasting about as long as a wham-bam-thank-you-sir, Margo's latest summer conquest involved a guy so ordinary he was almost extraordinary—Jonathan Ballister from Des Moines, Iowa, of all places. A mere three hundred and fifty miles, Margo had insisted; less than six hours of highway driving from his portal in Iowa to hers in St. Louis. A flash-in-the pan romance like this was never destined to last. Somehow this one would mercifully wiggle its way out of her life before inflicting too much damage on the poor guy. Margo knew it; I knew it. Not that I would have confronted Margo with this, my big sis who may be older but claims she's three sizes smaller. I say two, not that a few inches here or there should matter in the overall scheme of life.

After Margo's mamma's boy fiasco in Florence and my heartbreaking romance in Cinque Terre, we'd agreed to restructure the remainder of our extended vacation. Having experienced the brief joy of independent traveling, my plan had been to continue on my own —as in minus Margo and Jonathan, who were hell-bent on making Monaco and the South of France their next destination.

Before going our separate ways, we'd opted for a stopover in Portofino, that wonderful Italian Riviera resort frequented by the Rich and Famous. However, when we were there, the beautiful people were nowhere to be seen unless they'd disguised themselves as ordinary tourists. Like the three of us seated at one of the ultra-pricey outdoor *ristoranti* facing Portofino's harbor, the blue of its water reflecting the same blue in the sky overhead. Equally impressive was the array of yachts and other sea-worthy crafts crowding the marina. They came in assorted sizes and price ranges, none of which would've attracted a species of unattached males who would've been attracted to me. Or Margo, for that matter, an unbiased observation I knew better than to share with her, in spite of her enviable figure and a face rivaling that of a younger Katie Holmes.

She forced a delicate frown without wrinkling her brow while sliding one finger up and down the menu. "It's all so yummy, I can't decide."

"A no-brainer for me," Jonathan said after a single glance at the menu. "I'm going top-of-the-line with the sea bass."

Margo's finger came to an abrupt stop and joined its mates for a drum-tapping on the crisp white tablecloth. "Mm, I'm still thinking, what with these outrageous prices."

"Forget the price," he said. "This one's on me. Same goes for you, El."

"Jonathan!" Margo pursed her lips into a fake pout. "We can't let you do that, not after paying for our overnight stay."

"Hey, what are friends for," he said.

I shifted my rear end and squared my shoulders against the chair's back. "I for one am perfectly capable of paying my own way."

Margo projected her sweetest smile and slammed one sandaled foot into my unsuspecting shin. "El, please, if it makes Jonathan happy, let him do this."

Hello, Margo the Passive-Aggressive. Big sis had not lost her touch. She knew how to work her latest conquest, a guy I'd rejected for being cornier than the corn growing in Iowa, the state Jonathan claimed as his roots. For the record, my earlier rejection of him may've been a slight exaggeration, Truth be told, during my first few days in Cinque Terre I'd been the focus of a potential triangle, with Jonathan and an Italian businessman better suited to my personal expectations. Or so I thought at the time. But that was then and this was now. Now as in Margo appointing Jonathan to the role of current squeeze. Again, her words not mine.

I picked up the menu, perused it without comment. When the waiter came, I ordered the least expensive item—pasta with basil pesto sauce. Margo selected the lobster and Jonathan stayed with his original choice. Based on the waiter's recommendation, he ordered a bottle of Vermentino, a bianco so pleasant we finished it before our main entrees arrived. Jonathan the Generous asked the waiter to bring a second bottle, prompting Margo to plant a fat kiss on his lips while I fanned myself and listened to a tenor at the neighboring table belt out an amazing "O Solo Mio." Could life have gotten any better than this? For me, yes.

After finishing our meal around mid-afternoon, we'd digressed into a trio of monkeys stifling yawns. Jonathan to the rescue; he ordered a round of espressos.

"Just can't get enough of this glorious Mediterranean sun," Margo said. She stretched out one tanned arm in Jonathan's direction.

He opened the palm of her hand and pressed his lips to her delicate wrist. "Then you're okay with going to Monaco."

"Absolutely, you never know. We might run into Prince Albert."

"Prince Who?" he asked. "You mean the guy in the tobacco can?"

To which Margo laughed herself silly, not a good omen for Jonathan who remained oblivious to the trace of annoyance lingering on her face after the laughter had faded away.

He was, however, all for the French Riviera, in particular Cannes and Nice. "Who knows, we might rub elbows with some famous movie stars. You'd like that, wouldn't you, babe?"

Margo flinched. She dropped her arm, leaving Jonathan's finger stranded in mid-air.

"El, what about you?" she asked. "You can come with us, of course. And if you prefer a more cultural experience, we could head inland." She paused before snapping two fingers. "To Grasse or Vence where ... you know, those artists—"

"Matisse and Picasso among others," I said.

"Hey, you do know a lot," Jonathan said.

Evidently more than he did, which confirmed my initial assessment of Jonathan when we first met on a motorboat cruise along the coast of Cinque Terre. Less than three weeks ago and yet it seemed more like a lifetime. In some ways for me, it had been.

Any other time, as in prior to Cinque Terre, I would've said yes to Margo's invitation. But since then I'd grown up, wised up, and looked up to myself with a happy face. Going where I pleased when I pleased defined the new me. No worrying about anyone other than myself. Which, after all, was the purpose of American anytime vacations or for European holidays in late summer, as in August where we now found ourselves.

The new independent me, a definite plus for Margo and her latest squeeze. Their French Riviera destinations I would save for another trip. Maybe next year if I played my cards right—give up certain luxuries such as … hold on, something besides food and rent and the gym membership. Oh, right, the gym I never got around to joining. Yes, that would make the ideal sacrifice, one I had yet to experience. Perhaps I'd walk instead, a practical choice for the remainder of my vacation, one I'd extended while still in Cinque Terre. Don't get me started on the reasons; but due to an extreme case of first-love naivety I had since blossomed with confidence and expectations of my life taking a turn for the better.

Besides Cinque Terre, I'd already played the *turista* in Rome and Florence, most of it with Margo at my side; more like me at her side since I'd started our Italian adventure as a first-class wuss. Now I wanted nothing more than two glorious weeks exploring the remote villages of Northern Italy, especially the one Mom's mom had emigrated from. Nonnie Clarita, as we call her. My big mistake was sharing this intention with Margo.

"What a mar-r-ve-lous idea," she said while stirring two sugar cubes into her espresso. "Why didn't I think of it before you?"

"Uh … because you wanted to soak up more of this incredible Mediterranean sun."

"True, but I'm certainly open to other options. You know me. Nothing I do or say is ever set in stone."

"Really, I hadn't noticed."

"Me-ow!" She curled one hand into a cat's paw and clawed at the air between us.

"Ladies, please," Jonathan said. He took Margo's hand, uncurled her long fingers, and kissed the tips.

"Oh, Jonathan, that's so sweet." Margo pulled her hand away from his lips and patted his cheek. "Would you mind terribly if we switched from the Riviera to the boonies of Northern Italy?"

"Hey, babe, whatever makes you happy."

What about me and my happiness I couldn't help but think. The wuss in me surfaced again. No way could I bring myself to convince Margo otherwise.

She snapped her fingers. "El, get out the map."

My hands were shaking when I pulled it from the side pocket of my purse. Jonathan moved our espresso cups to one side and I opened our Italian road map onto the table.

He leaned in and asked, "Where?"

"Somewhere around here." I tapped my finger on *Torino*. "Above Turin," I said, using the English version.

Jonathan shifted his finger northward until it landed on a mountain range. "What have we here … the Alps."

"Where?" Margo got up and leaned over Jonathan and me.

"Here," I said, nudging Jonathan's finger to the side in order to give Margo a better view.

Margo clapped her hands. "The Alps, yes, now we're talking."

"Did I say anything about the Alps?"

"No, El, but you know and I know that you would have if Jonathan hadn't mentioned it first."

3
MARGO ON ELLEN

Hmm, did I detect as edgy resistance from El? Come on. All I did was suggest Jonathan and I tag along with her since we were wavering on thoughts of Monaco and Provence. True to her nature, El agreed to our making it a threesome. But then this dreadful image popped into my head, the three of us strolling around one sleepy little village after the other and not having anyone to talk to except each other. Please, that we could do back home. How many ways are there to say boring, how many ways to inject a dollop of excitement? I sat down and put one hand over Jonathan's, the other over El's. My next words caught her totally off guard.

"How about we compromise?"

The look on El's face said more than the two words she spoke with raised brows. "Such as?"

"Such as *Mont Blanc*, can it get any better than the French Alps?"

"How about *Monte Bianco* in the Italian Alps," El shot back.

As if one side mattered more than the other, it was all about semantics.

"We can do both," Jonathan chimed in. While El and I had been going head to head, he'd been thumbing through his travel guide. "It's less than a one-hour drive from Courmayeur in Italy to Chamonix in France. I mean by way of this tunnel through the Alps." He showed us the travel guide photo.

"Thanks for the geography lesson," El said.

Oops, big sis to the rescue. I tried to smooth things over. "Jonathan, sweetie, in case you forgot, El makes her living as a middle school librarian. She also considers herself somewhat of an authority on Italy."

"How can I forget what I didn't know before," he said.

I pinched his cheek. Okay, maybe a little harder than I should have, prompting El to give me one of those looks I refused to acknowledge. Jonathan, poor baby, leaned back as if fearful of what might come next.

"Ow-w," he said. "Don't play so rough."

"You didn't complain about my rough play last night."

El, who lacks my sense of bawdy sensibility, covered her ears and said, "Please, this is way more information than I need to know."

Feeling a slight tinge of guilt, I leaned over, closing the space Jonathan had made between us. This time I patted his cheek, a light touch followed by a nibble on his ear followed by a big fat kiss on his lips.

El cleared her throat before issuing a warning too *Mom-ish* for words. "This may be Italy," she said, "the land of all things romantic, but people are staring."

"Sorry, I keep forgetting about your years in the convent."

"You were a nun, El?" Again, he leaned back.

"More like a failed postulant," I said. "Not that it matters."

"Please, I can speak for myself," El said. "There's no shame in leaving before the final vows."

"Our mother would beg to differ," I reminded her.

"I don't answer to our mother. Nor have I for a number of years."

"Uh, ladies ... girls," Jonathan said. He held up the guidebook and waved it like a red flag. "How 'bout we map out our route?"

"For starters, we'll need a bigger car," El said.

Oh, yeah, the car, it was perfect for El and me. Just the thought of adding Jonathan made me feel the squeeze, a little too tight for my comfort zone, in more ways than one.

4
BR-R, HOW WARM IS IT?

There we were, three of us jammed into the little Fiat Margo and I had rented weeks before. Jonathan, on the other hand, had given up his rental before going to the pedestrian-friendly Cinque Terre. And now Margo had let him commandeer the wheel of our rental, what with him being a man from Iowa and all that salt-of-the-earth macho stuff. Never mind that I had chauffeured Margo and myself from Rome to Florence without a single major problem. Never mind that I had undertaken a solo run from Florence to La Spezia with only one incident that later evolved into an unforeseen major problem. None of which mattered with the addition of Jonathan.

Our new arrangement involved Margo taking her rightful place beside Jonathan, and me getting exiled to the backseat, surrounded by more luggage than any one man or woman should ever need, unless they happened to be Steven Tyler or Paris Hilton. Add to the cargo bin Margo's latest purchases along the Italian Riviera and I found myself flirting with a serious attack of claustrophobia. Hello, iPod. I plugged in the earphones and tortured myself even more with some Katy Perry, as if I had anything to roar about.

On the outskirts of Genoa we located our car rental agency and switched to this bigger car, a mid-size Fiat, but still in my name. As with our earlier drive consisting of two occupants, Margo assumed her role of navigator to help Jonathan find his way north while I went back to my iPod, closed my eyes, and without realizing it, let Justin Timberlake suck me into his broken romance. Just what I needed: a reminder of my own heartbreaker. I'd vowed to erase Whatshisname from my memory. His face too, easier said than done. Harder yet was recalling the way he'd touched me, not only physically but emotionally which hurt to the depths of my soul. First love, for me a late, late bloomer. I'd come to Italy a virgin but would not be leaving as one. Hmm, maybe I'd have to come clean at Customs. Or Passport Control. Maybe there'd be a stamp indicating my new status.

Enough with the pity party, I opened my eyes to enjoy the passing scene. Imagine my surprise on seeing a road sign indicating we were now in France rather than Genoa in the opposite direction. Don't ask me how this happened since I wasn't the one driving, which is not to say I would've done any better. I yanked out the earphones and edged forward. Margo must've dozed off because she jerked to attention when I tapped her shoulder. Another sign came into view.

"Jonathan, we're in France," Margo sort of yelled. "What were you thinking?"

"What was I thinking? Where have you been? I only went where you told me to go."

"Pull over to the side so we can regroup," I said.

"To the side, to the side where?" he asked.

"Oh for God's sake, alongside the toll gate," Margo said. She held that thought until he edged our car off the road. "Okay, now turn around, and go back the way we came."

"Margo, think. I can't turn around. Not only is it illegal, we'll be going the wrong way."

"Do you have a better idea?"

"No, but—"

"No *buts*, dammit, just do it. El and I did a couple of times, right El."

"Uh ... we might've."

I sat back, berating myself for ever agreeing to my role as third wheel. After two more wrong exits and two illegal back-ups, we finally managed to get back on course.

"Stop at the next Autogrill," Margo said while fanning her face with the guide book, its corners curled up and edges frayed from wear and tear. "I am so feeling an undeniable urge."

Already, please. Margo's sudden urge could only mean one thing. She slid one hand across the seat and squeezed Jonathan's thigh, to which he responded by allowing the vehicle's two right tires to drift off the autostrada. The car bounced over the bumpy service lane until Jonathan eased back onto the pavement.

"Shall I drive?" was the best I could manage.

"No, no, we're … I'm fine."

"Maybe later," Margo said.

"Yeah, right."

"Sorry, El, I didn't mean you."

How true. Margo unbuckled her seatbelt, moved closer to Jonathan, and wiggled her tongue in his ear. Really, here? Rather than laugh or groan or bury my face, I silently prayed for the next Autogrill, which soon appeared like an oasis in the desert, and considering the front-seat love fest, not one minute too soon.

After taking a much needed potty break in the immaculate restroom, I strolled around the convenience section, aisle after aisle of what counted as imported Italian back home—a variety of crackers, pasta, sweets, sauces, and olive oil. Meanwhile Margo was off somewhere satisfying her *maybe-later* urge with Jonathan. When the lovebirds made their return to the real world, it was with her face flushed and him adjusting his fly and backside. No one seemed to notice except me. After all, we were in Italy.

"Where'd you go?" I couldn't resist asking.

Margo shot me her Mona Lisa smile before she said, "To this darling storage room next to the kitchen."

I shook my head. "And no one stopped you or said anything."

"El, please, give us some credit. Jonathan tipped the guy in charge of those yummy panini I'd love to sample but—"

"But won't because it's not worth the calories."

"You could take a page from my book … sorry; no more nagging. Back to the little kitchen nook, it was so-o romantic."

"Really?"

"Of course, why would you think otherwise?"

"I keep picturing jars of olives, stacks of bread, fat grissini."

"Bingo! While you're at it, picture … never mind, we don't have time for this. Anyway, Jonathan is such a sweetheart."

"So you've mentioned before."

Jonathan having a few bucks sweetened the pot, somewhat. He did treat us to coffee: espresso for Margo and me; cappuccino for himself. We stood at a small round table, and I stretched my legs that were still cramped from being squished in the back seat, though not as bad as they'd been prior to our upgrading to the larger Fiat. Before we left our auto oasis, I made my only purchase, a bag of Italian candies filled with liquor and individually wrapped in foil.

"Today on the lips; tomorrow the hips," Margo said on our way out.

Of course, that didn't stop her from divvying up the bag three ways as soon as we got settled in the car. More for her lips meant less on my hips.

Three hours later and a total devouring of the Italian candies brought us face-to-face with the snow-capped Alps separating Italy from France, a range extending as far as I could see from one end to the other and beyond in either direction. I rolled down the backseat window, closed my eyes, and breathed in air so fresh it cleared my sinuses. Then Margo cleared her throat.

"Ahem … El, would you mind rolling up the window—I am positively freezing."

"At seventy degrees outside, I don't think so."

"Nevertheless …"

"Okay, okay." One push of a button closed the window, allowing me to focus on the road signs. "There's the Courmayeur exit."

"Do we for sure want to stop here," Margo said instead of asked.

"I'd like to," was my comeback.

"Let's do France first and catch Courmayeur on our return."

"Whatever, but I do need to use the facilities before we go through the tunnel."

"Really, El, wouldn't you rather wait until Chamonix."

"I could use a break too," Jonathan said as he exited into the last rest area before entering France.

Thank you, Jonathan.

As with the other public facilities I'd used in Italy, this restroom was immaculate and … down-to-earth, a throwback to times past with several stalls distinguished by squat-down toilets. In other words, footrests flanking porcelain vessels fitted flush into the floor. The primitive varieties were located in the unoccupied stalls, that is, until Margo insisted we step inside and experience them first-hand. Make that foot; better yet, feet, one on either side of the porcelain. Face the rear wall and squat. Used toilet paper goes in the waste basket, not the vessel. Yuck.

"Oh, El, don't you just love this," Margo called out from the stall next to mine. "It's so … hmm … so Old World."

Leave it to Margo, what more could I say except, "Where's the flush button?"

∞∞∞∞

After bypassing Courmayeur to please Margo, we arrived mid-afternoon at the tunnel connecting *Monte Bianco* in Italy to *Mont Blanc* in France. Jonathan forked out fifty-four euros for a round-trip ticket and we were allowed to enter the tunnel. The speed-monitored drive took about forty minutes and provided the perfect experience—in a singular oh-so-welcomed word: uneventful.

A few more miles into France soon brought us to our destination, a charming alpine village. *Where shall we stay in Chamonix* soon evolved into our primary topic of conversation.

"Any ideas?" Margo asked while Jonathan cruised up one street and down the other.

"Sorry, babe. Only got two hands and one head, which means I can't drive and make important decisions at the same time."

Patience, this too will pass, I told myself, as will all things Margo. "At least park the car so we can find a decent place to eat," I said. "After that, we'll decide between a hotel and a *pensione*." Good for me, I'd taken charge and made a reasonable suggestion no one bothered to challenge.

The restaurant we agreed on can only be described as French Tourist specializing in omelets and crepes. We followed our waiter's suggestion and ordered two omelets—one cheese, one spinach—plus strawberry-filled crepes, portions substantial enough to share.

"And this *vin blanc*," Jonathan the Generous said, pointing to one of the higher priced white wines listed on the menu.

"An excellent choice," Margo said, echoing the last words from our waiter. She blew Jonathan a kiss from her fingertips. "Let's hear it for the guy from Iowa."

"Thank you, Jonathan," was all he heard from me. Margo felt it necessary to compensate for my three words by leaning over and planting a way-too-intimate kiss on his puckered lips. Okay, nobody noticed, or seemed to care, except me. After all, we were in France.

No complaints about the food or the wine or the chalet-type hotel Jonathan later selected. Located in the heart of Chamonix, the hotel was quite comfortable, more so with me having a room to myself, one I insisted on paying for with my own credit card, thank you very much. I took a quick nap before changing into a glam outfit Margo had passed on to me during our recent stay in Monterosso El Mare. One glance in the mirror told me the frilly thing actually looked half-way decent on my body, given it was meant to be worn loose and did not cover my knees. Oh my, if the convent's mother superior could've seen me that evening, I'd still be doing penance.

Although the sun had barely set, a Do Not Disturb sign hung on the doorknob of the room Margo and Jonathan were sharing. How lucky could I get, a whole evening on my own to explore the upscale village of Chamonix, just as I'd done weeks before in Florence when Margo deserted me for her then boy-toy, a handsome young mime who later deserted her for reasons she had yet to explain to my satisfaction. My own failed romance was still too painful for revisiting in my thoughts so I hit the streets instead.

After two blocks of window-shopping and no buying, I heard the music of Bruno Mars coming from a nearby bar. I wandered inside to find a collage of psychedelic lighting and twenty-something patrons dancing alone or as couples who needed to get a room. At thirty-two I felt ancient and must've looked out of place, but no more so than an absurd silver-haired guy whose face was obscured by the flashing lights and a pair of oversized tinted specs. Without saying a word, he grabbed my hand and pulled me onto the already crowded dance floor.

"I ... I'm not much of a dancer," I told him more than once. But did he listen, no. Or maybe he couldn't hear me over the music. Instead he kept his head down, body bent, and with his hand still clutching my hand, he bumped his hip into mine. Five bumps later he turned and wiggled his rear end against mine. Not a pretty sight, nor a feel-good moment. In fact, our performance bordered on ludicrous since he couldn't dance any better than I could. After bumping his way around to face me—actually my heaving tatas—he lifted both hands to my cheeks and squeezed until my mouth opened. Eyes closed, he stuck his tongue down my throat. I was seriously ready to chomp down on the damn thing when he finally withdrew it.

I gasped and I gagged until my breath returned to normal, allowing me to choke out words that in no way sounded as though they came from my mouth. "You've got some nerve. We don't even know each other."

With that he laughed, pulled off his glasses, and said, "You do now, pleased to make your acquaintance."

Pleased? Not for long. Although I couldn't make out his face, my ears confirmed what I already suspected. There was no denying the familiar voice. I reached out, as if to caress his cheek, but then moved my hand upward to the silver hair. One twist of my fingers put the wig in my hand, only to have him rescue his prop and plop it back on his head. Lopsided, making it all the more ridiculous.

I debated between a nasty slap and a good laugh, and settled for the no-brainer. "Jonathan, is that you?"

His eyes flew open, his jaw dropped. Just as the music came to an end, he found his voice and yelled, "Oh my God! I didn't realize you were you, El. I swear I didn't."

"That's for sure." I turned to leave and felt the tentative touch of his hand on my shoulder. I shook it off, like I would've a pesky mosquito.

"I'm so sorry, El. Please don't tell Margo."

"Tell her what, Jonathan? I have no idea what you're talking about."

The next morning Margo showed up for breakfast without Jonathan. In fact, she'd beat me to the small dining room and was already stirring sugar in her cappuccino when I sat across from her and asked if Jonathan had slept in.

"You won't believe this," Margo said, "but after you and I split yesterday afternoon, I was so exhausted I fell asleep after one magic moment with Jonathan. Or maybe there were two, I don't recall. When I woke up early this morning—with the worse headache of my life—Jonathan was preparing to leave, of all things. Sometime during the night it seems he got a phone call from Iowa, an emergency in the family business requiring his immediate attention back home.

"Aw, that's too bad." I may have misspoken but sometimes a misspoken word or four makes more sense than a truth hurting to the quick.

As for Margo, she seemed more relieved than disappointed. Since Jonathan had paid for two additional nights on their room, I moved in with her and we spent the next two days sightseeing. We even rode the ski-lift, an awesome delight in the summer since a winter ride would've required my half-hearted attempt to ski. In these Alps, no way! Not after my embarrassing failure on the bunny slopes of Colorado a few seasons before.

5
BETTER CALL NONNIE

"We should call Nonnie Clarita," I told Margo as we climbed into the mid-sized Fiat that Jonathan had upgraded for our extended holiday. Thank you again, Jonathan. His betrayal would remain safe with me, as long as he didn't come panting after Margo any time in the near future. Or Margo didn't figure out his betrayal on her own, a sixth sense she'd groomed over the years.

Our last day in Chamonix, we'd already checked out of the hotel, both of us ready to move on. I took my rightful place behind the wheel; Margo assumed her usual shotgun position as navigator. Since Margo only hears what she wants to hear—what our mother calls selective hearing—I repeated my earlier comment. "We should call Nonnie."

Margo wrinkled her nose. She brushed a strand of hair from her face. "I hate involving Nonnie. You know what a *testa dura* the woman can be."

"And how she prides herself on being one," I said. "Let's not forget that hard heads run in the family."

"Speak for yourself, El."

"I am, which is why our number one priority should be chatting with Nonnie. She can pave the way for us. After all, Margo, we're the outsiders. Just because we're American doesn't mean we can invade a strange village and expect a huggy welcome without having a local connection."

"Hmm, I'm not sure our phone even works here in Chamonix," Margo said while tapping the screen. "Guess I should've charged it last night."

"We'll buy a new one, on my Visa."

Now *that* comment Margo heard, a perfect example of her selective hearing. "Wow," she said. "This from Miss Tighter-Than-Tight, in more ways—"

"Don't even think about going there. We're getting a new phone."

"In that case, we should wait until Italy. Courmayeur would be the logical place."

"Yes, Margo, whatever you say, Margo."

"Don't get sassy with me, young lady."

"Okay, I had that coming. But calling me sassy makes you sound just like Nonnie."

"Ugh, perish the thought," Margo said.

Our give and take prompted a series of giggles and me hooking pinkies with Margo, the Savino sisterly way of calling a truce.

∞∞∞

Some things in life were never meant to be shared and I don't mean men. Not that Margo and I had ever crossed into the love-triangle mine field, at least not yet. Nor were we about to share another phone, not after Margo's lack of communication almost got her killed in Monterosso El Mare. So, while poking around in Courmayeur, we each bought our own phone. The clerk spoke decent English and set up our new purchases with premium calling plans since neither Margo nor I wanted to mess with running out of juice or minutes. Back in the parking area, we assumed our positions in the car and using Margo's new phone, made the dreaded yet necessary call

"What if Mom answers?" Margo asked while pressing the speaker option.

"At this hour, I don't think so. It's Thursday, she always has lunch with Kat." Kat Dorchester was Mom's Best Friend Forever, before the words evolved into BFF. Every woman, no matter how old, needs a BFF. Not that I considered fifty-eight old, nor did Mom look her age but attitude-wise, she'd not adjusted well to the twenty-first century. On the other hand, although eighty-something Nonnie had surpassed the best years of most lives, she didn't seem old, just steadfast and in many ways more open to change than our rigid mother.

After Nonnie answered on the third ring, Margo got the conversation off to a confusing start with, "Guess what, Nonnie."

"Who the hell is this?" she asked in her familiar Italian accent, one that conjured up images of her ageless beauty—high cheekbones, dark eyes shaped like almonds, well-defined lips without the usual cosmetic enhancements.

"Who do you think," Margo said. "How many people call you Nonnie?"

"Just my two granddaughters and they're both in Italy. God only knows doing what."

I'd had enough and spoke up. "Nonnie, hi, it's me, Ellen. I'm with Margo and we're calling all the way from … Italy." I didn't bother going into the Monte Bianco detour.

"Ellen and Margo, why didn't you say so from the beginning instead of making me guess. It's not like we're competing on one of those silly game shows. Talk fast; this has to be costing you a bundle."

"Don't worry about the money," I said.

"If I don't, who will," Nonnie said. "Your ma can't come to the phone. She's—"

"Yeah, we know. It's Thursday," Margo said. "Guess what?"

"You're getting married. Well, it's about time, given your … never mind."

"Sorry, Nonnie," Margo said with a laugh. "I'm still looking for my Mr. Right."

"Good luck with that. How about this instead? Ellen's going back to the nunnery."

"Never going to happen," I said. "Here's the thing. Since Margo and I are here in Italy, we've decided to visit your village."

"My village," Nonnie said in a voice reeking with suspicion. "What village?"

"The one you grew up in," Margo said. "We want to walk the streets you walked."

"You think I was a streetwalker? Show some respect."

"Now, Nonnie, you know me better than that."

"Yeah, yeah, just kidding. But I just don't get the village thing. Why now?"

"What better time," I chimed in. "We have some days to kill before heading home."

"No-o-o, you don't say." She paused, not a good sign.

"And we really want to see the house you grew up in."

"No you don't ... I don't know ... call back tomorrow."

"Nonnie!" Margo said. "We thought you'd be crazy for the idea."

"Shush, give me a minute. I'm thinking."

Margo raised an eyebrow. I resisted rolling my eyes. Silence filled the Fiat. I pressed the down button for windows, allowing the crisp mountain air inside.

"Hello, Nonnie," Margo said. "Are you still there?"

"I'm *here*, if that's what you mean. Trust me, you won't like it *there*. Talk about nothing to do. *There* in no way compares to St. Louis. No Cardinals baseball, no Forest Park, no shiny Arch or fake riverboat casinos that can't find their way up and down the Mississippi."

"Neither one of us gamble, Nonnie," Margo said.

"No, but I do ... not that anybody cares one way or the other."

"We're tired of touring," I said. "We need some quiet time."

"Maybe you need quiet but Margo won't last more than a day or two. From what I've heard, Italy's nothing like it was in my day. Back then we danced the night away. Worked like dogs the next day so we could dance again at night. Or tried to when the Germans weren't watching our every move."

"Like Nonnie, like me," Margo said.

Okay, now. Drum roll for my eye roll.

"Dancing was a long time ago," Nonnie said. "Now those same people are probably sitting around, coughing up their guts, complaining about sore knees and bad backs that went out and didn't come back. That is, if those old farts are still looking at the green side of the grass. Talk about boring."

"There's no talking us out of this," Margo said. "With or without your blessing, Ellen and I are going to Pont Canavese."

Not the way to handle Nonnie. I motioned for Margo to put a lid on it.

"Nonnie, it's me, Ellen. What about the cousin who used to send Christmas cards."

"*Used to* … and finally stopped because I didn't send any cards to her nor did I care if she sent any to me. A very distant cousin, I might add. We hardly share a drop of the same blood. In fact, I doubt we were even related."

"Would you mind calling her, at least let her know we're coming."

"How long have you known me, Ellen?"

"My whole life." I could not recall when she hadn't live with our family, from the time Margo and I were little kids. Now she lived with our widowed mom, which relieved Margo and me from having to worry about either of them.

"And when did you ever hear me call Donata on the telephone? I don't even have her number."

"Just give us her address," Margo said. "That I know you have."

"Directions to her house would be nice," I added.

"What do think I am, one of those smart computers? It's been forever and a day since I last saw the woman. It's not like we're best friends."

"Not so fast, Nonnie," I said. "What about Donata's maiden or married name. I used to know her married name from the return address on her envelopes but I'm drawing a blank."

"Her husband died which might mean the married name no longer counts in Italy."

"Think, Nonnie, think."

"Oh, for God's sake, if you insist on going to Pont, just hang around the main piazza and ask the first person who looks friendly, but not too friendly. Watch yourself, Margo. Don't do anything to embarrass the family. Ellen, I ain't worried about. Her beauty comes from within. Right, Ellen? Ain't that what your ma ... look, I gotta go."

"But Nonnie—"

"Somebody's knocking at the door. *Ciao,* Margo. You too, Ellen."

End of conversation, before Margo or I had a chance to say our goodbyes. Oh well, there'd always be tomorrow. And the day after, I had a feeling our trans-Atlantic conversations with Nonnie were just getting started.

6
PONT CANAVESE

"Blessed Mother, I just can't get enough of this," El said from her position in the driver's seat.

"So far so good, I haven't got us lost ... yet," I replied, in spite of El droning on and on with a travel monologue I found myself half-way enjoying. But after a while the pre-occupied mind can only absorb so much and her words, however interesting, were reduced to sound bites.

"Medieval defines every region of Italy ... majestic mountains ... boot tip ... silhouetted villages ... rugged hills ... towering cliffs ... Mediterranean Sea ... Ligurian ... Adriatic ... same sea, different locations."

"Need I remind you whom it is you're talking to? Me, Margo Savino, not your sixth graders back in St. Louis."

"Sorry, I keep forgetting you're not that into history and scenery."

"This much I do know, we've got the Italian Alps to our back."

"Otherwise known as the French Alps, the Swiss Alps, or the Austrian Alps, etcetera," El said, "depending on the country the Alps happen to be spanning and from which side of the span you're viewing."

"Don't get me started, Miss Know-It-All."

Strange, how Miss Know-It-All had barely said a word or two about

Jonathan's sudden departure. As for me, I couldn't dump this nagging feeling about El knowing more than she'd let on, which, for the moment, relieved me from having to share a slew of nitty-gritty details with her. Humiliating disclosures didn't suit my personality. Still, I couldn't help but revisit those details clogging my brain before I put them to rest. I leaned back, closed my eyes, and faked a quick snooze.

The nerve of Jonathan, going out for the evening in Chamonix while I'd pretended to be asleep. And for good reason: it was the only way I could have time to myself. Okay, so maybe he felt the same about me, which I found hard to believe after the way he'd carried on earlier that day. I swear the man could not keep his hands off me, especially my best parts. Yeah, I know—me, me, me, it's always about me, always has been. As for Mr. Butthead, he didn't know how lucky he was to have had me, me, and me. If only for a short time ... ugh!

It's weird how the mind can wander. Mine had traveled all the way back to Chamonix until I heard El say we'd entered the outskirts of Pont Canavese. Or, Pont as Nonnie referred to the village she didn't want us visiting.

"Where have you been?" El asked.

"My own little world but I'm back now."

Looking ahead, I saw this medieval village with mighty towers jutting out between spans of red tile roofs. Picture postcard perfect, you bet, with all the potential for a shitload of endless ho-hum as opposed to El's time-out for get-over-first-love therapy. Okay, I admit to insinuating myself into her recovery but in doing so I also counted on Jonathan tagging along as my faithful companion. Ugh! Huge mistake on my part. Although I may've been down, I most definitely did not count myself out, not by a landslide. As for the local manpower, please let there be at least three single hetero guys, preferably under the age of thirty-nine, two for me and one to keep El occupied. *How occupied* would be her problem, not mine.

"Below us ... below us flows the Soana River, a ... a tributary of the Orco," El said as we headed across the sturdy bridge. Shoulders hunched, she gripped the steering wheel as if it might go spastic and plunge us into the Soano's rushing waters.

"Relax," I said, faking an open-wide yawn. "The bridge won't collapse under our weight, especially since you've lost ... how many pounds?"

"Not now, Margo."

"Then how about this: In case you didn't already know, Pont means bridge in Italian, I guess in French too since we're so close to the border."

"Uh-huh," she replied, only then loosening her white-knuckle grip as we rolled onto solid ground, a road as modern as any in Smalltown, USA, but this one leading to Pont's city center. Or, *centro* as the Italians say.

"Chen tro," I pronounced for El, who repeated it to my satisfaction.

From what little I could see of Pont Canavese up close, not exactly a tourist mecca, which at that point did not present a problem. Nor would I let it for the next few days. The buildings were a mix of modernized old and older than dust, the streets a mix of generous two-lanes and narrow one-lanes. There seemed to be a decent amount of activity, mainly pedestrian shoppers demanding their fair share of pavement from impatient motorists driving efficient vehicles designed for Italian roads and hot-headed temperaments. No gas guzzlers here, not at the price of petro per liter. Not one guy close to my age. Not to worry, at least for the moment, most of the eligibles were probably working. Or sleeping, if they worked second or third shifts.

Picturing Nonnie walking these streets as a teenager, or whatever Italians called that age group seventy years ago, blew my mind. Having never seen photos of her early years in Italy, I kept drawing a blank. I could not imagine her ever being a young girl, a young married, a young anything. Nor had I ever seen any photos of her and Grandpa Riva. Such a tragedy, he died before Mom took her first breath. Nonnie never talked about John Riva. Nor did she talk about Italy or her parents. Of course, El and I never asked. Perhaps we should have.

Finding the right hotel in Pont turned out to be a no-brainer since El and I had our pick of one, a decent location with its own well-stocked bar that started calling my name as soon as I poked my head inside. Not the caliber of hotels Chamonix offered but so affordable we took the last two single rooms, which I considered a colossal blessing. As did El, judging from the smile she didn't bother hiding. On the down side, neither of us realized those last two rooms meant sharing a bath down the hall with other guests.

7
DONATA

The next morning after breakfast El and I were killing time in the hotel dining room, indulging ourselves with endless cups of Americano coffee instead of the Diet Coke we'd both requested but the hotel didn't have. Half dazed, I'd been watching a breeze ruffle the curtains of an open window and realized the air conditioning hadn't been turned on. Or perhaps it wasn't working. Either way, I didn't miss it.

"*La dolce vita* is one thing but this is getting ridiculous," El said while playing with her coffee spoon.

I executed half a yawn. "Whatever, the sweet life works for me."

"Only if we're living it, not sitting here talking about it."

"Why, El, I do believe the higher elevation has scrambled your brain. You've morphed into the Holiday Police."

"Guilty as charged and not one bit ashamed. We need to get our butts in gear."

"If you insist."

"I do. And if I were you—thank God I'm not—I'd leave those Jimmy Choos in your room."

Some of the finer things in life El just didn't get. I set her straight with one of them. "Italian men, any men for that matter, prefer to make passes at girls who wear high heels or in rare exceptions, ultra-sexy flats."

"Whatever," El said. "But don't get all whiney on me about your feet hurting. Now, let's stick to the plan and make Donata our first priority."

"Need I remind you that Nonnie did not share Donata's last name with us. Perhaps she figured you, being the brilliant one, would eventually remember it without resorting to desperate measures."

"I'm going to ignore that. Think, Margo, think." El put on her best librarian face, lips pursed and brow furrowed. "How many females named Donata can there be in a village this size?"

"I don't know; how big is Pont?"

"Under four thousand," El said. She heaved an exasperated sigh reserved for yours truly. "Ask our waitress if she knows an older woman named Donata."

I did, in my best Italian. To which the waitress explained in her broken English that she'd recently arrived from Ukraine and only knew a few people, not one of them named Donata. At least I think that's what she said. And since the hotel proprietor had skipped town for the day, I couldn't ask her. The cleaning lady I flagged down in the hallway also came from Ukraine and only knew the same people the waitress knew. Both women were blonde and built like Amazons, not the typical workers I'd envisioned for a hotel in Italy. Back in the dining room, three tables filled with non-Italian Europeans didn't have a clue what I was talking about and made me wonder what they were doing in this remote village.

Sure, Pont Canavese reeked of Old World charm, sitting in a valley with lush green mountains on either side and two parallel rivers with water tumbling over jagged rocks ranging from mere pebbles to centuries-old boulders. For most people a scene such as this would've been enough. For me, enough was never enough.

"I vote for going to the main piazza," El said. "Just like Nonnie told us. Any idea as to how we get there?"

"Do you see the village map taped to my forehead?" I snapped at her. "Sorry, you didn't have that coming. I'm more than a little cranky this morning."

El ignored my apology and half-assed excuse, making me feel even crappier. Instead she came back at me with a comment smacking of insincerity: "It's a shame Jonathan had to leave."

"Really? More like a relief," I said, giving her the benefit of a doubt. "Those last few days with him turned out to be a wake-up call for me. Putting it in as few words as possible, Jonathan most definitely was not my type."

"He seemed like a nice-enough guy."

"You think? Hmm, as I recall, you introduced Jonathan to me. What a crock, me scooping up one of your rejects, not that you've had many nice guys in your life. Or bad boys. Sorry, El."

"Comment ignored, apology accepted. Nice guys can be ... annoying at times. Besides when I first met Jonathan, someone else was actively pursuing me."

"He who shall continue to remain nameless."

"At least for now," El said.

Nice diversion on her part. Whatever El might've known about Jonathan did not show on her face; and for me, he was fast becoming a distant memory.

Our Ukrainian waitress came by and using my so-so Italian, I asked her about the village's main piazza. She replied in her so-so broken English, giving a simple set of instructions both El and I understood.

∞∞∞

El and I soon found ourselves parked on a concrete bench at the Piazza Craveri, watching pigeons snap up bits and pieces from the ground cover, after a not-so-far walk that quickly lost its European charm. Talk about pain, on a scale of one to ten with ten being the worst, my killer ten had rebelled against the Jimmy Choos molded into my unhappy feet. El, on the other hand, had pampered her tootsies with a pair of cushioned shoes, what old ladies wear on their morning walks through suburban malls, or so I've been told since I wouldn't be caught dead there before the stores opened. She pulled out a pair of flats from her purse and handed them to me. After dumping my Choos into her purse, I slipped on the flats. "Ah-h, little sis, my feet thank you profusely."

"Until next time, will you ever learn, I think not. El pressed two fingers from each hand into her temples, held them there for about twenty seconds. "For the life of me, I cannot recall Donata's last name. Maybe we should call Nonnie again."

I glanced at the time on my cellphone. "Let's see. It's ten in the morning here, which makes it three in the morning back home. Now there's a bonding moment guaranteed to put Nonnie in a good mood."

"The woman never sleeps, or so she says."

"How true but Mom does. A phone call at this ungodly hour would mess up her whole day. Of course, we wouldn't be around to witness her displeasure; and Nonnie, as we both know, can hold her own against anybody."

"Speaking of dear ol' Mom, we haven't spoken to her since leaving Rome," El said. "On the other hand, it's not like we're expected to check in."

"She has her own life, for which we should both be thankful. Besides, what would we tell her? That you lost your—"

"Keep it up, Margo, and I'll call Mom right now. We'll see what she has to say about your mamma's boy in Florence."

"Our mother, her mother, his mother," I said. "What's with the maternal flap?"

We'd been so busy outdoing each other I didn't notice the man standing nearby until I heard him clear his throat in a way that reminded me of Jonathan clearing his.

"Excuse me, *signorini*," the man said in English. "I could not help but overhear, even though I did not understand most of what you said. You are American, sì?"

He looked mid-fiftyish and introduced himself as Filippo Sasso. El and I gave our names and explained our nonna used to live in Pont. "Many years ago my family lived in Faiallo," he said, motioning to an area beyond the village. "High in the hills but I grew up here in Pont. Your nonna is still of this world?"

"To the fullest, every day," I said, speaking each word distinctly. "She went to America around 1948. Her family name is Fantino, Clarita Fantino but we don't know where she lived. Or if any of the family is still alive. For sure her parents are both dead and to my knowledge she didn't have any brothers or sisters."

"Fantino ... Fantino." He rubbed his chin and rubbed some more. "The name is familiar from long ago. You should visit the cemetery before you leave."

"Perhaps start with the living," I said, making El cringe.

"Nonnie Clarita had a good friend she wants us to visit," El said. "Her name is Donata ... Donata ... uh ... Margo, help me out, please."

Before I could cough up the name I didn't know, Filippo said it for me. "Do you mean Donata Abba?"

"Si," I replied with feigned relief. "Donata Abba, of course, by any chance do you know her? Better yet, where she lives?"

He nodded from El to me. "*Si, si, la casa di Abba* is not far from the piazza. Signora Abba is expecting you?"

"Not exactly," I said. To which Filippo twisted his mouth and pondered the situation.

"Donata will be pleased we came all this way to visit her," El said.

I followed up with a cheesy wink, confirming Nonnie's cheesy assessment of me.

"I will take you to Donata." Filippo lifted his shoulders and opened his palms. "But after that, who can say what kind of welcome she will give you."

El and I stood up at the same time. With Filippo sandwiched between us we left the piazza and headed toward a narrow street lined with two-story buildings. Most had been updated with stucco covering their original stone exterior, Filippo told us when he stopped to run his hand over the surface of one structure. Similar to what we'd seen throughout Italy but with subtle colors instead of the bright hues of yellow, terra-cotta, and mustard prevalent on the Mediterranean coast.

"Is Pont considered part of the Alps?" I asked, referring to the mountainous area surrounding the village.

"More like the foothills," he said. "But high enough to put you in the morning clouds and send a chill through your bones nine months of the year." He paused before asking, "How long will you stay in Pont?"

"We haven't decided," El said.

"Is good you came at this time of the year," he said. "In the summer there is much to do. Many people return to their family homes in the countryside instead of fighting the heat of Torino. In Torino people find work. Here they find pleasure."

"What do the Italians around here do for fun," I couldn't resist asking. "Other than eating, I mean, not that there's anything wrong with a nice bowl of risotto."

Filippo chuckled. "Good food opens the door to all things good, Signorina Margo."

"Please call me Margo. And my sister ... Elena."

El opened her mouth to object but Filippo spoke first. "Ah, Elena in the Italian way, is good, si?"

Not in the Cinque Terre wake of El's bruised ego, a romance that promised more than it could've ever delivered. She let her next words escape through the thin line of determined lips. "If you don't mind, I prefer Ellen in the American way."

I mouthed a sorry to her. Wounded hearts were tough buggers to heal.

"Then Ellen it is. I like the American way too." Filippo turned to me. "You asked about entertainment. For us, each day that passes is entertaining—one lived and loved to its fullest. Is it not the same in America?"

"Most Americans have a short attention span," El said.

"I do not understand."

"Some of us crave excitement and diversion," I chimed in. "Right now, every day and most nights."

"Ah, with time that will change. How long did you say you're planning to stay?"

Again, how many times would he ask and what difference did it make. Relax, I told myself and answered with a faint smile. "I suppose it will depend on the number of friends we make."

"Making friends will take time, signorina."

"Margo," I reminded him.

"Si, Margo. Speaking our language would help."

"I speak enough Italian to get by."

"Which is more than I can say," El said. "Do you know if Signora Abba speaks English?"

"Maybe so, maybe not," he replied with a seesaw of one hand. "But I think maybe her grandson speaks good English."

"He lives nearby?"

"No, no, Pio Gavello lives with his nonna. He is all she has and she is all he has. His mamma—God rest her soul—sleeps in the cemetery."

El muffled a giggle and shook her head. *Thanks for the awkward moment, sis.*

"This amuses you, signorina?" Filippo asked.

"No, no, *mi dispiace*," El apologized, using one of the few Italian phrases she spoke fluently and for good reason. "It's a sister thing between Margo and me. I meant no disrespect."

Oh, yeah, she meant the Italian *mamma mia* culture. Shades of my last romance with a mamma's boy, a humiliating mistake I did not plan on repeating in the near future, if ever. Italian nonnas would be even more protective when it came to grandsons they'd spoiled since birth. Not that I was revving up for another holiday romance. Not with thoughts of Jonathan from Des Moines still jerking my chain. Although I must admit, giving him the heave-ho didn't hurt me nearly as much as it had hurt him, given his hound dog demeanor. Whatever was he thinking, cheating on me before I had a chance to cheat on him. Talk about nerve. Never would I have been so bold in Italy, miles away from my U.S. comfort zone. Unless some irresistible hunk swept me into his arms and carried me off to his man cave carved in the mountains ... okay, foothills. Fat chance of a cave happening in the short time we planned on being here.

Filippo stopped in front of a four-family building made of stone aged to muted shades of marbleized gray streaked with green moss. Pink geraniums tumbled from flower boxes attached to the underside of the front windows. "This is the house of Donata Abba, also known as Donata Bartolini, widow of Giuseppe Bartolini," he said. "The signora lives on the ground level." He knocked once on a solid door painted a deep shade of green. He waited and knocked a second time. Soon after, the door opened.

Donata Abba, I presumed correctly. The woman stood taller than me, thinner too. What is it with these Italians who live for the next meal yet somehow manage to maintain their twenty-something weight. Her back was bent slightly with age but no more than Nonnie Clarita's. Strands of white hair mixed with the gray, a stylish cut parted on the side that flattered her lined face without overpowering it. On seeing Filippo tip his cap, she smiled. "*Buongiorno,*" Donata said, and continued in Italian I understood with no problem. "What brings you to my house this day?"

Filippo tipped his hat a second time and returned her greeting. He motioned to El and me, introduced us by name. "The signorini are from America. They are the granddaughters of Clarita Fantino."

Donata folded her arms. She looked us over and having dismissed the smile reserved for Filippo, she said, "I speak a little English."

Phew, what a relief, considering my labored Italian was iffy at best and sometimes wore me out just thinking about my next sentence.

"Then you know our nonna," El said.

"Clarita, si, from long ago."

"We thought you were related," I said.

She answered with a shrug. "Not exactly but what does it matter after all this time. Please to come in."

"I will go now," Filippo said. "The three of you have much to discuss."

"Nonsense," Donata said. "You'll stay for the wine, si?"

Her words came across more as a command than an invitation. Filippo removed his cap to expose dark hair streaked with gray. He followed us inside where the living and dining areas were combined to make one large room, its focal point a pine table so old it must've served hundreds of diners over several centuries. Again, no air conditioning and no need for it. The room smelled of times past, slightly damp and musky but not in an unpleasant way.

"Sit, sit," Donata said, motioning us to the table. She brought out four short glasses and a jug of wine with no label, a homebrew reminding me of what Nonnie Clarita often brought back from her visits to Southern Illinois. After pouring a round, Donata sat down and lifted her glass.

"*Salute!*" she said, to which the rest of us echoed her cheers.

As usual, El waited for me to go first. I swirled my glass with the confidence of a wine connoisseur, sucked in the aroma, and took a sip. Those in the know would've sloshed it around in their mouth before swallowing. Not me, no way would I have insulted our hostess by questioning the wine she offered. I closed my eyes and let the wine slip down my throat, all the while enjoying it to the max. Before taking another sip, I shot a glance to El and gave her a subtle thumbs-up.

Donata was already pouring another round for herself and Filippo, who had two fingers leveled against his glass. When the wine reached that point, Filippo said, "*Basta,* enough." He tossed the wine down in a single motion, pushed back his chair, and got up.

"*Grazie,* Donata," he said with a slight bow to her and then to us. "Buongiorno, signorini."

So we were back to being called signorini, oh well. "Perhaps you could show us the village," I said with my best smile. "We could meet tomorrow if it's convenient for you."

"Filippo is a busy man," Donata said, "a married man."

"Buongiorno," he said for the second time. He backed away, turned, and nearly tripped over his chair while hurrying to the door.

"Mi dispiace, signora," I said to be polite.

"No need to apologize. Soon my grandson will be home. Whatever you want to see, he will show you."

"We don't wish to impose, signora." El said with her best convent demeanor.

"Call me Donata. Everyone calls me Donata." She lifted her glass and took a generous sip.

"Thank you ... Donata," El said. "Before I forget, Nonnie Clarita sends her love."

Donata kept the glass pressed to her lips longer than necessary before setting it down. "She is well?"

"Except for a touch of arthritis, yes," I replied.

"Is the same with me," Donata said. She leaned forward and rubbed her lower back. "Clarita and I, we once had many things in common, at times too much. What about your *mamma*?" She emphasized both ems in the Italian version of mamma, giving each consonant equal value unlike most Americans who slurred double consonants. "Your mamma, she came here once, back in … I forget."

Mom, of course, I'd forgotten about Mom having come to Pont. El and I should've called back and talked to her instead of Nonnie. Too late, we'd made it here on our own. Okay, with help from Filippo.

"That's right," El said. "Mom was eighteen at the time, and just out of high school. It must've been around 1973."

"Now what was her name; it's been so long." Donata showed me her palm, fingers pointing upward to indicate she wanted no help recalling. "Antonia, si, but everyone called her Toni. A girl like that I would not forget, especially one so … pretty."

El and I exchanged glances, both knowing what the other must've been thinking. Not what Donata had said about our mother at eighteen but the way she said it; and perhaps what she left unsaid. In any case, all thoughts of our All-American Mom ended with the opening and closing of Donata's front door.

No mistaking the thirty-something man who walked in and headed straight for his nonna. She'd already gotten to her feet, as did El and I. No taller than Donata, he leaned into her, kissed both cheeks, and stepped back. Donata projected a toothy smile, her first since El and I came into her house. Her moment of nonna pride gave me a chance to peruse the object of her affection from head to toe. Nice, if you like the interesting mix of emerald eyes over strong cheekbones, a nose not too big for his face, and auburn hair skimming an up-turned shirt collar, which at that moment I most certainly did. She introduced us and explained our relationship to Clarita Fantino.

"Should I know her?" Pio Gavello asked in English better than Donata's.

"No, Clarita is before your time. But your mamma often spoke of Clarita's daughter, Toni Riva."

"Ah-h, that Toni," he said. "Toni from America, Mamma did mention her even though Toni was a few years older."

"I'm sorry about your mamma," El said. As did I, which seemed kind of odd since we'd only met Pio three minutes before and neither of us had even heard of the woman until Filippo mentioned her passing.

"Grazie," Pio said, lowering his auburn eyelashes. "God in his mercy did not let her suffer too long. Now there is only me, and my nonna."

Don't get me started on The Italian Way. I forced myself not to look at El. Another misplaced snicker we did not need.

"You'll take *le sorelle* around," Donata ordered Pio as if we Savino sisters weren't standing next to her. She went on to speak in the Piemontese dialect that sounded like a cross between Italian and French with many of the ending vowels omitted. Most of what they said I couldn't understand because they were talking too fast although I did understand the dialect when Nonnie communicated with her Italian friends living in Southern Illinois. While Donata dominated what was supposed to be a two-way conversation, Pio held up his end with a mouth twisted to one side, his head bouncing up and down in rhythm to every *"Sì,"* and *"Sì, sì,"* he gave back to her.

Now I was beginning to have my doubts. No way would I allow El and myself to be foisted onto an unwilling host, hunk or otherwise. "Really, this is not necessary," I said in English, pronouncing each word with care. "My sister and I can get around on our own. All we need are a few addresses and instructions on how to get from here to there."

"No, no ... er ... uh ... Margo ... is no problem." His voice, a melodic tenor, turned me on. His words turned me off. "I was merely confirming what my nonna expects ... I mean, would like me to do ... for you ... and your sister ...." He popped the heel of his hand to his forehead. "Mi dispiace ... already I forgot your ... her name."

"My name is Ellen."

"Is good," he said with a slight smile, "but in Italy we say Elena. Is okay with you?"

Oh brother, we didn't need to go there again. The mere mention of Elena had to bring back some ugly memories from El's Cinque Terre fiasco. I braced myself for her possible meltdown.

"Elena, it has a certain something," she said, returning a smile I'd not seen since events preceding that same fiasco. "Yes, Elena would be fine."

Give me a break, especially since she'd told Filippo not to call her Elena. After locating her foot under the table, I rammed it with mine and then stood up. As always, El followed my lead and got to her feet.

"We should go now," I said. "Grazie for the lovely visit, Donata."

"And for the wine," El said. "And for offering up Pio."

"Is no sacrifice," Donata said. "You're staying at the hotel, si?"

El raised her brow. "Well, yes but—"

"Pont is a small village," Pio said, again with a smile. "When two strangers check into our only hotel or any pensione—everybody knows within hours. I pick you up at nine, si?"

"*Perfetto,*" El said, circling her thumb and forefinger. "Tomorrow morning at nine will be perfect."

"No, no, I mean this evening at nine. You want to see how we live, yes? At night we drink wine, just as we do in the day, only more of it. And we dance. I take you to do the wine and the dance, your sister too." He looked at me. "Sorry, already I forgot—"

"Margo, my name is Margo." Jeez.

8
YOU, ME

That evening in the hotel bar El and I distinguished ourselves as the only barflies—make that patrons—occupying two of the six stools. There we sat, gazing at mirrored shelves filled with assorted aperitifs, cordials, spirits, and wine while listening to overhead fans circulating air warmer than we could've found outside. The silence proved more annoying than deafening as we shared a carafe of the house red, me tapping one foot and El chewing on her cuticles.

"Will you please stop that disgusting habit," I told her.

"Only if you give your foot a rest," she said with an air of nonchalance.

"What time is it?"

"What? Don't tell me you're too lazy to check your cell phone."

"That's why Mom gave me you, little sis."

El looked beyond my shoulder to the clock hanging on a paneled wall. "Nine-fifteen, Pio should be here any minute."

"Oh, right, I keep forgetting. You've known this Pio for … let me think … all of ten minutes, fifteen tops."

"May I remind you where we are," El said. "In Italy, where most Italians are notorious for their tardiness, so let's cut Pio some slack."

"Wasn't it Mussolini who set his *paesani* straight, got the railroads running on time? Or, else?" I ran one finger across my throat.

El lifted her glass to me. "Brava and thank you for the history lesson. I am truly impressed."

"And hopefully amused," I heard Pio say. "Mi dispiace, an emergency came up."

Screw the emergency, I thought. El and I wiggled out of our bar stools. We exchanged a brush of cheek-to-cheek kisses, as if we'd known Pio longer than the afternoon's brief encounter.

"Is good I brought a friend with me." Pio gestured a hand wave over his shoulder, inviting another thirty-something for a meet and greet. A little rough around the edges and in need of a shave but not bad for a spur-of-the-moment blind date Pio introduced as Amadeo. No last name since it wouldn't have mattered anyway.

Nor was there any point in looking at El to know she must've tensed up over the prospect of a blind date. Unlike me, she hated surprises. Our next surprise came when we walked out of the hotel. There, parked in the open area were two motorini, Vespas to be precise. Other than a dance partner for El, who wasn't crazy about dancing, another reason to bring an extra guy since three on one Vespa would've meant for a crowded ride wherever we went.

"Uh, we have a car," I said. "It's big enough for the four of us."

"But not as much fun," Pio said with a cautionary forefinger moving sideways. He did the unexpected and took El's hand. "Elena goes with me."

Amadeo pointed to his scooter, and being a man of few words, said only two, "You, me."

Really, now *I* hated surprises. A tough break for me, an even tougher one for El. She'd be on her own, having recently entered the big girl arena in Cinque Terre. So quit worrying I told myself. Still, I gave her a thumbs-up, to which she responded with a half-hearted wiggle of four fingers. Amadeo handed one helmet to me and covered his mass of wild hair with a second helmet. I slid onto the motorini seat, scooted back, and spread my legs for a less than perfect stranger. Amadeo positioned himself in front of me and from over his shoulder, he said, "*Scusi.*" I guess his way of apologizing for me having to snuggle against the T-shirt stretched across his broad shoulders.

Leading the way, we made a quick U-turn and headed down the street, away from the village center. After crossing the Soana River, we turned right and sped into the unfamiliar, at least for El and me. The cool night air smacked my face, forcing me to lean even closer to Amadeo, this guy I'd only met minutes before. Over the years I'd ridden on a few motorcycles but never one I would describe as more scooter than Harley. As for El, I could only imagine how terrified the poor thing must've been. I turned my head in time to see her and Pio passing us on the left. This time, El gave me a thumbs-up, along with a big shitty grin I should've welcomed but felt an unexpected tinge of jealousy.

Relax, I told myself. How lucky could El and I get, not a care in the world as we cruised into the great unknown of our ancestors. After skirting the edge of open land, we slowed down for the next village. Amadeo turned his head and said, "Cuorgnè," pronouncing the village name as *Cone yay'*. A half circle through the roundabout brought us back to the main road, a piece of cake for anyone acquainted with the concept, one that still baffled El and me. I tapped Amadeo on the shoulder and using my outside voice, I asked, "How much longer?"

He answered with a shrug, which could've been interpreted as, "I don't know," or "I have no idea what the Americana is saying," or, "Shut uppa your face."

As soon as we put Cuorgnè behind us, we entered the village of Castellamonte and continued following Pio's tail lights through a series of dark streets until those tail lights grew smaller and faded into the night. Minutes later, Amadeo turned into a large parking area filled with assorted vehicles and scooters. After pulling into a narrow slot, he killed the motor, stepped onto the pavement, and helped me separate my ass from his Vespa. Having found my feet, I willed them to move, only then realizing it would be with stiff hips and unsteady legs, definitely not the impression I wanted to make, nor should have given a second thought to, considering the inadequate lighting responsible for creating more shadows than visibility. A few parking slots closer to the action we came upon El and Pio leaning against his Vespa, arms folded as if they'd been waiting an eternity.

Pio gave Amadeo a playful tap on the chin, and said something in Italian I didn't quite understand. To which Amadeo laughed and tapped him back.

"No fair," I said. "English, please."

"Would not be fair to Amadeo," Pio replied. "His English is not as good as mine."

End of discussion, Amadeo came first. After a few steps I latched onto El's arm, my way of slowing her down while the guys up ahead put some space between us. "Is this for real or what," I mumbled to her.

"What did you expect," she mumbled back. "After all, we are in Italy. And you do speak Italian."

"Just enough to get by," I said with a snort.

"Getting by should be enough to keep us out of trouble."

We followed Pio and Amadeo toward the sound of music blaring from a gigantic tent that took me by surprise, the kind of surprise I enjoyed. When we passed through a well-lit area, I lowered my voice and spoke from the corner of my mouth. "Get a load of those tight asses."

"Knock it off, Margo."

Not realizing the guys had stopped, we almost plowed into them.

"No fair." Pio wagged his finger at El and me, mostly me. "We cannot hear you."

"You weren't supposed to," I said.

"Ha! How you say ... you got me there. But not to worry, Amadeo will treat you okay. He is a good dancer."

"You, me," Amadeo said again. He took my hand and Pio took El's. I would've preferred holding hands with Pio but that would've left El with Amadeo and given the language barrier, I wasn't sure she could handle him.

The four of us walked into the crowded tent where long-haired musicians on stage were performing something very macho Italiano. Music I couldn't recall having heard before. As soon as their set ended, a DJ took over, the canvas arena providing surprisingly good acoustics. I shook my booty and said, "Name that tune." Pio told me it was *"Far l'amore"* and asked if I liked Raffaella Carr. "Absolutely, she makes me want to dance." One could only hope he would take the hint.

While Amadeo made himself scarce, Pio found a table near the dance floor and waited until El and I sat down before he joined us.

"I'm not much of a dancer," El said with the apologetic look she'd mastered over the years. My poor sis, the family dance genes had danced right past her two left feet.

"Is good," Pio said, tapping his chest with two sets of slender fingers. "I am an excellent teacher."

"Don't mind me," I said with a wave of one hand. "Go, dance. I'll just sit here by myself."

"No, no," Pio said. "Is not polite *Italiani*. We wait for Amadeo. You like him, si?"

"I don't know him. Nor did I know you had this in mind."

Pio leaned forward, his face inches from mine. "Explain, please."

"No offense, Pio, but I don't like being passed around like ... like some—"

"What? Is better you should insult my nonna? Refuse her hospitality? Refuse the friendship of Amadeo?"

"No, of course not, it's just—"

"Amadeo is a good man, an honest man. No touching without *permesso*. You understand."

Sure I did. Get the two *Americane* drunk and show them what Italians call macho. As if I didn't already know and on certain occasions had enjoyed. Okay, what with El shooting me daggers and kicking me under the table, I may have jumped the gun in challenging a guy I barely knew.

As soon as Amadeo came back with a jug of wine and four glasses, Pio stood up, taking El with him. Off they went to dance. Amadeo didn't have to practice his macho persuasiveness on me. Instead he wiggled his fingers and motioned his head toward the dancers. I held my head high and walked onto the floor unassisted.

Another surprise, unlike the first, this one super nice. Amadeo turned out to be a terrific dancer, making the next two hours pass so fast I didn't have time to stew over the guy who chose El over me, a rejection I had not seen coming. Nor one our mother would've believed. Nor did I have any intentions of telling her. After consuming two jugs of wine, the four of us were still heating up the dance floor while the crowd had dwindled to a precious few. Make that *a sweaty few*, given the lack of air circulation. Back to the plus side, my blind date's English had improved beyond a simple *you and me*.

"Your hair smells good," Amadeo whispered during the oh-so-romantic *"Tu Per Me."* He shifted his weight and pulled me closer to him. "You want to see my bed?"

Si, si, I almost said but held back, along with the yawn threatening to escape from my mouth. "Maybe another time," I did manage to say. "We really should be going." I stepped away from him, made my way to the table where El was laughing with Pio, and said, "I'm exhausted. Are you ready to go?"

The laughter came to an abrupt end. "Uh … I guess I am if you are."

Okay, so she didn't seem as ready as I was; but staying any longer would've led to where the evening didn't need to end, at least in my case. Whoa, since when did I turn down the chance to connect with a half-way decent Italian, one who could dance better than any American who'd ever twirled me around the floor. It must have been the jug wine. Yeah, blame it on the wine.

∞∞∞∞

On the way back to Pont I leaned into Amadeo again and closed my eyes to air that felt ten degrees cooler than our earlier ride. Instead of focusing on the fun evening my thoughts drifted to Nonnie Clarita, her fondness for dancing the night away, which she rarely did anymore in America, what with most of her old farts having given in to bad knees, bad backs, or bad hearts. Here in Italy El and I still didn't know where Nonnie once lived or anything about the family she rarely discussed. Nor did Mom talk about her time in Italy, which, the more I thought about it, seemed rather odd since the two of them seldom ran out of the usual chitchat.

Tomorrow, more like later in the morning, El and I would get down to business, focus on our visit to this area yet-to-be-discovered by tourists whose families had not emigrated from here. Otherwise, El would never move on, never get over her Cinque Terre disaster, although tonight did seem like a step in the right direction. Make that *a dance step*. And, yes, I was happy for her. For me too. Amadeo turned out to be an okay guy.

Back in Pont, Amadeo helped me off the Vespa and unbuckled my helmet. After walking me to the hotel door, he surprised me by asking if he could see *my* bed.

"No, no," I said with a laugh. "But grazie for the less-than-subtle pick-up line. Tonight my bed is only for sleeping. Perhaps another time."

"You promise?" he asked.

To which I responded by holding his whiskery face between my hands and planting a kiss on his lips, along with the sweet and salty taste of my tongue.

And way better than the cheek-to-cheek El exchanged with Pio. Serves him right for choosing her over me.

9
PHOTO FROM THE PAST

There I was, the new Ellen Savino, my second resurrection in less than a month, one that almost felt sacrilegious had I allowed myself to dwell on past ill-timed transgressions. I couldn't speak for Margo but last night had boosted my level of confidence a notch or two. Dancing with Pio, no way could it have compared to the heart pounding of first love I'd found in Cinque Terre, but that didn't stop me from having a good time. And riding behind Pio on that sweet Vespa had made me feel years younger, those all-important years I'd given up to the convent. No regrets for attempting the religious life, but some years later I was still trying to catch up with the rest of a world that had been moving too fast for me.

As for Margo, she'd behaved herself with Amadeo and any other guy who happened to brush up against her. And yes, there'd been at least two, which relieved me from having to defend her actions to strangers, more like locals since we were most definitely the strangers. *Le due donne americane*, as I heard someone refer to Margo and me, the two American women. *Women*, only a word but it felt … too mature for thirty-somethings, at least in our part of the world. But this was Italy. Where women weren't afraid to be women and men had always thought of themselves as macho men.

This morning's breakfast consisted of the typical Italian we'd found from Rome to Florence to Cinque Terre and now Pont Canavese: cappuccino, crusty bread, and soft cheese served in the hotel's dining room. Neither of us had much to say, a typical breakfast for me anywhere but a rarity for Margo who always had something to say and often with her mouth full even though not one morsel of food or drink exited it while she pontificated on this or that, as only she can. I didn't push her for conversation; some words are better left unsaid, especially those involving two sisters and one guy … er, man. Amadeo didn't count. I'd seen her eyeing Pio from the moment he walked into Donata's house. What he saw in me instead of her, I didn't have the foggiest. Nor did I expect anything to come of it. Summer romances, I'd had my fill of one. A man, not a guy, I should never have let him break my heart.

Having nothing better to do, Margo and I agreed on a long walk around the village, again with few words spoken between us. We soon wound up in Piazza Craveri, same place as the day before. We sat on the same bench, watching some of the same people come and go. One who came and stayed was Filippo Sasso. He tipped his hat and I scooted over, allowing him space to sit between Margo and me.

"Your visit with Donata Abba was good?" he asked.

"Si, grazie," Margo said.

"And you, Elena? You danced nice with Pio?"

"You know about that?"

"Pont sees all and hears all," Filippo said. "This can be good if you ever need help."

"And not so good if you want privacy," Margo grumbled.

"Is different in America?" Filippo asked.

"No, the same."

"Do not be offended. In Pont you and Elena are … how you say, persons of interest."

"What brings you here today?" Margo asked, much to my embarrassment. Pont was, after all, Filippo's village, his right to be wherever, whenever.

"Donata said you would be here. She invites you to visit again, now."

"Well, we wouldn't want to disappoint Donata," Margo said. She got up, knowing I would follow.

"Are you coming," I asked Filippo?

"Better you should go without me. You know the way, si?"

∞∞∞

Fifteen minutes later Margo and I were again making ourselves comfortable around Donata Abba's time-worn table instead of the sofa or chairs reserved for more formal gatherings and those whose status had not yet been determined. Nonnie Clarita would've been pleased, or should've been. Nonnie thrived on the unpredictable, in particular when it originated from her end. The same could've been said for Donata, at least from what little she'd revealed about herself. Having hauled out a large box crammed with old photographs, she sat across from Margo and me while shuffling through stack after stack, muttering to herself until she finally located the object of her search.

"This," she said, pushing a black and white photo in our direction.

Margo picked up the photo and together we looked at two girls standing in front of a stone wall, between them a teenage boy who didn't look old enough to be carrying the rifle slung across his shoulder. In the lower white border of the photograph, a date written in faded ink—1944.

"This is me ... *a sinistra*, on the left," Donata said. "The other girl is Clarita Fantino. Both of us fourteen but she was older by six months."

Never would I have guessed the girl with the Mona Lisa smile to be our Nonnie Clarita. Clearly, God had passed the best of her genes onto Mom and then Margo. The boy had deep-set, brooding eyes and was taller than either girl. He wore trousers too big for his slender frame, a grayish shirt with the sleeves rolled up. Dark shaggy hair hung below a cap cocked to the side of his head. He stood close to Clarita, their shoulders barely touching, with Donata positioned a good six inches to his left, as if an uncomfortable afterthought who'd insinuated herself into the picture. Or been invited, perhaps by the amateur photographer. Donata wore a print dress; Clarita, a dirndl skirt and white blouse. Clothes that spoke of hard times.

"And the boy ... young man?" Margo asked.

"No longer a boy, Stefano was barely sixteen and with the *Resistenza*, although this I did not know at the time."

"He was your brother?" I asked.

Donata sort of laughed. "No-o-o, but had I been sixteen instead of fourteen, we might have been more than friends. Even though Clarita looked older and behaved older, she did not have as much sense as I did. There came a time, after this picture, when she lived and breathed Stefano Rosina, in her mind, that is. I think she would have died for him. And maybe he would have for her, God only knows."

"Our nonnie," Margo said, "no way."

"You think Clarita Fantino was always old?"

"Of course not, she'll always be young to us." I opened my wallet; removed the glam photo Margo had insisted Nonnie get for her eightieth birthday, and passed it across the table.

Donata did more than look at the headshot; she studied it. "Humph. Clarita's hair was never that light. She dyes it, si?"

"Doesn't everyone," Margo said with a smile reminding me of Nonnie at fourteen.

"Not me." Donata patted her hair. "A few gray hairs do not stop the men from coming around."

Oh brother, I couldn't help but think. Just what we needed: an aging prima donna.

"Whatever happened to Stefano Rosina?" Margo asked.

Donata lifted her chin. "He comes around from time to time."

"That's so sweet," I said.

"Not always." She yawned, one hand making a half-hearted attempt to cover her mouth. "Please excuse. I must take my morning rest before I start to prepare dinner."

Eleven o'clock. She meant her mid-day meal, no doubt as substantial as what Nonnie still prepared, but what most Americans consumed later in the day, closer to evening.

"You'll stay, of course," Donata said. "Pio will soon be home."

"Grazie, but another time." Margo got up, leaving no doubt as to her intentions. "We have other plans."

I raised my brow, and mouthed two words. "We do?"

49

Margo nodded with her eyes. We'd been around Italians so long their subtle gestures were starting to rub off on us.

"Then come back this evening," Donata said, "around eight o'clock if you wish to meet Stefano."

∞∞∞

After we left Donata's, I stopped along the road to check the time on my cell phone.

"Are you thinking what I'm thinking?" Margo asked.

"It's four in the morning St. Louis time, too early to call Nonnie."

"Right, Nonnie in a bad mood makes for a very bad nonna." I lifted my head to the bluer-than-blue sky, the perfect day for an excursion into the mountains. "How about we drive up to Ceresole Reale and continue on through the Gran Paradiso?"

"Never heard of either one," Margo said.

"Then you're in for a treat, according to my research and the guidebook Jonathan left behind."

"Jonathan?" Margo asked with her I-couldn't-care-less look.

"You know, Jonathan from Iowa."

"A guy so ordinary he bordered on the extraordinary." Margo thought a minute, her way of letting go, worse yet, hanging on. "Okay, Miss Librarian," she said. "Let's go back to the hotel and get the car. You drive; I'll navigate."

Same as always but Margo saying the words made it official.

10
GRAN PARADISO

A day as sunny as this may've been par for the course in Northern Italy but nothing smacked of ordinary for Margo and me during our drive to Gran Paradiso National Park. "The park is located high in the Graian Alps, Italy's mountain range in the western Alps," she said, having made that discovery while thumbing through Jonathan's guide book. I already knew about the Graian Alps connection but refrained from mentioning it so as not to discourage Margo from further geographic tidbits.

We followed an upward route lined with campgrounds similar to those back home, and rustic trattorias situated beside the Orco River. Along the way we stopped at the resort village of Ceresole Reale. More to the point, a flock of sheep crossing the road stopped us.

"Photo op," Margo yelled. She hopped out and snapped away, graceful as ever in the practical shoes she'd borrowed from me, one of only two walking pairs I'd packed for the trip. I parked along the roadside and together we checked out the few shops appealing to tourists. After browsing the limited options for souvenirs, we wound up with a handful of postcards the shop clerk offered to mail at no extra charge beyond the postage. Now that was my idea of service.

On the road again, we began circling the mountain, climbing higher and higher with each hairpin turn as Margo kept up her familiar chant of, "Photo op ... quick. Pull over. Now, El. Dammit now."

If only there had been convenient pullovers wide enough to

accommodate Margo's constant demands. Patience, eventually it paid off to my relief and her Type-A personality. With each stop, both of us got out, me gazing in awe while Margo snapped one photo after another of the lakes below, so blue they looked as if nature had painted them into the lush evergreens of distant slopes and valleys. The cooler temperatures of higher altitudes kept me alert and wanting more. Good thing I'd thought to bring the binoculars because they revealed several mountain goats licking salt off the brick wall of the dam, a practice I thought only occurred during the cold of winter but what did I know about the ways of alpine ibex.

Memo to Self:

1. *Yes, boys and girls, I saw ibex in the Italian Alps.*
2. *I also danced the night away, with a hunky Italian guy.*
3. *Don't ask what I did in Cinque Terre. You're too young.*
4. *I know, it is possible to have your sixth-grade heart broken.*
5. *Life can be a b-i-t-c-h at any age.*

Continuing upward, we became part of the clouds, a scary feeling on the outside curves with steep drop-offs capable of sending us directly to hell. Forget about any stopover in limbo or purgatory. Near the pinnacle I noticed a few vehicles parked alongside a little trattoria, the only visible eatery since circling the mountain.

"No," Margo said before I had a chance to open my mouth. "Save your appetite for later."

"Did I say anything about eating?"

"You didn't have to," she said. "I heard your stomach growling."

"Well, excuse me for expressing my hunger in a manner I did not initiate on my own. But since we're on the subject, I'd settle for a nice cup of hot chocolate."

"Control yourself, El. Think about the gorgeous scenery. We're sitting on top of Italy and we will never witness a sight such as this again."

"Since when did you develop an appreciation of God's natural treasures?"

"Get real. There's more to me than fashion and Jimmy Choo and sexy guys."

"If you say so."

With Margo, arguing only led to more arguing since she had to have the last word. That is, unless I wore her down before she did me. Not a good situation with either of us behind the wheel. I circled through the parking area and was ready to exit onto the main road when Margo told me to pull over. More like ordered, so I did.

"What now," I said, switching off the ignition. "Don't tell me you want to drive."

"No, I want to … I need to … talk."

"Over coffee? We wouldn't have to eat if we went inside."

"Forget about going inside; forget the hot chocolate. Or espresso or cappuccino. What I have to say won't take long."

Oh, oh, I thought with a lump growing in my throat. This cannot be good. When Margo had something important to say, it always evolved into more time than she estimated.

"It's about Jonathan," Margo said. "I haven't been totally upfront with you."

Dear God, confession time. I scooted the car seat back a notch or two and prepared myself for the curse of an awkward situation. Blessing Margo with the sign of the cross bordered on hypocrisy so I gestured for her to go ahead and then tucked both sets of fingertips under my thighs. Hmm, they seemed to have lost another inch or two, a testament to the Italian experience, of feet hitting cobblestones more often than auto pedals.

"El, are you listening?" I heard Margo ask, her voice sounding as if it came from another dimension.

"Every word," I said, surprising myself. "You were talking about our first evening in Chamonix. About Jonathan being obnoxious at times, his obsessive horniness getting on your nerves so you pretended to be asleep and he snuck out, leaving you alone in the hotel room, the dirty bastard."

"Right," Margo said. "As soon as the door closed behind Jonathan, I switched on the TV and watched a foreign movie—don't ask me the name because I've already forgotten it—but oh my, what a triple-decker sizzler. Then I tried reading the travel guide. Imagine that with a forty-watt bulb stuck in the bedside lamp. I was ready to turn out the damn light when in walked Jonathan, his face flushed with the cheater guilt I'd seen in my own mirror over the years, and on more than one bad boy. Not that there's anything wrong with bad boys, if they're being bad with me. This, however, had not been the case with Jonathan."

How well I knew but didn't dare hijack Margo's story.

"By any chance do you have a cigarette?" Margo asked.

Me, of all people. I'd never learned to inhale and hadn't bought a pack of cigarettes in years.

"Never mind," she went on. "I'm not going there again. Anyway, Jonathan walked in. Sitting catawampus on his head was this ridiculous gray toupee—what a pathetic riot. As soon as I asked him about it, he grabbed the silly-ass rug and stuffed it into the wastebasket, all the while giving me a weird excuse about some guy in a bar sticking the damn thing on his head.

Margo turned to me. "Can you imagine Jonathan trying to weasel out, such colossal bull shit."

"Well, I hardly knew him."

"Neither did I," Margo said, "for which I blame myself not you."

"So, what happened next?"

"I mumbled a good night, slid under the covers, and turned to face the wall. Although my eyes were squeezed shut, I sensed him moving closer to the bed, heard the clink of his belt buckle, the slide of his zipper, his jeans drop to the floor. I told him my head had been hurting for hours, a truthful statement if ever there was. He had the nerve to ask if this meant no sex tonight. I rolled back to face him. 'Yes and no. It means no sex tonight or any other night in the near or distant future.'

"Then he said something about there being a silly misunderstanding between him and … and …which is when he stopped talking and my eyes opened wide. I sat up, leaned forward, and tried to ignore the denim puddled around his ankles. Instead I cut to the chase with a straight-forward question. 'Between you and who … whom?'

"Jonathan said between him and nobody … that he was just thinking out loud. You know, El, I thought about his comment for about twenty seconds, long enough for one hell of a bell to go off in my head. 'You'd better not be referring to my sister,' I told him.

"The blood left his face, turning it a pasty gray in the dim light while his mouth stumbled around for the right words which amounted to, 'For God's sake, El of all people? You think I'd ... what the hell, give me some credit.'

" 'If not El, then who?' I asked.

" 'Who, what?' he said in the high-pitched voice of a lie. 'I don't know what you're talking about.'

"That's when I noticed the lipstick on his shirt. I reached over, stretched his shirt to the side so he could see what I saw. Jonathan rubbing the stain only made it worse, as if I gave a shit one way or the other. He said some broad had crashed into him. An accident he didn't see coming, what with the place being so crowded. I wanted to know what place and told him not to lie to me.

"He bent over, pulled up his jeans, and said, 'Just a place, a no-name place that doesn't matter.'

"I smelled cheap perfume ... make that cologne ... and asked him if it came from the same broad. 'Probably, I can't say for sure,' he said. 'How the hell should I know and what's with the third degree. It's not like we're in a committed relationship or even close to one.'

"Boy, did he ever get that right. My fingers turned into claws as they crumpled the bed sheet like discount wrapping paper. I told him to get the hell out. He thought I meant that very night."

"How awful, more like awkward," I said, picturing that scene in my head.

"Awful for me, for sure. But as you well know, I'm not a heartless bitch. I gave Jonathan until morning."

"Did he say anything about the car?" I asked.

"You bet he did. 'Get real,' I told him. 'If it hadn't been for El letting you tag along with her and me, we wouldn't have upgraded to a bigger car.' He started whining about having paid the difference. 'For a car still in El's name,' I said. 'You are so on your own, just like before.'

"I yanked one blanket off of the bed, tossed it in his direction, and gave him a *good night, sleep tight*. And I do mean tight, as in the bathtub since his only other choice would've been the floor. Too bad he blew what could've been a nice bubbly together. All things considered, I actually slept quite well that night. Can't say the same for Jonathan but don't know for sure. When I woke up the next morning, he was gone. Hmm, given the hour, I guess he hired a car to drive him wherever. Some things just weren't meant to be, at least for the long haul."

"Come on, Margo. Don't be too hard on Jonathan. After all, if it hadn't been for him, you might've died that awful day in Cinque Terre."

"Yeah, and if it hadn't been for you, I wouldn't have been in that awful pickle to begin with."

"You don't have to remind me. On the other hand, had you stuck to our original plan, I wouldn't have gotten myself mixed up with the gypsies."

"Whatever. I'll always carry a soft spot for Jonathan. But for now, listening to my head instead of my heart makes more sense, don't you think?"

"You bet," I pushed my seat forward and leaned toward the ignition, only to have Margo brush my hand away.

"I'm not finished, El. Back to that night in Chamonix, you know what I think?"

My mouth went dry. It always does when Margo suspects me of doing her wrong "Hmm, what *do* you think." I drummed two fingers on the steering wheel while contemplating my next words. "Well, it seems to me you covered just about everything, at least the important stuff."

"Except for the broad he bumped into that night. The broad was you, wasn't it, El."

That's when I told Margo my side of the story, basically confirming what Jonathan had told her but with the straight and skinny of my perspective.

"Why you little shit!" was all she said.

"I didn't know the idiot was Jonathan. I swear I didn't. Nor did he know the broad was me. When we discovered who the other was, we were both mortified, Jonathan more so than me. The whole thing was over, just like that." I snapped my fingers. "On the other hand, as you well know, I do not wear cheap cologne. Or any cologne, I'm just saying."

Margo sighed. "He was such an ordinary jerk."

"You got that right."

11
OUR DAY SO FAR

Margo and I returned to our hotel around five in the afternoon, which made it around ten in the morning St. Louis time. Perfect for a conversation with Nonnie Clarita, as long as we sat near the window in my room for optimal cell phone reception. After the usual admonition for wasting our money on long distance charges, Nonnie hemmed and hawed and said Mom had gone shopping with Kat Dorchester. To which Margo gave a single 'yes' pump with her arm and I told Nonnie we were staying in Pont Canavese.

"Margo must be bored silly," Nonnie said. "One or two more days in Pont and you will be too, missy."

Missy, she hadn't called me missy in years, not since I left the convent. Mom hadn't been quite so forgiving with the name calling. But enough of what had been an unnerving period of my life. This day I considered an enjoyable one, especially after relieving myself of the Jonathan misunderstanding.

"So far, so good," Margo chimed in. "We drove up to Ceresole Reale and Gran Paradiso today."

"Uh-huh, I hear Lake Como to the east is pretty nice," Nonnie said. "You should leave Pont and go there instead."

"Maybe in a few days," Margo said.

I shook my head so hard it almost fell off my neck. "Margo's just kidding, Nonnie."

"Well, how's this for not kidding: George Clooney's got himself a fancy place in Como. A guy like him, a girl like you, by that I mean Margo. Sorry, Ellen. God gave you the brains, which ain't so bad if you know how to use them."

As if I hadn't heard that one before. I didn't bother going into George's many relationships that didn't pan out. Or the unlikelihood of him ever connecting with Margo.

"Hello, anybody there?" Nonnie said. "If not, I'm hanging up."

"No, no, we're still here," I said. "Get this. Last night we went dancing."

"Not in Pont, unless there's a *festa* I don't know about, which I doubt since nothing ever changes in Italy. Or if it does, it takes a good seventy-five years and I've only been gone … let's see, sixty-three or four, more or less. What the hell, who's counting."

"We went to … I think Castellamonte," Margo said, "behind two guys driving motorini."

"What? Are you out of your mind? First, those scooters will kill you faster than inhaling cigarette smoke. Second, you met somebody already?"

"One of them is the grandson of your good friend Donata," I said.

"You saw Donata? I told you not to bother."

"It was no bother," Margo said. "Some guy named Filippo took us to meet her."

"Filippo who?"

"Uh … he didn't say or maybe he did and I forgot."

"Stay away from strangers or anybody who doesn't give his last name."

"It's Sasso," I said. "Filippo Sasso."

"You don't say. Any relation to Lucca Sasso?"

"We just met. These things take time."

"Find out and let me know. The mamma died, right?"

"If you mean Pio's mother, yes," Margo said. "He lives with Donata."

"Okay, so you met Donata. You met her grandson. Now stay away from them and from Pont."

"Donata treated us well. In fact, she invited us back."

I heard Nonnie blow a raspberry as only she could and resisted the urge to wipe virtual spit from my phone. "What a couple of dopes you two are," she said. "Don't believe a word the woman says. You hear me?"

Bringing up Stefano Rosina—for now not a good idea. With Nonnie on a roll such as this, ending our conversation made better sense. "Sorry, Nonnie, it's these mountains," I said, scratching the phone with my fingernails. "We must have a bad connection."

"Did you hear me? Dammit, I know you did. Do not believe Donata Abba. The woman is lying through her crooked teeth and forked tongue."

"Gotta go, love you," Margo said.

"Love you, Nonnie."

∞∞∞∞

That evening Margo pressed the buzzer at Donata's house while I shifted from one foot to the other, hoping it would be Pio who opened the door and invited us inside. No such luck, it was Donata, her hair carefully groomed, face touched-up with just enough mascara and lipstick to make a noticeable difference. She motioned Margo and me to the leather sofa and selected a chair from the dining table for herself. She sat facing us, her back rigid, ankles crossed, and hands folded. But only for a brief moment until she opened one hand and gestured in our direction.

"So, what did Clarita say when you called her?"

"Uh, I'm not sure what you mean," I said.

"You called her, sì? Told her you talked to Donata, sì?"

"Well, yes, but …."

"Did you mention Stefano Rosina?" Before either of us could answer, Donata checked her wristwatch, and said, "No, I did not think so." She got up, went to the window, and pushed an edge of lace curtain to one side. "Good, he is here."

She opened the door *before* he knocked. Or, maybe he wasn't expected to knock before entering. They did kiss, but in the Italian way, cheek-to-cheek with a slight brush of the lips. He stood several inches taller than Donata. Steel gray hair flared back from a bronzed face and rested on the starched collar of his white shirt. Considering Nonnie Clarita's age and Stefano a few years older, he had aged remarkably well and could've passed for a man in his early seventies.

I couldn't help but recall the 1944 photograph Donata had showed Margo and me earlier that day, three young people on the verge of adulthood, their lives disrupted in ways no one could have anticipated. Nonnie with Stefano Rosina in today's world, highly unlikely. But the two octogenarians standing before me made a handsome couple, which didn't seem to be the case back then. To be fair, I couldn't imagine Nonnie in a serious relationship with any man, although she did date on occasion.

What Margo was thinking, I had no idea, but she did grab my hand. Hers felt damp. Not a good sign. One could only hope she wouldn't make a move on Nonnie's old flame. Not that I would've put such an abomination past Margo, considering her brief encounter with an even older gent in Cinque Terre, Monterosso El Mare to be precise. Which is not to say Margo didn't go for younger guys too; case in point, the mamma's boy in Florence we'd agreed not to discuss. Just as we'd agreed not to discuss my failed romance that started in La Spezia, blossomed in Cinque Terre and ended back in La Spezia.

Margo slid her hand away from mine. We got up like twins joined at the hip; and without waiting for Donata's inviting gesture, moved closer to her and Stefano Rosina. We stood in respectful silence while Donata did all the talking, in Italian with an occasional nod from him. Twice, she mentioned Clarita, prompting Stefano to wrinkle his brow and glance toward Margo and me. I smiled, but got nothing in return.

"This is so-o awkward," Margo whispered. "Maybe we shouldn't have come."

Some words are better left unsaid, especially when overheard by the one person who shouldn't have heard them because Margo's last words prompted a response from Donata. "Is good you came. Stefano knew you were in Pont but did not expect to meet you here."

He stepped forward, extended his hand to Margo and then to me. He said our names before we did and introduced himself in English better than Donata's or Pio's.

"Your nonna, she is good?"

"Better than good," Margo said. "She's terrific and beautiful."

Talk about awkward. Stefano narrowed his eyes to Margo, as if searching for his past in her lovely face.

12
FIRST IMPRESSIONS

Over the years I've known more than my share of men, been tighter than a Brazilian butt lift with some of them, but never had a man stared into my face with the intensity of Stefano Rosina. "Did you find what you're looking for?" I asked him.

A typical gasp of disapproval erupted from El, one I ignored.

"*Scusi, signorina,*" Stefano Rosina said. "I could not help but think of Clarita Fantino."

"You think I look like her?"

Stefano stepped back and gave some thought to my question while rubbing his chin. "There is a resemblance to Clarita but only slight. To your mamma, maybe so ..." he rocked his hand, "maybe not."

"You've met our mother?" I asked.

"Long ago," Stefano said. "We did not ... how you say ... connect."

"Well, at times Mom can be intimidating ... you know, scary."

"Not with me. And your pappa?"

"Prostate cancer, he passed five years ago."

"May he rest in peace," Stefano crossed himself, as did Donata. He shifted his attention to El. "This one looks like ... nobody I ever knew."

El's face turned red and she stammered her usual, "I ... I'm sorry."

Sorry! I didn't know whether to bop El or this Stefano Rosina. It was one thing for me to insult her, more like a give-and-take game of sisterly ping-pong, but a complete stranger insulting either El or me was most definitely an unmitigated no-no.

"No need to apologize," Stefano told El. "You are every bit as *bella* as your sister, but she is not you and you are not her. Is good the difference, si?"

If you say so, Stefano, I thought but held my tongue. While he continued his line of Italian bullshit, Donata moved to the table, opened a bottle of red wine, and poured four glasses. She called us over and gestured where we should sit—Stefano and me on one side; El and her on the other. After the usual *salute* we settled back to enjoy the wine along with a platter of soft cheeses, figs, and sliced melons the Italians prefer serving at room temperature instead of chilled.

"Quit your bitching. It's the Italian way," Nonnie Clarita would've said had she been sitting beside me. But she wasn't and for sure she would not have approved of El and me poking our noses into her past, which made it all the more tempting for us.

"Clarita, did she ever marry ... again?" Stefano asked in an off-hand way that didn't fool me, or anyone else at the table.

"Never found the right man," I said while El fumbled around in her purse. She pulled out Nonnie's photo and handed it to him.

Stefano held the photo in the palm of his large hand, fingers caressing the border as if he could transport her into the room.

"Humph," Donata muttered. "As you can see, Clarita colors her hair."

"On Clarita it looks good," Stefano replied.

"But would not have on me or so you said."

"And what I meant. You are what you are and will always be—*bella, bella.*"

"*Bella, bella,* pfft ... you tell that to all the women."

"Not any more. In the winter of my life I only tell that to the woman sitting before me." He took her hand and kissed the fingertips, a gesture she seemed to enjoy but only for a brief moment before jerking her hand back. Knowing men as I do, I thought his behavior was as much for my benefit and El's as for Donata's.

"Tell them." Donata pointed to El and me. "The daughters of Clarita's daughter want to know about their nonna."

"Clarita's story is for her to tell, not me."

"She has told them nothing."

"Then why should I?"

"If not you, then who," Donata said. "Coming from me would not be the same."

I nudged my foot against El's; she nudged back while Donata and Stefano continued their accelerated exchange.

"At one time Clarita was a friend to you," Stefano told Donata.

"And to you so much more," she said. "Stefano and Clarita ... Clarita and Stefano ... you and your secrets, you and your lies, I no longer existed." She blew unsaid words of anger from the fingertips he'd kissed moments before.

Such resentment Stefano must've heard *ad nauseam* over the years. A slight smile crept over his lips when he asked, "You want me to leave?"

"Si, if you have nothing more to say, you should go home."

"Who said anything about going home?"

"You came tonight to talk about your precious Clarita, so talk."

"I came because you invited me. Clarita would not like me talking behind her back. Nor would you."

Phew, enough with the bickering was my thought. I said my next words with a straight face. "I don't think Nonnie Clarita would mind. After all, she sent us here." Okay, that may not have been a totally accurate assessment of our being there. Nor of Nonnie's feelings, which explained why El was digging the heel of her shoe into the arch of my foot.

"You think?" Stefano asked me.

"I am positively certain." More or less, if I counted the time Nonnie spoke about confession being good for the soul. Or maybe that had been Mom since she took a more serious view of traditional Catholicism, especially where El had been concerned. Not that anything had been said about confession, more like setting the family record straight. Truth be known, until that moment I'd never given much thought as to why or how Nonnie had immigrated to America. And if El had, she did not mention it to me.

"Okay, you want to hear about Clarita and me," Stefano said. "Then I will tell you my story ... which may not agree with her story but mine you heard from me and before anyone else. Donata set the jug in front of him. He filled our glasses, emptied his, and refilled it again before saying another word. "When I think back to those days of my youth, I cannot recall a time when Clarita was not a part of it, which does not mean I always liked her."

"But you always loved her," Donata said.

"If you know so much, maybe you should tell my story."

"Mi dispiace," Donata said with arms crossing her chest. "I will keep my mouth shut."

"Grazie, this is very generous of you. Now where was I?"

"You always loved Clarita," El said, parroting Donata's earlier comment.

"Did I say that?" Stefano asked.

"You did," Donata said. "More than once."

"Not that I recall."

"Careful, Pinocchio. Your nose is growing again."

"Look who's calling the kettle black."

"This is about Clarita. Clarita. Clarita. Everybody loved Clarita, even me. She was my best friend, the sister I never had. We were like this." Donata clasped the fingers of both hands together. "All that changed when Clarita turned fifteen before me and you saw her in a new way." Donata separated her hands, leaned across the table, and shook one forefinger in his face. "That's all I got to say."

"Good. Or not so good, maybe I should go." Stefano pushed back his chair. His arm brushed against mine as he started to get up.

"You leave now; do not come back," Donata said. "Not tomorrow, not ever."

He heaved a great sigh and repositioned his narrow hips back onto the chair. "Okay, I will talk but only if you promise to shut up."

"I will shut up if you promise to tell only the truth."

"Donata, Donata … have I ever lied to you?"

She held up both hands. "*Uno, due, tre* … wait, I must remove my shoes for more counting."

"Okay, okay, but first more vino, *per favore*."

While Stefano tapped his fingers on the table, Donata filled our glasses again. After taking a generous sip, he set his glass down. "Now where was I?"

"Nowhere, that's where." Donata stood up. She leaned across the table and snatched his glass away. "Go home, Stefano. You are too old for fairy tales and you make me sick."

"Sit down and shut your mouth. I am ready to talk about Clarita."

I put my right hand over his left, a sharp contrast of mine tanned and wrinkle-free against his lined with blue veins threatening to pop through skin as taut as leather. Now it was my eyes that held his when I spoke. "Please, Stefano."

"For you, Margo, and for your sister, I will proceed." Another sip, he cleared his throat. "As I said before, I cannot recall a time when Clarita was not part of my young life. And even though she has been gone from Italy for sixty-five years, not a single day passes without my thinking of her." He hesitated, glancing in Donata's direction. "Which is not to say I am incapable of thinking about anyone else; in fact, sometimes I think of Donata when we are not together. And always I think of my late wife, God rest her soul."

Donata waved him away like a bothersome mosquito. After draining his glass, he tapped it with three horizontal fingers. She poured wine to the level of his forefinger. He slid his fingertips onto her hand and she jerked it away. He ran his tongue over his lips, as if trying to capture a moment from long ago.

"*Basta*, enough," Donata said. "How many times must I sit through the love-sick story of your youth?"

"But you wanted me to tell it."

"Not this way—you know better." She stood up. "You should go, Stefano. And please, take the granddaughters of Clarita with you. My head hurts from all this talk. No, no, better yet, I will take myself to bed."

"At this hour?" Stefano said. "It would be a first."

"To bed does not mean to sleep."

"Si, this I know."

"But you do not know everything." Again, Donata waved one arm into a broad gesture. "The three of you, stay as long as you please. If you go before Pio comes home, leave a light burning for him."

Pio, I hadn't given him a thought and considering the circumstances, Donata's parting was not as awkward as it might've been. Exchanging cheek-to-cheek kisses does have a useful purpose after all, a way of soothing over words spoken in haste or anger. Or cruelty disguised as teasing, which may've defined Stefano Rosina although I didn't know him well enough to make a fair assessment.

After Donata left, Stefano opened another bottle of wine, offered refills which El and I both refused, at least for the moment. We sat back and let him continue. "Now where was I?" he asked.

"Your first kiss," El said, which surprised me. Brava for her not wasting any time.

"Si, so sweet, as was every kiss that followed," Stefano said. "Our kisses soon progressed to the ... how you say ... a friendlier level. The details matter to only me and perhaps to Clarita, although I cannot speak for her after the passing of so many years." He paused for a moment. "Out of respect for Clarita, I will not share those moments with the two of you."

"I'm sure Nonnie wouldn't mind." An incredible stretch, I know, but curiosity had always been one of my weaknesses.

"Better those details should come from her then," Stefano said.

"She'd like us to hear your version." I said, "That's the Nonnie we know." *Forgive me, Nonnie. Not only am I deceitful but also a shameless liar.*

Stefano's silence told us what not to expect.

"That's it?" I asked. "This is what Donata wanted you to tell us but couldn't stick around to hear?"

"You want to hear more?" Stefano asked. "Without the passion of my youth but with the yearning I still feel when speaking of our time together."

"Only if there's a point to all of this," El said.

Speak for yourself, I so wanted to tell her. She was still feeling the sting of her first broken heart. For me, there'd been so many I'd lost count. "Please go on," I told Stefano.

Naturally, Stefano's cooperation required more wine. El and I waited while he poured himself another three fingers and after a lift of his brow, we allowed him to refill our glasses as well.

13
STEFANO'S STORY

"In 1944 the world was filled with the chaos of a violent war and Italy had already sided with Hitler. Me, I was sixteen, more than a boy but not quite a man. My eyes had been following Clarita Fantino for some time, watching as she became not quite a woman but no longer a girl. It was as if the mythological gods had cast a spell on me, luring me deeper and deeper into the web they were weaving on behalf of Clarita. In my heart I wanted to believe she felt the same about me although during that year of transition neither of us spoke of this to the other.

"Fortunately, I was too young to be conscripted into the Italian army. Instead I followed my heart and joined the *partigiani*, a secret known only to those who were also involved. As a runner for the partigiani and in turn The Resistance, my duties were unpredictable but allowed me considerable freedom from my widowed mamma. Good thing she supported the cause and what I was doing when away from home. Many things I chose not to tell her. To have done otherwise would have destroyed her faith in me, her only child to have survived infancy. Such are the ways of war.

"Shortly after Clarita's fifteenth birthday I asked my trusted friend Tommaso Arnetti to deliver a note to her, one I had written in my best penmanship. To this day I still recall my words to Clarita:

Tonight when all is dark,
When your mamma and pappa are sound asleep,

Meet me in the stable beneath your house.
Only to talk, nothing more.

"Later, Tommaso, who everyone called Tommi, apologized when he explained how Clarita had read the note and then tore the damn thing into little pieces, right there in front of him. So I sent him with another note and after that another, each time my words pleading a little harder and promising not to touch Clarita or to disrespect her in any way. Every note Clarita read before destroying while Tommi stood by. After the sixth rejected note I no longer trusted Tommi and delivered the next one myself. And what did Clarita do? Tore up the note without even reading it. She demanded I speak directly to her. Only on *hearing* what I had to say did she agree to meet me at the stable.

"Our meetings started out with the innocence of a newborn lamb taking its first steps. Clarita and I would lean our backs against the stone foundation and take in the fragrance of hay mixed with the good earth. Always I brought a special treat to share, beginning with chocolate that did not agree with her. Later, fruit, nuts, or berries—perhaps a bunch of wild flowers picked earlier in the day. We talked about our daily lives. We talked about our dreams for the future after the war ended, how Mussolini would feel the crush of defeat he well deserved, unlike our beloved Italy he'd brought to ruin.

"Our first kiss was so natural it came without warning, so memorable I can still taste the sweetness of her lips. I continued to leave my home each night, alternating between my duties with the partigiani and those precious hours with Clarita. The stable animals sensed not only our growing passion but our need for quiet so as not to alarm Clarita's parents. So much to learn and so little time, *mamma mia*! Clarita and I could not get enough of each other. To this day my heart still aches just thinking about her. But then our little world came crashing down when Clarita's parents found out she'd been meeting someone, although his name they did not know.

"Clarita's pappa turned into a bloodhound on a mission, a crippled one at that, having been shot the previous year in his ass—pardon my vulgar language—while serving with the Italian army in Greece. I can still see Vito Fantino sniffing around Pont, casually asking about this young man and that young man—those on leave from the military or those yet to be drafted— and if any of them had been seen talking or flirting with the village girls. Perhaps his daughter Clarita? To my everlasting regret I should have come forward instead of taking the coward's way out by remaining silent.

"One villager, who should have known better, offered a possible name, that of Tommaso Arnetti. The same Tommi who delivered my messages to Clarita until I no longer needed him, no longer trusted him, even though I considered him the type never to be interested in girls. But what did I know then? Only that the expression on Vito Fantino's face did not change that day as he limped away from the Piazza Craveri.

"Weeks later while on leave from the army, Cosimo Arnetti found his son hanging from a rafter in the family stable. For God's sake, Tommi was no more than sixteen years old. Cosimo nearly went insane with grief. He could not believe his son would take his own life. Nor did the padre of San Costanzo who gave Tommi a proper funeral Mass and burial in the cemetery. One week after they put Tommi in the ground, his mamma collapsed with a seizure that could only be explained as a broken heart. She died within twenty-four hours. Another funeral, the endless mourning, not once during this time did Clarita and I speak to each other. Nor to my knowledge did Clarita's pappa or mamma speak to her about Tommi.

"From there, things only got worse. Two weeks after Aida Arnetti's funeral, Vito's wife Bruna—Clarita's mamma—went to the stable and found Vito dead. Rammed in his heart was the *balla gancio*, a large hook he used for baling hay. Later that same day Cosimo Arnetti's battered body showed up at Cuorgnè, sprawled across boulders in the River Soana."

Listening to Stefano describe four deaths in a matter of weeks, three of them under violent circumstances, made me cringe, especially the part about Nonnie's father, our great-grandfather. El must've felt the same way, having screwed up her face into one of utter disgust.

"Oh, no," I said. "Nonnie Clarita never told us any of this. How tragic. It sounds like something the Mafia would have done."

Stefano gestured a no-no with his forefinger. "No Mafia then; no Mafia now. Not here. Mafia does not come this far north. Sometimes they dump a body or two in the north but always the connection goes back to Sicily."

"So who killed Nonnie's father?" I asked.

"Is still an unsolved crime, although at the time many believed Vito was responsible for Tommi's death. As for the death of Cosimo Arnetti, a domino effect of unexplained events intertwined and eventually forgotten. Life goes on, one by one leaving to history those who knew more but did not speak up when it would have mattered, just as I did not."

"How unfortunate," El said. "Nonnie rarely talked about her parents or how they died. Nor did I think to ask."

"In Italy some believe it is not polite to question the details of death," Stefano said. "For me, it depends on the circumstances."

"Hmm," I said. "Nonnie did mention something about her mother having a heart condition."

"*Impossibile,*" Stefano said. "The woman had no heart. Bruna Fantino outlived most of her neighbors and the few friends she supposedly had. After the funeral of Vito, I confessed my sins to Don Luigi, the padre who buried him as well as Tommi and his parents, even though some believed Cosimo was responsible for his own death, a matter the padre again ignored and the police did not pursue. As part of my penance Don Luigi insisted I tell Mamma Bruna about Clarita and me, and beg her forgiveness for all the grief my actions had brought to so many people. After doing so, I asked her permission to marry Clarita but Mamma Bruna had other ideas. She refused to let me near Clarita and kept the stable door padlocked at night.

"I continued my work with the partigiani and occasionally saw Clarita walk through the village. At first she did not look in my direction, making me think I was dead to her. Then, one Sunday after Mass our eyes met and I knew she wanted me as much as I wanted her. That night on my way home from delivering a message, I could stand it no more. I climbed into her bedroom window and from there into her bed. We stayed in each other's arms until dawn, ever so quiet so as not to wake Bruna who was snoring louder than any partigiano I'd ever heard during an overnight mission. After that night in Clarita's bed I met her in the woods, in the stable of my house, anywhere we could be alone.

"The war came to an end and slowly life returned to what became a new normal. I mean no disrespect but a death in Bruna's family became for me a gift from the gods. As soon as Bruna left for Novara to attend what promised to be a lengthy wake and funeral, I contacted Clarita. We agreed to meet in Ceresole Reale. For her, a short distance by bus and for me an even shorter distance on the horse I borrowed from a man who owed me a favor. Five glorious nights and five glorious days Clarita and I stayed in the remote cabin of the friend of a friend.

"One day we ventured out, on horseback to attend the *carnivale* in Ceresole. It was there a gypsy invited us into her trailer and after much coaxing, convinced Clarita and me to pose for her. Images in charcoal that would've made my mamma blush and Clarita's mamma rip out my heart.

Although we did not tell this gypsy the circumstances for our being in Ceresole, she insisted we stay in her trailer until the fair closed for the evening, in case anyone from the surrounding villages recognized us or questioned our youthful appearance. The gypsy sprinkled her magic over Clarita and me, spoke mumble jumble in a foreign language. I think Romani. Back in the cabin we made love as never before and later cried at the thought of never seeing each other again. In the middle of the night we returned to the gypsy and she made things right by us.

"In the morning before we parted, I begged Clarita to run away with me but she refused to leave Bruna so soon after her pappa's death. Weeks later, Clarita stopped speaking to me altogether. Our separation lasted almost two years, twenty months to be exact. Dear God, twenty months without my arms wrapped around her, twenty months without my lips pressed against hers. During those months I courted the village girls, kissed many of them, took a few of them to the next step, but never with the desire I'd felt for Clarita.

"To my surprise on the day Clarita turned eighteen, Bruna invited me to their home for a dinner celebration. Just the three of us, make that four; Donata showed up, which annoyed both Clarita and me—don't tell Donata I said that. Is difficult for me to remember the details of that celebration—what we talked about or how Clarita fixed her hair or the dress she wore. But this much I do know: only one of us almost died from food poisoning and that person was me."

"Are you sure it was food poisoning?" El asked. "Perhaps a virus—"

Stefano tapped his chest. "Please, Stefano Rosina knows the difference, even then I knew. While I went through hell battling demons of the devil, sprawled out on my sweat-soaked mattress and evacuating from both ends, the she-devil Bruna sent Clarita away, to live in America with friends. Or perhaps relatives, their names Bruna kept from me. How the woman managed to get the required paperwork so soon after the war, I do not know. Maybe Isabella Rocco oiled a few squeaky wheels to make this happen."

"Isabella Rocco," El said, "that name sounds familiar."

"She was one of the few women Bruna Fantino accepted without question. Or, who accepted Bruna. But that was Isabella. During the war, the Piemontesi considered Isabella Rocco a living saint. Not only did she aide the partigiani but also the Italian soldiers and their families, all of whom suffered. Before and after the war some of Isabella's family went to live in America."

"I wonder where they settled," El said.

"Clarita would know."

"You mentioned the gypsy making things right," El said.

"At the time, si, but not for long."

"I don't understand."

"Nor do I expect that you should." He stood up. "Is time we should go, si? Come, I will walk with you."

I put my hand on Stefano's arm, still muscular for a man his age. "Don't bother. El and I know the way."

"Ah, but I insist. Pont Canavese may seem idyllic, and in many ways this holds true, but dark, lonely streets and the quiet of night still invite the unknown or the unwelcomed."

14
REFLECTIONS

Family skeletons—not what I had expected—no wonder Nonnie Clarita didn't want Margo and me poking our noses into her Italian past, the life she'd left behind, hoping for a better one in America. Or so we thought. Little did we know Nonnie had also left behind her first love, perhaps the love of her life, or not. Aside from my years in the convent and my recent heartbreaker in Cinque Terre, I'd still been around enough men not to believe everything they implied or inferred. Or for that matter what women implied or inferred. After a while, memories tend to grow fuzzy and the keepers of those memories only recall what they choose to recall—usually the best and the worst with the in-betweens becoming non-descript gray matter.

Nonnie never had much to say about her late husband, our grandpa, which didn't make him a bad person or a good person but rather, an unforgettable one. In any case, whatever the reason for her leaving Italy turned out to be a plus for Margo and me. Otherwise, we would've been … nothing, not here or there or anywhere, not even the proverbial twinkle in God's eye.

Our walk back to the hotel with Nonnie's first love became a pleasant distraction, with Stefano stopping to chat with every person along the way, always introducing Margo and me to the older villagers who remembered Clarita Fantino. Or those too young but who'd been acquainted with the family name, which now carried a much different meaning after learning how Nonnie Clarita's father had died. Make that been murdered. Tried, but not in a court of law. Found guilty, but not by a jury of his peers. And executed by a person or persons unknown, for a crime or crimes the man may not have committed.

Okay, so color me naïve, a bland shade of indecisive beige for wanting to believe beyond the obvious. I couldn't help thinking about those recent deaths in Monterosso El Mare, the obvious not necessarily the reality, and me in no position to make the distinction between the two or to convince anyone in authority of my concerns. Maybe that had been the case here in Pont Canavese, an unresolved mystery from long ago, the obvious not necessarily the reality.

As for Nonnie and her ill-fated romance, hardly worth anyone dying for, especially the wrong person, a boy at that, supposedly killed for something he didn't even do. And even if he had, he didn't deserve to die for doing what all teenage boys dream about doing. The injustice of it all, the domino effect of senseless tragedies, no wonder Nonnie didn't want us anywhere near Pont Canavese. Times and morals and what's considered acceptable certainly had changed over the past sixty-plus years. Or had they? Somehow I had the feeling Stefano Rosina may've told us the story he wanted us to believe but not necessarily the whole story.

Memo to Self:

1. *Discuss mysterious deaths with Margo.*
2. *Try to resolve said mysteries before leaving Italy.*
3. *Enlist help from anyone with half a memory.*
4. *Or, from someone who once knew anyone with half a memory,*
5. *Believe only half of what we are told.*
6. *Above all else, convince Nonnie to come clean with us.*

We were nearing our hotel when a man I'd not seen before stepped out from the shadows of two buildings. Stefano stopped so quickly I almost stumbled over my own feet before slipping one hand through the curve of his arm. Margo and I must've been in sync because she did the same from Stefano's other side. Together she and I had steeled ourselves for what— the possibility of this stranger snatching our purses or ripping a stiletto through Stefano's gut? Or cutting his throat from ear to ear, as if I hadn't seen the result of that already in Cinque Terre. While I considered belting out a scream bordering on hysteria, a cooler head than mine prevailed. Stefano shook himself loose from Margo and me so he could bear-hug this stranger grinning like a Cheshire cat. The two men released their grip and Stefano introduced us.

"My only son," he said with a choke in his voice. "Franco's mamma died too young and too long ago."

Franco Rosina I would've put in the vicinity of mid-fifties. Though not a younger version of his father, he did stand about the same height, but his hair was reddish brown, his eyes a dark shade of blue.

"These signorini are the *nipoti* of Clarita Fantino," Stefano said.

Franco shook my hand first, then Margo's. Nice, at least it didn't require me having to lean in for the proverbial Italian hug, so awkward when meeting a stranger for the first time. And often thereafter, some people just weren't worth the effort although Margo the proverbial hugger would probably disagree.

"Welcome to Pont," Franco Rosina said in English as good as Stefano's. "You're staying long?"

"We only arrived yesterday," Margo said. "Or was it the day before … we've been gone so long."

"From St. Louis, si," Franco said, to which I nodded in agreement.

We started walking again, the Rosina men on either side of Margo and me, which didn't present a space problem with none-existent sidewalks getting in the way.

"I suppose we really should check out the family while we're here," Margo said.

"Is good to start in the cemetery," Franco replied with a smile.

"Or, by talking to people who live in the area," I said.

"Si, anything you want to know—"

"I already told them," Stefano said.

"Ah-h, but, Pappa, every story has more than one side."

"You are so right," Margo said as we arrived at the hotel. "And here we are, safe, sound, and not one hair out of place. Nice meeting both of you."

She held out her hand to Franco for another sturdy grip. After shaking my hand, he stepped aside, allowing Stefano to hug Margo and me. Not too long, or too tight, but just right. Nice cologne I hadn't noticed before. At least he wasn't wearing Gucci. No more Gucci for me, no more reminders of Cinque Terre, no more what might've been but never would be.

∞∞∞

"So, what do you think?" Margo said while following me into my hotel room.

I stifled the yawn I truly felt. "About what?"

"Jeez, about tonight, about Stefano Rosina and our very own Nonnie Clarita, about their teenage romance. Nonnie's father found dead with a hook in his heart. Stefano's friend found dead, hanging from the rafters. Two grieving parents dead, one under mysterious circumstances. I could go on and on."

"Or, we could save some time and call Nonnie again. Get her version."

"Not on your life," Margo said. "You know as well as I do that her version would be no version."

"Maybe we should give it a rest."

"Seriously, you think?"

"No, just for tonight," I said through a yawn refusing to be stifled. "Trying to keep up with Stefano and his vino has made me so sleepy I can't think straight."

"You are so right, again." Margo opened the door and stepped into the hall. "We'll digest tonight and discuss tomorrow. Meet me in the dining room at eight o'clock."

She didn't wait for an answer, nor did I feel compelled to give her one. During this past month in Italy we'd been meeting every morning around eight, in whatever dining room of whatever hotel we were occupying. Not counting Cinque Terre since we'd stayed in an apartment part of the time and a villa the rest. Just thinking about Cinque Terre pained me, even though I knew time would heal all pain, no matter how long it might take.

A splash of cool tap water on my face worked as well as any slap, whatever it took to rid myself of him ... my first love. Okay, so water on the face didn't work. Instead, I walked down the hall to the common bathroom and subjected myself to a cold shower. Not by choice, I might add. Back in my room I considered calling the desk clerk, who'd have to call the maintenance man, who was probably at home doing what all Italian men do at the end of each day. Hot water issues would have to wait until morning.

After slipping into the just-in-case naughty nightie Margo had foisted on me in Cinque Terre, I slid under the covers and closed my eyes. Visions of Nonnie Clarita popped into my head. Make that visions of Clarita Fantino, the young girl of fourteen standing on one side of Stefano Rosina, her friend, Donata Abba flanking Stefano's other side. I could not imagine Clarita of long ago having come from parents unlike any I'd known in America. Her pappa capable of killing an innocent boy, her mamma capable of poisoning Clarita's lover—what kind of madness had been considered the norm back then? And how much of Stefano's story was factual and how much his fictionalized account, rationalized over the years to make it more palatable.

Memories to die for—however good, however bad—were tough enough to swallow, but making sense of them on too much wine and too little sleep didn't seem worth the effort I couldn't muster. One final yawn did the trick, putting me out for the night, my salvation a dark place without dreams and other distractions.

15
TAKING CHARGE

I'd been sitting in the dining room for a good fifteen minutes, drumming my fingers on the table while waiting for El to show up. El, who usually obsessed over the sin of tardiness, except during those romantic intervals in Cinque Terre, which didn't count since she'd been crazy in love at a moment so brief in time I doubt she even remembered it. Yeah, right. Knowing El, she would've remembered. A guy like her first love would've been difficult to forget, even though he was most definitely not my type, at least in the physical sense. Still, he did have a certain sophistication and demeanor lacking in most American men I'd encountered over the years. Although in all fairness, I'm the last person who should be criticizing others.

Donata's grandson I'd given up on, what with Pio showing more interest in El than me. Talk about a blow to my not-so-fragile ego, which El had never challenged in the past and for good reason. At least she had the decency to pretend Pio choosing her over me had been nothing more than a matter of convenience, as to who happened to be standing closer to him before we hopped on those Vespas. Which brings me to Pio's friend, Amadeo, an acceptable guy in a spur-of-the-moment pinch. And yes, Amadeo did pinch my ass the other night. In a cute sort of way I might have encouraged without realizing it. Okay, so maybe I did but at the last minute decided not to follow through with anything more. After all, even I possessed some standards, one of which was to avoid behaving in a manner capable of bringing disgrace to the family name. Fat chance of that happening here in Pont since the Fantino family of long ago had already set the disgrace bar way over my head.

On the other hand, this son of Stefano Rosina may've been out of my age-appropriate range but as a short-term possibility he did intrigue me, in an earthy sort of way, unlike the Florentine mamma's boy who could not get over himself. Damn, I'd promised myself to never, ever think of him again unless I became truly desperate. Which I was not, nor did I intend to reach that point before making a few adjustments in my attitude.

"Buongiorno," I heard El say, in a voice so cheerful it grated on my nerves, much like the old-fashioned box grater Nonnie insisted on using when doing a number on hard cheese. Not a good way to start a morning such as this, what with skeletons sneaking out of the family closet. I managed to crack half a smile and return El's greeting when she plopped down across from me.

Within a minute or so, our Ukrainian waitress appeared with two cups of creamy cappuccino and the usual breakfast goodies—some packaged in cellophane; others, such as slices of day-old bread, scattered in the basket. Since we would be interacting with our waitress for a few more mornings, a courteous exchange seemed in order. I asked her name. *"Nome?"*

"Ivanna." She pointed to the other Ukrainian, who was cleaning the entryway, and then using that same finger, tapped her chest and said, "Sasha, *mia sorella.*"

"Your sister," I said before making a similar gesture to El. *"Mia sorella."*

"Ah-h." Ivanna shook her head as she leveled one finger to my face and then to El's.

"Si, we don't look alike," I said.

"Or act alike," El said. "Do you know Pio Gavello?"

Ivanna smiled again. "Si, is ... good."

End of the getting acquainted game, Ivanna made herself scarce. Which pleased El, who'd been shifting from one butt-cheek to the other as if she'd transported her mind to another realm.

"Hello, anybody home? Out with whatever's bugging you."

"How intuitive of you." El pulled out her little red notebook and flipped open to a page of precise notes written in the proper penmanship of her convent days.

Wanting a closer look, I snapped my fingers and opened my hand, expecting her to lay the notebook in my palm. Instead, she leaned back, clutching her words as if I might eat them in place of the Melba toast sitting on my plate.

"Please, Margo. Do not rush me."

"Whatever." I threw up my hands. "Take your time but make it quick."

"It's not like we have a full day planned. One thing's for sure: not another visit with Donata. Awkward, to say the least."

"Agree, but what about Pio?" I asked without trying to sound smarmy.

"If we run into him, great. If he comes looking for us, even better."

"Agree, with or without Amadeo."

"You have to admit Amadeo is kind of cute."

"In a scruffy sort of way," I said. "Perhaps you'd like to switch."

"What are we playing, musical Vespas. To be fair, it's not like I picked Pio for myself."

"This is true." *Grr*, did she have to rub salt in my wounded pride. A pregnant pause followed so I switched back to our original discussion. "So, what's with the red book secrets that must've kept you awake all night?"

"Should've but didn't, I slept like a baby but woke up early." El released the notebook from her chest, opened it again, and took thirty seconds to ponder her notes. "And, in my humble opinion I think we owe it to the Fantino family—Nonnie's father and our—"

"Don't forget Mom. She comes before us."

"Of course, Mom too; I didn't mean to overlook her."

"As if she'd ever stand for that."

"Anyway, we owe to our Fantino side of the family to find out what really happened those many years ago. Not only to our great-grandfather Vito Fantino but also to the unfortunate kid …uh—"

"Tommi," I said. "Tommi Arnetti."

"You remembered his name. That is so ... so humane of you."

"I do have a heart, you know. Unlike our great-grandmother Bruna, at least according to Stefano Rosina. His story leads me to believe there's more to it than he's telling."

"Which leads me to the second thing on my list," El said. "Hear me out before you say *no*."

"You think we should do some investigating on our own."

"Just to pass the time away until something better comes along. It's not like I expect to dig up any information that hasn't already been unearthed."

"Agree," I said. "We'll do a little poking here, a little poking there. Ask a few questions."

"A local go-between or two would make life easier," El said. "Pio, unless you have someone else in mind." She reached for a third slice of bread, giving me an excuse to slap her hand. "Ouch, what the—"

"Doesn't Pio have a job?" I asked. "It's not like he can spend all day hanging out with us."

"It's not like we have a pool of bystanders to choose from."

"But you are right about more than one person—maybe Filippo Sasso."

"Or ... I hate bringing this up," El said, "but another phone call to Nonnie might unravel a few tangles in the family web."

"Not unless you agree to do all the talking, endure all the abuse, take responsibility for the heart attack she'll either fake or instigate. Choose your poison: whatever it takes for Nonnie to lay another guilt trip on us."

"Give me some credit, Margo. I did learn a few things in the convent, for one, the subtle art of communicating."

"Didn't you take a vow of silence?"

"Never, you're thinking of the Carmelites and even they're allowed to speak on certain occasions." El stood up, purse in tow. "We should do this outside, no point in attracting more attention than we already have."

"Fat chance, there's no one in the dining room but the two of us."

"And we're wasting a gorgeous sunny day," El said. "Trust me, I've already been outside."

"Which explains why you were late for cappuccino."

"Look who's talking about me sounding like our mother," El countered. "*Andiamo*, let's go."

Damn, El got that right. Dear God, please don't let me turn into dear old mom, at least not now, in the prime of my life. I grabbed my purse and followed El out the door. After parking our sweet asses on the nearest bench, she pulled out her cell phone.

"Don't waste your time calling Nonnie," I said. "It's two in the morning there."

"Shoot, I keep forgetting." After dropping the phone back in her purse, she resurrected the little red notebook again. "Let's see now. What do we know so far?"

"Stefano Rosina had the hots for Clarita Fantino, who grew up faster than her friend Donata Abba, who had the hots for Stefano, who didn't give a rat's ass about Donata then but now he does."

"You make it sound so tawdry, Margo."

"*It's* called life, little sis. No different six-plus decades ago than in today's world."

"Except Stefano's messenger was found hanging from the rafters. Poor Tommi. His mother dies of a broken heart. His father goes ballistic and later dies under weird circumstances. Nonnie Clarita's father winds up dead—ugh. Her mother must've been a real bitch."

"Or so they say, make that Stefano says."

"You think Nonnie's mother may've had a heart after all?"

"Need I remind you of the many times my heart, or lack thereof, has been in question, not by me but by certain others, in particular, guys I may have dumped before they got around to dumping me. So-o, God must've … uh, might've blessed Bruna Fantino with some kind of heart, however shallow or confused or misunderstood."

"But what about Nonnie and Stefano? The woman could've shown some compassion toward two young lovers."

"Really, El. *The woman* had been recently widowed under horrific circumstances. Who can blame an angry lioness for protecting her violated cub? You do realize how young Clarita was—sixteen when the affair ended. Maybe Bruna figured Clarita needed a fresh start in America." The fine-tuned explanation I'd put so much effort into pontificating suddenly went south like flushed water swirling down one of Italy's premier toilets. Pay attention I wanted to tell El whose sleep-deprived eyes had drifted beyond my shoulder. I turned to see Filippo Sasso approaching us. Great, just what we needed. That is, if we played our cards right: a local escort for the day, one we didn't have to start with from scratch.

El and I stood to greet Filippo. We each leaned forward for a not-too-huggy Italian greeting, one I could live with and not be accused of stealing the man from his wife. After a brief discussion about how well we'd slept the night before and what a *bella* day it promised to be, I asked if, by any chance, he had some time to show us around.

"*Mia moglie* ... my wife, she spends this day with her mamma and pappa," he said with hand gestures punctuating his every word. "Whatever you want to see, I will show."

"Perhaps if we start with the cemetery," El said.

"A short walk from here," he said, having already taken the first step. "Come."

Along the way he pointed out several homes that might've sparked some interest had we been familiar with the owners' names. When we paused in the mini-tour so I could remove a pebble from my shoe, El told him about our going back to Donata's house the previous evening.

"Ah-h, is good she likes you. Me, she likes too. Donata not like everyone."

"What about Stefano?"

"Stefano Rosina was there too?" Filippo circled his thumb and forefinger. "Ah-h, *molto interessante*."

Very interesting, you bet. "Does Donata like Stefano?" I asked.

"*Si, molto, molto*, I think more like love. Does Stefano love Donata?

Maybe, but not as he once loved his wife. And before her, his first love. How you say, *l'amore della sua vita.*"

"The love of his life," I said.

"Si, but this you did not hear from me."

Having arrived at the cemetery, we took our time strolling up one aisle and down the other, intrigued by eight-foot-high marble walls containing the remains of generations of *Piemontesi* who once walked the streets of Pont Canavese and nearby villages.

"With land so precious, too much of it cannot be allotted to the dead," Filippo explained. "After so many years in the ground, we then move our beloved to the wall. This way is better to see them, better for them to see us."

Some of the walls were sectioned off for one or more families, with those deceased the longest installed closer to the top. Steel gates stretched across the individual crypts, as Filippo referred to them. Most were decorated with artificial floral arrangements. Filippo stopped in front of one crypt, opened the gate, and lifted one hand, placing it between the porcelain headshots of Lucca Sasso and Maria Bartolini Sasso. The man's hair was streaked with gray. His brooding eyes reminded me of Stefano's as a youth and those of the older adult I'd met the night before. Dark circles beneath the woman's eyes added years to her age. "My pappa, my mamma," Filippo said. "Say hello to the granddaughters of Clarita Fantino, Margo and Ellen … Elena."

I nudged El. We moved inside the crypt, placed one hand each next to Filippo's, and after a moment of silent respect, the three of us stepped back.

"Grazie," Filippo said, closing the gate. "Until the day Mamma died, she cooked and cleaned, always scrubbing a floor already clean. Pappa was eighteen years older but lived longer because he knew how to live. Six days a week he worked until sundown. At night he drank wine with his friends and played the ocarina. During the war—before Mamma—he became a respected *partigiano.*"

"You mean he fought with The Italian Resistance?" El asked.

"Si, as did many others. Some of them died. For Italy, a very bad war."

"You must be very proud of him," I said.

Filippo tapped a row of fingers to his heart. "If you stay long enough, I tell you the stories Pappa told me."

"We have time today," I said.

"For me, not so sure. First we see people in cemetery and talk of them. Is only right, si?"

We followed Filippo down another aisle of walled remains. Again, he stopped, this time in front of Vito Fantino and Bruna Coppa Fantino, who were situated near the top of one wall. Beneath them were names unfamiliar to me, perhaps part of their extended family.

"The mamma and pappa of your nonna," Filippo explained.

"A first for El and me, grazie." I wanted to run my fingers over their images but would've needed a ladder to get close enough. We stepped back for a better view and an impractical photo op. El held up her phone and took a few half-assed shots. No smiles from Vito or Bruna nor anyone else we'd seen at peace for a number of decades. As opposed to some of the more recently deceased still in the ground, some smiling for the camera as if they'd never intended on leaving this world for the next. El made the sign of the cross and pressed her opened palms together in prayer. Not to be outdone, I extended my right arm and blessed the remains of our great-grandparents.

"Tell us about Vito and Bruna Fantino," El said before I had a chance to speak up.

"As a young man, I knew Bruna well enough to fear her sharp tongue," Filippo said. "Vito was before my time. What I know of him came from the mouths of others."

"Not a problem," El said. "We'd still like to know anything you recall or may've been told."

Filippo told us what he'd heard about the mysterious deaths, a version similar to Stefano's, but then went on to include Lucca Sasso's perspective. "My pappa had great respect for Vito Fantino. He did not believe Vito would've killed the wrong boy for making love with Clarita. Nor would he have killed the right one—Stefano. Although Stefano was no longer a boy after he joined with the *partigiani*. In the way of war, boys become men before they are finished being boys."

"But Stefano just delivered messages for The Resistance," I said.

Filippo raised one eyebrow. "For which he could have been shot. Stefano did whatever the partigiani asked of him, same as my pappa."

"What about Vito Fantino?" I asked.

"Vito fought in the Italian army and almost lost his leg in Greece. Like many Italians, he hated Mussolini for siding with Hitler."

"Did your pappa ever say who might have killed Vito?"

"Only that it must have been someone Vito knew and perhaps trusted. Maybe an act of passion. Love or hate, both invite evil. Questions the police should've asked then but the Germans may not have considered important since they were in control."

Next stop, the Arnetti family, again high on the wall along with other family members. We stepped back so El could take individual shots of the parents, Cosimo and Aida. She lingered longer than necessary over Tommi's photo before clicking from several angles. Again, she crossed herself, lips moving in silent prayer.

"A handsome boy," she said. "And what a waste."

"Very sad," Filippo said, "even though their story ended before I came into the world."

"What about Donata's family?" I asked.

Before answering my question, Filippo answered his ringing phone. He listened more than he talked, all the while nodding. When the call ended, he apologized and said he needed to go home. "I will walk you back," he said. "Hotel is not far from my house."

El opened one hand, leaving the decision to me.

"Grazie, Filippo," I said. "But Elena and I prefer to stay a while longer. Not to worry, we will find our way back."

"Is sure?" he asked. "Then I go alone."

After directing us to Donata's family, he hurried down the aisle, leaving El and me on our own. I wouldn't have had it any other way.

The Abba, Bartolini, and Gavello families shared one crypt. Fairly new, which made me think the crypt may have been installed after the death of Donata's daughter, Rosa Gavello. El snapped more photos.

"For Nonnie," she said. "Before we leave Pont, remind me to get photos of Donata and Stefano and of all the people we've met."

"As in Pio," I couldn't resist saying.

"And Amadeo. Did I see him pinch you the other night?"

"Doesn't every guy? One more stop, and then we can leave."

After a careful retracing of aisles, we located members of the Rosina family, in particular Monica Ronchetti Rosina, wife of Stefano.

"Pretty," El said while focusing her camera phone. "But not as pretty as Nonnie."

"Which reminds me, have you ever seen a photo of Nonnie's husband?"

"Not a one," El said. "But I have to tell you, all this poking into Nonnie's past makes me feel like a shameless voyeur."

"Speak for yourself. I may've dragged my feet about coming here but I now consider myself a family historian."

"On a mission to bring justice to those who cannot speak for themselves. Thanks, Margo. I needed that."

∞∞∞

After leaving the cemetery, a quick stroll around the village brought us back to the hotel and our noonday meal. A mix of locals and obvious tourists filled the dining room, their cacophony of languages bouncing off one another, none of which came close to English. The bottle of wine we shared initiated a series of uncontrolled yawns so when El suggested an afternoon siesta, I couldn't think of a good reason to disagree. A nap in the middle of the day, give me a break. Such a luxury neither of us would have considered back home. What's more, I felt not one pang of guilt.

Four o'clock found us on a bench near our hotel and El again pulling out her cell phone. "Need I remind you about this call to Nonnie being your baby, not mine," I said. "Do not, I repeat, do not drag me into your conversation."

"And need I remind you, I am more than capable of handling this myself." While the phone was ringing, El turned on the speaker. On hearing the familiar *hello*, she said, "Nonnie! It's El again. And Margo."

Oh, yeah, El just had to drag me into this, in spite of my telling her otherwise. I poked her in the ribs before turning on my usual charm with a warm and fuzzy response. "Hi, Nonnie. Just so you know, this is not my idea. El insisted on calling you. I'm nothing more than an innocent bystander."

"Bystander, I don't get it. You're standing by her ... next to her ... or what? Take a load off and sit down so your feet don't get puffy. Your ankles too, men don't like fat ankles."

I pointed to the phone, mouthed the words, *go ahead*.

"Nonnie, it's Ellen again."

"What happened to Margo? Don't tell me she's sick."

"No, I just thought we could talk some more."

"So talk, it's not like I'm stopping you."

"You know I love you. Margo does too."

"Yeah, yeah, same here."

"How's Mom?" El asked.

"Like always, on the go. Get to the point, Ellen. I don't have all day."

"Er ... right. We wanted to ask you about Lucca Sasso." El gave me a thumbs-up.

"Everybody knew Lucca, him and that damn ocarina he played day and night."

"Would you consider him an honest man?" I asked.

"What kind of question is that? He fought with The Resistance. Isn't that enough? What do you want, a history lesson? This is costing you money and me time."

"Not to worry," El said. "Remember our telling you about Filippo?"

"Who the hell is Filippo?"

"Filippo Sasso," I said and continued in a precise manner, not wanting to consider the possibility of Nonnie suffering from short-term memory loss. Or long-term for that matter. "You know, the son of Lucca Sasso."

"Yeah, just playing with your head, Margo. What about Lucca's boy?"

"Filippo was kind enough to take us to the cemetery."

Silence, so deafening it hurt my ears. I was so on the verge of telling El to hang up but then she spoke up. "Nonnie, are you there?"

"Hell of a way to meet the family," she said. "You took pictures?"

"Lots of them," El said.

"Okay, you've met the family. You've seen the village. You're done. Time to move on."

"We met someone else," El said. "Stefano Rosina."

"Who?"

"You heard me: Stefano Rosina."

"Did I ... do I know him?"

Jeez, El. Give it a rest. I started to run my finger across my throat, her cue to shut up, but decided it would be beyond tacky, considering those deadly encounters in Cinque Terre, mine more so than El's. Although to be fair, I should give her some credit for contributing to my rescue. Jonathan too but him I so wanted to forget, at least for now. Enough, we needed to move forward. "Nonnie, it's me, Margo."

"Still on stand-by?"

"No, I ... we ... El and I need to talk with you about Stefano Rosina."

"Make it snappy. I'm due for my mid-morning constitution."

I took a deep breath and let the words spill from my mouth. "Stefano told us about the two of you, how you fell madly in love with each other. He told us about his friend Tommi, who supposedly hanged himself, a suspected suicide that really wasn't. He told us about the horrible way your father died. He told us about your mother, how mean she was to you and Stefano."

"Really? Well, let me tell you something, missy. You go back to this Stefano Rosina from long ago and give him a message from the Clarita

Fantino who used to be but is no more. Tell him as far as Clarita is concerned, Stefano Rosina can go straight to hell."

A click from Nonnie's phone ended the conversation.

"Well, missy, are you satisfied?" I asked El.

"Sort of, at least we know she's not carrying a torch for Stefano Rosina."

"Excuse me. Don't be so sure about that."

16
SPEAKING THE LANGUAGE

Margo had been right about Nonnie's smackdown of Stefano Rosina. Of course, I didn't admit this to Ms. Know-It-All. Instead I told her I needed a siesta before going out for the evening. More like some time alone to reflect on what I knew so far, not that Margo needed to know my every thought. Actually, she probably did know and needed her own time apart from me. She, on the other hand, did volunteer to track down Pio and enlist his help in our investigation. If that meant her turning on the Margo charm, and seducing the pants, as in jeans and briefs, off of Pio, more power to her. Having endured one holiday romance that ended on a sour note, I didn't have enough heart left to get involved in another.

This non-stop sisterly togetherness was getting out of hand. At a time such as this I could've used Jonathan or another guy on the order of Jonathan. Or Pio, or Amadeo. Not for myself, for Margo. Take your pick, Sis. Over the years her menagerie of this guy and that guy had served one essential purpose. They kept Margo and me away from each other, at least part of the time. So when we did get together, there'd be something new to talk about, new experiences to share since our last bout of togetherness had gone sour.

After the Florentine fiasco Margo and I had yet to reach the predictable sour stage, one I wanted to avoid until our return to the States. At which time we could go our separate ways until the next family holiday or family emergency or family disaster re-ignited the flame of our bond, demanding we behave like the loving Savino sisters our mother and nonna had always demanded of us.

Back at the hotel desk a message was waiting for me. From Pio, how nice … even nicer that he had written it in English, a decent cursive I read with no problem.

Can we dance again?
Or drink more wine?
Or both?
Please.
Amadeo and I will see
You and your sister
Tonight at nine.
Until then,
Pio

Friendship, no problem. Fun and flirting, no problem. I could deal with any of those. A sister more caring than I would've hurried out the door, tracked down Margo, and told her not to bother looking for Pio since we'd be seeing him and Amadeo later. But that's another problem with too much togetherness. Margo would've come back to the hotel with me. Or insisted I do another walk-around with her. My alone time would've evaporated like dust in the air, like the cloud settling over Pont Canavese had done earlier in the morning on my precious walk alone. So I hadn't done anything out of the ordinary then, or encountered anyone extraordinary. Margo and I were not connected at the hip and she didn't need to know my every move.

Later, more like early evening, I did meet up with Margo in the dining room for a four-course dinner, other than the light breakfast our only meal for the day, and unlike most Italians who preferred their main meal before two in the afternoon. "What are these?" Margo meant the white dice-sized cubes scattered around the antipasto platter sitting on our table. She popped a cube into her mouth, and gave it a satisfying chew before swallowing. "Not bad. I think I'll have another."

Knowing Margo, she would've eaten the entire batch if I hadn't grabbed a few for myself. Something about those morsels seemed familiar, like I should've known what I was eating but couldn't quite figure it out. The next time Ivanna passed by, I asked her about the last one left on our platter.

"*Lardo*," Ivanna said with a pinch to her belly and a snort from her nose. "From *animale*, sì?"

"Oh-h, lard, I should've guessed. We've been munching on cubes of pig fatback."

Margo gulped. A look of repulsion spread across her face. "Horrors of Beelzebub, we're going straight to hell."

"Perhaps when we get back to the states, you should check us into the Prima Donna Fat Farm."

"Get real, by then it'll be too late to repair the damage." Elbow on the table, Margo rubbed her eyes with the thumb and forefinger of one hand before she finally spoke. "Lardo, who'd've thought. Oh, well, it wasn't half bad, in fact, quite good."

"Which explains why you gorged yourself. On the plus side, pardon my pun, how about dancing off those extra calories later tonight?" I showed her Pio's message.

After a quick glance Margo shoved his note in my direction. "You could've said something before now. How long have you had this?"

"Don't get so touchy. The desk clerk handed it to me this afternoon. You'd already gone out."

"Whatever," Margo said. "But I, for one, am in no mood for another ride into the night."

"We don't have to dance. We could drink wine and pry information out of Pio."

"Hmm … a possibility if there's anything worth to pry from an empty head. Those unexplained deaths occurred decades before Pio was born. You and I too, which means we must be vigilant yet keep an open mind. I don't know about you but I'm starting to obsess about the Fantino name and what happened to Nonnie and her family those many years ago."

∞∞∞∞

Dusk had turned to dark while we waited outside the hotel. After the church bells ended their nine o'clock peal, Margo folded her arms and began tapping her foot. Ten minutes later I'd reached my limit and told her to knock it off. Another ten minutes passed before Pio and Amadeo arrived on their Vespas. They hopped off and walked toward us, only to have Margo greet them with a pouty face and lukewarm hug. Unlike my enthusiastic version, color me the forgiving kind.

I turned and spoke to her in a low voice. "Isn't tardiness the Italian way?"

"Maybe, but it's not the Margo way," she said. "It's one thing for me to be late but I don't like to be kept waiting."

"Is my fault," Amadeo said with a slight bow. "Mamma fell earlier today. Pappa took her to the *ospedale* … the hospital."

"Wait a minute," Margo said with a slight flair of one nostril. "Your English has improved considerably since the first time we met."

"Si, but only if I have something worthwhile to say."

An exchange such as this was not going to end well so I made it mine. "About your mamma, I hope it's nothing serious."

"A broken foot, a sprained wrist, painful, si, but she is home again."

"Good grief," Margo said in a tone more forgiving. "You didn't have to leave your mamma on our account."

"No problem, Pappa will look after Mamma."

Pio patted Amadeo's shoulder, and said, "Filippo is a good man."

"A good husband," Amadeo replied, "and a good pappa, I could not ask for more."

Margo and I looked at each other and spoke as one. "Filippo Sasso?"

"Si," Pio replied. "I thought you knew."

"Pio!" I said. "How would we know if you or Amadeo didn't tell us?"

"Mi dispiace. Here in Pont we forget that foreigners do not know what we know."

"Pio and I are cousins," Amadeo said with a grin, "more like brothers."

"Why didn't I think of that," Margo said. "And how are you cousins?"

Amadeo paused to gather his thoughts in English. "My mamma's zio … her uncle … married Pio's mamma. Sadly, both are now dead."

Pio crossed himself. "So, do you want the wine and dance? Or do you want the wine and talk?"

"Perhaps a quiet place for wine and talk," I said.

"Quiet I cannot promise," Pio said. "But I know a nice place not far from here. Is better we walk."

"Lead the way." The tone in Margo's voice had changed to a definite upbeat. I do believe my sister was revving herself up for an evening of interrogation, of squeezing any tidbit from Pio and now Amadeo.

The guys took us to a crowded trattoria near Piazza Craveri. As we passed by the bar, Pio waved to the bartender and ordered a bottle of the local wine. As soon as the waitress brought our order, Amadeo said something to her in Italian; probably that he'd take it from there because she backed off. One by one he filled and passed, the first glass to Margo, the second to me, and the third to Pio. After Amadeo had filled his, we all clicked with a "Salute!" One sip and one more, then Margo and I got down to business.

"We spent the morning with your pappa," Margo said, patting her lips. "He walked us around the cemetery."

"This I did not know," Amadeo said. "Nor did I tell him or my ... mother about me knowing the Savino sisters from America."

"Oh, dear, I hope we didn't embarrass you." Margo being Margo again, this time fishing for a compliment.

"No, no," Amadeo said. "Even though we are currently occupying the same house, I do not tell my parents everything. Yet, they always seem to find out. So, what did you think of our cemetery?"

"A great lesson in the local history," I said. "Filippo told us his father had been with The Resistance."

"Si, Lucca Sasso became a hero during the war, a partigiano who did not marry until years later. This I know not only from him but from others who lived during that time, many who have since died. My ... how you say ... my grandfather, my nonno was a legend, one who lived a long and healthy life. Never did the man stop talking, not until he took his last breath. His great pride was being part of the execution squad that shot Mussolini, although no one knows this for sure. Sometimes is best not to take credit unless ... unless ... help me out, Pio."

"Unless you are prepared for the consequences," Pio said.

"Si, grazie. What I mean is: revenge comes in many ways and from those we least suspect—the neighbor, the neighbor's brother who lives in the next village."

"Really," Margo said, "even after the passing of many years?"

"Not in my nonno's later years but certainly during the war and for a time after the war."

"What about our great-grandfather, Vito Fantino?" I asked. "He fought in Greece, got shot up and was sent home."

Amadeo nodded. "Si, si, Nonno Sasso often spoke of Vito Fantino."

"You know how Vito Fantino died?" Pio asked.

"Only what Stefano Rosina told us." I repeated Stefano's version, that is, the part about the hook embedded in Vito's heart, while Pio and Amadeo drank their wine and listened.

"We were wondering if you had anything to add," Margo said.

"You want to know what my nonno told me," Amadeo said. "Everything?"

"Everything," I repeated. "And don't be concerned about our feelings."

"No, no, no." Amadeo shook his forefinger at me. "First you must tell us *everything* Stefano told you."

"I'm not sure what you mean."

"Sure you do. Every story has a beginning," Pio said. "For Stefano's story, you only told us the end. We are not fools."

"Then you know about the young boy Tommi," Margo said.

"The suicide that was not a suicide," Amadeo said.

"And Stefano's romance?" Margo asked.

"Maybe so, maybe not."

"With our Nonnie Clarita," I said.

"Is that what he told you?"

"A tragedy for all concerned," I said, "Tommi and his family, Vito and his family, Stefano, of course. Did we leave anybody out?"

"Hmm." Amadeo ran a hand through his hair . "I tell you what I know, with help from Pio since his English is better than mine."

"Not always," Pio said. "Just so you know, I was not there when Lucca Sasso told Amadeo what Amadeo will now tell you."

"At the time Nonno Sasso was already older than the finest wine in all of Pont," Amadeo said. "But no older than Stefano Rosina is now."

17
THROUGH THE EYES OF LUCCA SASSO

And in the words of his grandson Amadeo Sasso

Since Lucca Sasso did not marry until later in life, he took a special interest in his godson Stefano Rosina, who had lost his own pappa at an early age. Stefano was no more than fourteen when Lucca brought him into the partigiani and from there, The Resistance. Young, yes, but Stefano was eager to learn, eager to do whatever the partigiani asked of him. The partigiani valued loyalty. They stood united as one and were determined to bring Mussolini to his knees for entering Italy into a shameful alliance with that monster Hitler. Because of Lucca, Stefano already knew how to shoot a rifle, as did most boys growing up in the foothills of the Alps. Lucca taught him to hunt rabbits and deer and cinghiale. But hunting a man, killing him to keep him from killing others, took special training and did not always require a gun. Guns make noise. Noise is not good when silence can save even more lives.

Stefano grew tall and took on the appearance of a young man, developed the feelings of a young man. He saw the village girls as young women. This is the nature of life as it should've been. But this was also in the time of war, and war forces young people to grow up faster than they otherwise would have. Although Pont produced many pretty girls then as now, Stefano focused his eyes on only one. When he first started working for The Resistance with Lucca, Stefano talked about many girls but the only thing he said about the rebellious Clarita was how she constantly challenged her domineering mamma.

Tommi Arnetti, on the other hand, did not seem interested in any village girl. Ah-h, but for Stefano Rosina, Tommi's eyes told a much different story. They followed Stefano's every move. Stefano took advantage of what he perceived as Tommi's loyalty, perhaps his infatuation, and convinced Tommi to deliver a series of notes for him. This Lucca knew from Stefano because he often told Stefano what to write although he did not see the final words. Nor did he know the notes were meant for Clarita Fantino, the young daughter of his good friend and partigiano sympathizer.

Clarita, being inexperienced in the ways of young stallions, thought Tommi had written the notes since they came to her unsigned. Now, Tommi was good-looking to a fault, with curly hair the color of straw and a smile that rarely left his face. Note after note Lucca helped Stefano write, all of which Tommi insisted the girl refused to answer. Stefano told Lucca he could stand it no more; he waited until dark and went to the girl's house.

Stefano stood in the shadows, on the chance she might come outside since in his notes that was what he had asked of her. After half an hour had passed, he was preparing to leave when he noticed Tommi approaching from the other direction, along with his dog, Nerone. Odd, Stefano thought since he'd not given Tommi a note to deliver for several days. Then, Clarita came out of her house, went down to the stable and opened the door. Tommi followed her inside, as if he'd done this many times before. Seeing what Stefano perceived as a betrayal made his head pound with rage. He threw up the wine souring in his stomach. Then tossed the polenta and rabbit, which Nerone ate with relish, plus some pieces of cooked meat Stefano always carried in his pocket. Whatever it took to fend off wild and domesticated animals. He fumed for another twenty minutes before Tommi left the stable and headed into the foggy night, unaware Stefano was following in the shadows.

Stefano waited until the next bend in the road before he stuck two fingers in his mouth and whistled as only he could. On hearing the distinctive sound, Tommi stopped but did not turn around. As soon as Stefano came face to face with Tommi, he wrapped one arm around Tommi's midsection and with the other, wrapped his fingers around the collar of Tommi's jacket. He lifted Tommi off of the ground and shook him like a rag doll, calling him a *bastardo* and a lying cheat for coming between him and Clarita. That's when Nerone went on the attack, pushing Tommi aside and knocking Stefano down before ripping into his chest. Tommi pulled Nerone from Stefano and helped him to his feet. When Tommi saw blood seeping through Stefano's shredded shirt, he begged his friend's forgiveness and asked for a chance to explain.

Tommi told Stefano that Clarita thought he, Tommi, had written the notes. 'And thought the words so perfect she allowed me to kiss her,' Tommi said. 'It was my first kiss and her first. After that I could not stay away from her. Hit me if you must. Make a fool of me to all of Pont. None of this will matter to me. I did not think it possible to love any girl the way I love her.'

Tommi's words set Stefano's head into another fierce pounding. Head held between his hands, he projected a silent scream only he could hear, so deafening his ears started ringing. More than anything he wanted to first kill Nerone, then break Tommi's face, flatten his nose across both cheeks. Instead he took a deep breath, tucked the remains of his shirt into his trousers, and said in a calm voice, 'Loving Clarita I can understand but did you *make love to her*?'

Stefano watched Tommi's face turn white against the gray fog. 'Not yet,' Tommi said. 'She is still … a virgin.'

Stefano asked how Tommie knew this and Tommi said because she told him. 'You spoke of such things with her?' Stefano yelled. He stuck his face in Tommi's. When Nerone growled, Stefano backed away, and said, 'Stay away from her, Tommi. Or else I will first take Nerone's head and then twist your scrawny neck until it pops.'

Amadeo paused. He took a deep breath and released it. "All of this Stefano Rosina relayed to Lucca Sasso the next evening. Only then did Lucca learn the girl's name. He ordered Stefano to stay away from Clarita but Stefano refused."

"Are you saying Stefano has been living a lie all these years?" I asked. "That he was responsible for Tommi's death?"

"Is not my place to say and every story has more than one side. I only tell you what my nonno told me and I'd never known him to tell a single lie."

"But he was quite old when he told you," Margo said.

"As I said before, not much older than Stefano Rosina is now. And yet you choose to believe Stefano's words over those of Lucca Sasso."

"I didn't say that." Margo said. "Nor did Stefano bring up the conflict with Tommi."

"It's all so confusing," I said. "I think we should talk with Nonnie Clarita."

"You've spoken to her about this before?" Pio asked.

"Not really," Margo said. "We think Nonnie might be in denial ... what I'm trying to say is—"

"Your nonna no longer remembers the past," Pio said.

"More likely, refuses to talk about it."

"Who can blame her," Amadeo said. "She made a new life in America. Stefano stayed in Italy. Some tragic events are better left to history."

"My Nonna Donata remembers the smallest of details," Pio said. "Or so she says. But I've noticed her stories change with the seasons and with certain cycles of the moon."

18
NONNIE CLARITA

Our evening with Pio and Amadeo ended around midnight, with nothing more than a friendly round of cheek-to-cheek kisses in front of the hotel. Perfect from my perspective although Margo might not have agreed.

"Next time we should dance," Amadeo said with a grin. "I like dancing better than talking."

"In Italy some people like sex better than dancing or talking," Pio said with a wink.

Margo laughed as only she could. "It's the same in America."

The best I could come up with was, "Watch it, Pio. We're practically cousins."

"Practically is not the same as blood-related. So, you are safe with me and I am safe with you, si?"

"Let's shelve the safety issues for another time." I faked a yawn, my mind already elsewhere.

"Well, I for one would love another night of dancing." Margo made an imaginary phone with her pinky and thumb, held it to her ear. "You have my number."

"Si," Amadeo said. "I have your number."

Pio held the door open while Margo and I walked into the hotel. "Stick to the plan," I whispered to her. "And don't you dare turn around."

"Please, what do you take me for?"

Never mind, I wasn't going there, not tonight. Instead, I suggested we call Nonnie.

"You took the words out of my mouth," Margo said. "But this time we take things nice and easy. Focus on one topic and not overwhelm her. It's about five in the afternoon St. Louis time."

"Your room?" I asked on entering the elevator.

"My room but you make the call."

∞∞∞

"Hi, Nonnie," I started out on the speaker phone. "It's me, Ellen. Margo's here too."

"Too bad your mom's not here. I'll tell her you called. Good—"

"No, no. Don't hang up. Margo and I want to talk to you."

"Again, good Lord, Ellen. We've talked more in the last two days than in the past two months before you left for Italy. No … make that four months. Yeah, four months, not that I miss you girls; I got my own life you know. It's not like I'm holed up in this immaculate, not-one-thing-out-of-place house night and day with nothing to do but watch TV. And even that's not as good as it used to be."

"Nonnie, you know we love you," I said.

"At least I'm not crocheting. Dear God, how I hated those damn crocheting sessions with the nuns. These fingers of mine were made for better things. Like sewing, dressmaking I mean. If it hadn't been for my little shop, your mom and me, we would've been on welfare."

"Hi, Nonnie, it's me, Margo."

"I figured as much. Get this, Margo: I'm thinking about taking up smoking again, which would give me a reason for going to Rudi's, you know that nice bar a few blocks over where you used to hang out."

"Only on certain occasions," Margo said, "and always with a date."

"Yeah, sure ... whatever. Anyway I could walk to Rudi's. Park myself on a stool, light up, and order a nice glass of Chianti. Or, maybe Barolo."

"I doubt Rudi carries Barolo," Margo said. "Not at those outrageous prices."

"You're not telling me anything I don't already know."

I poked Margo and motioned for her to move along.

Message received, maybe too loud and too clear since Margo raised her voice a few decibels. "Uh, Nonnie, would you mind if we discussed your social life after we get home?"

"No problem. Speaking of, I gotta go."

"No, no, don't do that," I said. "Actually, we called for a reason. About Lucca Sasso, just how well do you remember him?"

The other end went silent.

"Nonnie, are you there?" Margo asked.

"Where else but ... I'm thinking." More silence while Margo and I waited. "As I recall, he married late to someone much younger. Kind of mousey she was. You know the type, right El?"

Margo gave me a smarmy smile; I gave her a raspberry. "Not exactly, Nonnie," I said. "Go ahead."

"Lucca, Lucca, the man had a mouth that wouldn't give up. Yakkity yak, yakkity yak, but in public only about run-of-the-mill things; Lucca was no dummy. He also knew when to keep his trap shut."

"Would you consider him a truthful man?"

"Truthful, honest, what next and how should I know? It's not like Lucca and I were best friends. The man was old enough to be my father. He did get along with my mother, which is saying a lot. Pappa too, maybe pappa more so since they talked about politics and the war. Hitler and Mussolini and their kind, evil *bastardi* they hated more than anything else."

"There's something I need to ask you," I said, "and please don't hang up."

"That depends. Give it to me straight."

"And you give me a straight answer, okay?"

"About as straight as any answer you ever gave me." She executed a yawn loud enough to cross the Atlantic on its own. "Make it snappy, Ellen. My bedtime's around the corner."

Good grief. That sounded way too familiar, on the order of me with Pio. Turning into my mother was bad enough but my nonna, please.

"It's only five-thirty in St. Louis." Margo said.

And no time to challenge Nonnie's lame excuses. "About Tommi Arnetti," I said. "Did you have a teenage fling with him?"

Silence, again. I braced myself for the inevitable click from the other end, followed by a dial tone.

"Nonnie, are you there?" Margo asked. "You know there's nothing you've ever done that could be worse than anything I've ever done. I told you things I would never have told Mom. Even to this day."

Really, Margo told Nonnie those dirty little secrets capable of turning my face fifty shades of red?

"You're talking long ago and far away, at least from where I now sit," Nonnie said. "Why in God's name would you want to know what I've spent a lifetime trying to forget?"

"Because we don't think Tommi killed himself," Margo said.

"Neither did anyone else. So what's your point?"

"Nor do we think your father killed Tommi."

"Nonnie, are you still with us?" I asked.

"Pappa was a good man," she said with a catch in her voice. "He didn't deserve to die the way he did."

"So-o, since El and I are here in Pont, we want to find out who killed Tommi and your father."

"As if anybody cares in today's world."

"We do and you do," I said. "Which is all that really matters."

"Speak for yourself, Ellen. No one knows what I think or care about."

"Sorry, Nonnie, sometimes El gets carried away. Anyway, back to Tommi. By any chance did you … er, uh … have an affair with him? You know, as in … sleep with him."

"That depends on your definition of sleep, as the saying goes. It's not like he climbed into my bed with my parents in the same house. We were both young and naïve, Tommi more so than me. Or maybe it was the other way around, God only knows. To this day just thinking about him pains me, such a sweet boy."

"Then you did have sex with him," Margo said, to which I sucked in my breath.

"Whoa," Nonnie said. "Why don't you say what you're really thinking? I'd have to give some thought to that. Whatever went on between us … like I said, happened a long time ago."

"And Stefano Rosina?" I asked.

"So we're back to Stefano again."

"Please, don't make us beg," Margo said. "Or believe only what Stefano said because we haven't heard your side."

"Stefano was another story. Stefano and I might've loved each other. At least I think I loved him. Yeah, I suppose I did. Or maybe there came a time when I hated him more than I loved him. Or, maybe I hated him after I loved him."

"Tell us what happened between you and Stefano and Tommi."

"Slow down, you're throwing too much at me. I gotta think this through. Call back tomorrow morning, around ten, after your mom's gone."

A quick calculation gave me five in the evening, Italy time.

"How is Mom?" Margo asked.

"Doing her thing, I guess, just like always. You know your mom. One minute she's a saint; the next minute, the bride of Frankenstein. Make that widow even though your dad didn't have an ounce of monster blood in him. In fact, he was the most okay guy I've ever known."

19
FRANCO ROSINA

The next morning neither El nor I had much to say while we sipped our steaming *cappuccini* in the hotel dining room. Things looked up when Ivanna brought a basket of assorted breads and packaged cheeses. "You again," I said with a laugh. "Don't you ever go home?"

"This my home," Ivanna said, motioning downward with her forefinger. I pictured a room next to the furnace. She pulled a folded note from her apron pocket and handed to me. "From Franco," she added before moving on to the next table.

El wrinkled her brow. "Do we know a Franco?"

I squeezed my eyes shut and circled one forefinger around my temple. "Hmm, let me think … Franco, Franco. Franco Rosina, Stefano's son, would be my guess." I opened my eyes and then the note, giving it a quick glance. "An invitation to join him for lunch, he'll meet us outside the hotel at noon."

"Do we have other plans?" El asked with a grin.

"Other than hanging out in the piazza with locals we don't know but who know us, no."

"I wonder if he'll come alone," El said. "Or if he'll bring Stefano."

"Stefano we could do without. I wonder where Franco will take us."

∞∞∞∞

Franco Rosina arrived promptly at noon, on foot and accompanied by bells chiming from the nearby church. As with our first meeting, instead of the usual hugs, he held out his hand for a friendly shake, and said, "I was not sure you would agree to my invitation."

"It was very kind of you," El said, to which I agreed with a smile.

"If you please, we will walk. Is not far from here."

His interpretation of *not far* may've been somewhat relative but what the hell, if it meant a good meal awaited us, who was I to balk. Taking the same route El and I had walked with Filippo Sasso, we now hurried to keep up with Franco Rosina who was proving himself a man of few words. After we crossed the bridge and then the main road, Franco slowed down as we approached the cemetery.

"No need to stop," I said between a huff and a puff. "We've already fulfilled our cemetery duty."

"Si, this I know," Franco said.

"Why am I not surprised? In a village this small news travels fast."

"Is the same in America, is it not?" He didn't wait for an answer. "One visit to the cemetery may not be enough. Perhaps another time."

"Maybe," El said. "Depending on how long we stay."

"Whatever you are looking for may take longer than a few days."

"Just what is it we're looking for?" I asked.

Franco answered with no answer. Another time for grave gazing seemed a reasonable alternative since my stomach was hell-bent on sending me undeniable pangs of hunger. What was it with this food obsession in Italy; back in St. Louis, I could go all day without thinking about my next meal. That is, unless my next meal involved one hot guy with deep pockets and an upscale restaurant followed by a luscious skin-on-skin dessert. That next meal would not be this one.

We walked a while longer, passing a number of houses clustered in groups of four or more, which Franco explained were occupied by several generations of the same family. Nice or not so nice, depending on whether the inhabitants were still speaking to each other. The neighborhood in which El and I grew up consisted of Italian-Americans who originated from Southern Italy and tended to be wound tighter than those from the North. Or so I thought before coming to Pont and learning about my own family.

Franco slowed his pace and turned down a side road. It led to a cul-de-sac containing eight or nine structures with clay-tiled roofs, single and multi-family homes, most of which had been updated. To my relief and that of my feet, he stopped in front of the first property, a single-family dwelling with two levels of stucco exterior and below those, what once had been a stable.

"My house," Franco said, motioning to it. "Is not so old, I think no more than two hundred and sixty years. Please to come inside with me."

"Your wife will be going to lunch with us?" El asked.

Way to go, sis. Even I had this one figured out.

"No wife, just me," Franco said with a face registering no emotion. "Like my pappa, I too lost my wife some years ago. Not to worry, however. Although I like to eat, I do not bite ... my friends. Cooking for friends and new acquaintances gives me pleasure. And them, I hope."

"Oh, then we're eating in," I said.

"Is a problem?" Franco wrinkled his brow.

"Not at all," El replied. "We're flattered to be counted among your favored group. Right, Margo?"

"Absolutely. Thank you, Franco."

Manly best described Franco's place, with its walls made of polished knotty pine and a furniture mix of old and modern, an open plan encompassing the living, dining, and kitchen area. *Cucino di Franco*, though compact, presented as modern a kitchen as any I'd seen in middle-class America. Red enameled cabinetry, a five-burner gas range, what more could any home cook have wanted. Not that I put myself in such an unobtainable, undesirable category. Thanks but no thanks, not after the devastating spaghetti fiasco I'd experienced during my recent stay in Florence.

Franco's kitchen countertop was lined with a variety of tomatoes—oddly-shaped pinkish red, hardball-sized intense red, and deep maroon bordering on black. Also green, yellow, and red peppers, perfect. And, yes, a full-size fridge topped by a decent freezer. Freezer, as in ice cubes, hopefully an endless supply. I licked my lips. Ice, oh yes, give me lots of ice covered with water or coke or Italian soda. The very thought of ice had elevated me to Italian heaven.

"Please to sit," Franco said. He gestured to the sleek contemporary chairs surrounding a dark wood table, its uneven top worn and dented from generations of serious use. Four place mats were positioned at either end and on the sides where El and I now sat. I was tempted to ask if Franco had invited anyone else but didn't want to hear him say his father. Or, if I had asked, did not want Franco to feel pressured into inviting Stefano. Instead I played it safe and kept my mouth shut.

As with any respectable Italian host, Franco opened a bottle of red wine, filled three goblets, and initiated the usual salute. After one quick sip he said, "Your mother, she is good?"

"You know our mother?" El asked.

A warm smile crept across Franco's thin lips. "From long ago when she came here, 1973, I think. It would've been impossible not to know her." He paused. "This I do not mean as an insult. Nor to ... how you say ... to disparage her. I was eighteen, she was eighteen. And prettier than any cinema star I had ever seen. But never did she flaunt her beauty. When she walked down the streets of Pont Canavese, every head turned. All the young men wanted to be around her and that made all the young women jealous."

Our mother, really? The uptight, anal-retentive Antonia Riva Savino, I found it hard to believe Franco's words, just as I'd found it hard to believe his father's. Good grief, surely the son of Stefano Rosina hadn't messed around with the daughter of Clarita Fantino ... our mother who never messed up; or if she had, would never have admitted it. One glance at El told me what she might've been thinking—perhaps recalling Mom's quick temper or her never-ending demand for perfection.

As for our host Franco Rosina, I could not resist asking, "Did you take her out, you know, date her?"

He measured his words before speaking. "She stayed in Pont about two months. We did ... how you say ... fun things together."

"Such as?" El asked.

"*Scusi*," he said. "You must be feeling the hunger."

What timing and how true. Franco went to the kitchen area and started prepping while El and I watched from a safe distance, as in one requiring no intervention. After slicing half a loaf of bread, he brought the slices to the table and spread them out on the extra mat he moved to the center. Way to go and halleluiah, there'd only be the three of us eating. He opened a can of tuna packed in olive oil and emptied the entire contents into a bowl, then sharpened his knife and wiped it clean. He chopped a few tomatoes and peppers into bite-size pieces, added them to the tuna, and splashed everything with more olive oil, the juice of a lemon, salt, a few grinds of fresh pepper, and fresh herbs. How easy was that? Easy enough for me to forget by tomorrow morning. He divided his easier-than easy creation onto three plates and set them on the table mats.

"With bubbles or *naturale*?" he asked, referring to the bottled water.

"*Naturale*," I said. "For El and me."

"Lots of ice, si," he said with a grin. After taking care of our icy water, Franco surprised me by blessing his antipasto with the sign of the cross. "*Mangiamo*," he said with a flourish of one hand before sitting down.

Ah-h, the ice water, it tasted almost as good as a dish so simple even El could've prepared it. Rather than appear too bossy, I instead said, "When we get home, El, check out any restaurants serving … this … uh, dish."

El stiffened her back, same as Mom would've done. "Really, do I look like your personal assistant?"

"I teach if you like," Franco said.

"Absolutely," I replied, grateful for the kind rescue. "Before we go back, how nice of you to offer."

After two bites, El put down her fork. She sipped some wine, followed up with water, and then asked, "Were there other young men … or boys … besides you?"

Franco thought a minute. He tore off a chunk of bread, used it to soak up the miniature puddle of olive oil lingering on his plate. "Is hard to say, she had things to do, same as me."

"And what did the two of you do together?" El asked.

"Perhaps you should ask your mother."

Not going to happen, at least not via long-distance phone. "I'm asking you, Franco," El said. "You must've invited us here for a reason."

He scooted his chair back and started to get up. "Is time I prepare the *primo*—the pasta."

"Sit, Franco. And for now, forget the pasta. Or else Margo and I are leaving."

"That's right," I said, backing up El. "Tell us everything now or we are so out of here."

Having lost all interest in the antipasto on my plate or the promise of pasta yet to come, I poured more wine into Franco's glass, then El's and mine.

"How much my pappa told you I do not know," Franco said. "But let me say this: I did not find Bruna Fantino as wicked as Pappa believed her to be. She possessed a good heart some of the time. But not all of the time, although who among us does."

"What a relief," I said. "One can only hope others will think as kindly of me after I hang up my Jimmy Choos for the last time."

"Your Jimmy what?" Franco lifted his shoulders. "Sorry, my English is not so good."

"Margo, please." El gave me the prim look of her convent days. "Let Franco continue."

"Si, before my memory grows colder than it already is. Unlike that of my pappa who recalls every significant detail of his life, or so he tells me."

"Whatever involves our family, we want to know," El said. "However painful hearing it may be to us."

"No one lives a long life without knowing pain," Franco said. "Bruna Fantino, she needed the ears of true family more than those of her neighbors. Unfortunately, the only family she had left was the daughter who had been living in America since the late forties when Bruna sent her away."

"And why did Bruna send Clarita away?" I asked.

"That is a question only Clarita can answer in today's world. As for Bruna, sometimes voices speak from the grave or in other ways when we least expect them. Now do you want my story? If so, you must listen and not interrupt."

"Sorry, please continue."

"Grazie, Margo."

While Franco paused to gather his thoughts, I took another sip of his irresistible wine, as did El, not that either of us needed an excuse. Okay, maybe not El, who'd shown her usual restrain, but my eyelids were fighting with each other to stay open. Had Franco suggested a nap instead of a walk back in time, I'd have agreed in a St. Louis minute. Instead, I could only hope whatever he had to say would make me forget about the yawn I so wanted to deliver. Discipline, if only I had El's. She reached over, put one hand on Franco's, and urged him to continue.

20
TONI RIVA

According to Franco, in 1973 Bruna Fantino sent a letter to her daughter in America, insisting she come home for a long visit. Clarita, a self-employed widow, could not afford the loss of income so she agreed to send her daughter instead. These family details Franco learned from Filippo Sasso on their way to the train station in *la macchina*, the automobile Filippo had borrowed from his pappa Lucca. It was a summer day that felt more like early spring even though droplets of sweat had fallen from Filippo's brow and stained the collar of his shirt.

Filippo made a hard shift into the Fiat's first gear and said, 'Since Bruna Fantino considers my pappa her convenient savior, she expects me to look after the American *nipote*. An impossible demand, you know how jealous Nora gets when I so much as glance at another girl.'

Franco gave him a playful poke to the arm. 'Come on, a smart guy like you can work things out.'

Filippo pleaded as only he could. 'Not when it comes to Nora, I need your help.'

Franco looked from El to me. He tapped the fingers of one hand against his chest. "*My help*, you have to understand. I loved Filippo like a brother, helped him out in the past, but this time he'd gone too far. Me, Franco Rosina, only son of Stefano Rosina, Stefano who despised Bruna Fantino as much as she despised him, looking out for the daughter of Clarita Fantino,

Stefano's lost love that Bruna had sent away years before, all this because Filippo did not have the courage to speak up and just ... say ... no. I told Filippo that Bruna would kill me when she found out who I was. And then after killing me, she'd have my pappa thrown in jail for giving me the life he had forced her to destroy."

"You opened up Pandora's Box," I said. "Let all the demons out."

And so he did.

After pulling into the railroad station, Filippo told Franco to relax. 'Bruna does not need to know every little detail of her nipote's free time,' he went on to say while parking the car. 'Besides, I can pay you.'

Money ... the very mention of it was enough to convince Franco. He shook Filippo's hand after Filippo stuffed his with lire, enough to equal one hundred American dollars, at the time a small fortune for both of them. After getting out of the car, they waited on the platform until the train came into view. As soon as it stopped, the door opened and out flew a leather shoulder bag, landing at Franco's feet. Only one passenger followed that bag onto the platform.

"Mamma mia, never had I seen an American such as this," Franco told El and me. He gave us a detailed picture of this daughter of Bruna Fantino's daughter, how she looked like no other young woman in Pont or Cuorgnè or the villages in either direction. Dark hair fell below her shoulders and was secured by a piece of cloth around her forehead. She wore flared pants low on the curve of her hips and a yellow tee shirt as bright as the sun peeking out from behind the clouds, as if the sun's only reason for being there was to spread its light on her. Those eyes—blue with amber specks. Lips painted a soft pink. Around her neck hung a long gold chain and from the chain a jeweled crucifix, as if warding off any guy harboring impure thoughts.

Filippo welcomed her in better English than Franco had expected but not as good as his. The daughter of Clarita's daughter put one hand on her hip and said, 'You must be Fil.'

He replied with a slight bow. '*Filippo* Sasso, here at the request of Bruna Fantino.'

Her blue eyes narrowed as she spoke her next words. 'Right ... Fil. And my name, as I'm sure you already know, is Antonia Riva but I answer to Toni.' She turned to Franco. 'And you are?'

He told her his given name but for her, an *Americana*, he would answer to Frank. She cocked her head to one side. 'What? No last name?'

After swallowing the lump in his throat, he managed to say, 'My name is Franco ... Franco Rosina.' The hard slap he expected from her did not cross his face. Instead, a sweet laughter erupted from her mouth, followed by words tumbling out too fast for him to understand. 'Please to speak slowly,' he said. 'My English is not so good.'

She picked up her bag and slung it over her shoulder. 'If you say so. Shall we go?'

Filippo did not move. 'Pardon,' he said. 'First we must explain.'

Not *we*, Franco told us. He let Filippo do the talking. That much Filippo owed him, and the lire already tucked in his pocket. After Filippo finished connecting Franco to his father Stefano and Stefano to Toni's mother Clarita and Clarita's mother Bruna to Stefano, Toni cocked her head for a second time and looked from Filippo to Franco before she spoke. 'So how is this supposed to work?'

Filippo cleared his throat and swallowed whatever words had been stuck in it. A few seconds passed before he brought them up to say, 'Perhaps you have some ideas, Toni Riva. But if you must speak American, slow down so we can understand you.'

'Right,' Toni said. 'So let me see if I've got this straight. You, Fil, picked the one guy with a last name I've never heard before today—a name my grandma supposedly despises—and I'm supposed to let him be my pretend boyfriend so your girlfriend won't get jealous.'

Filippo hung his head. He kicked a stone from the platform and said nothing. So Franco found the courage to say, 'Is a problem, si, but not to worry. We—Filippo and me—will think of something.'

Toni rolled her eyes. 'No, you won't. I am perfectly capable of finding my own friends. But thanks anyway.' She put one hand over her mouth and held back a yawn. 'Can we go now? I am so wiped out.'

Franco described how Filippo's face turned red as a *pomodoro*, he meant tomato. Filippo yanked on his shirt collar like it was a rope around the neck of a condemned man. 'But … but … your nonna,' he said.

Toni took Filippo's face between her hands and kissed him on the lips, to his horror and at the time, to Franco's envy. 'Don't you worry about Granny,' she said, 'I'll take care of her.'

Really? Our straight-arrow, anal retentive mom, a one-time brazen hippy, or at least dressed like one and acting like one, who would've thought. Certainly not her clueless daughters. El grabbed the wine; she emptied the contents into our three glasses.

"Please forgive our boldness," I told Franco, my comment putting a smile on his face as he uncorked another bottle. Ready to go at a moment's notice.

He raised his yet-to-be-emptied glass and said, "I did not think it possible for Toni or anyone else to take care of her *granny,* a word I'd only heard for the first time and quickly figured out."

To appease Filippo and to uphold his end of an unrealistic bargain, Franco accompanied him and Toni to Bruna Fantino's house. He remained in the car while Filippo walked Toni to the entrance. As soon as Bruna opened the door and saw Toni, she released a flood of tears that surprised Franco, considering her reputation as a woman who never cried, a peculiarity in the alpine foothills where a woman without tears was rarer than a morning without fog.

Later that day Franco returned the money Filippo had paid him at the station, which only seemed fair and reaffirmed their friendship of many years. Three days passed before his next meeting with Filippo. Again Filippo pressed the lire into his palm. And told Franco that Bruna Fantino wanted to meet him at her house. Just Franco, not Filippo.

Franco's knees were shaking when he knocked on Bruna Fantino's door, not out of fear but in anticipation of seeing Toni Riva again. To his surprise it was Toni who opened the door and winked when he asked permission to enter. 'Only because my nonna insists,' she said, allowing him inside.

There sat Bruna, in a chair as rigid as her back. She did not stand but motioned for Franco to sit across from her and Toni next to her. Two against one, so far Franco felt he had done nothing wrong. 'We will speak in Piemontese,' Bruna said, already using the dialect Franco had learned as a young child. She gestured toward Toni. 'Even though the nipote may not understand every word.'

Toni smiled and said, 'Love you, Granny.'

Bruna pressed two fingers to her lips, a nice way of telling Toni to be quiet. To Franco she said, 'You are the son of Stefano Rosina, si?'

He told her yes, and dared to add that Stefano Rosina was a good father. Bruna curled her lip, reminding him of a wolf protecting its young. 'Basta!' she said. 'I did not invite you here to argue the merits of a man who ruined my life and that of my family.'

Franco started to speak. Bruna showed him her upright palm. 'Antonia, the daughter of my daughter, has come all the way from America to take care of me, against my wishes because now I must take care of her as well as myself. Even though God has punished me for living too long and every bone in my body cries out for the mercy it seldom receives, I must allow myself some solitude, a morsel of time away from Antonia. She has begged to stay with me every hour of every day but an act that selfish on my part would surely be considered a terrible sin.'

Toni wiped the single tear rolling down her cheek. She patted her heart and then her nonna's hand as the old woman spoke again. 'Filippo Sasso has explained his affair of the heart, one I find ridiculous but must respect because I am a right and just person. At Filippo's encouragement, several young men have stopped by to meet Antonia. But I fear for her … I mean their … ability to behave in a manner that would not bring shame to our good name. What more could I do, other than weep and pray for God to take me now. Then someone, whose name I do not recall, mentioned the son of Stefano Rosina, a name Antonia abhorred, having already heard it from … others.'

Bruna leaned over and wagged her finger in Franco's direction. 'Of course, Antonio rejected you; but I, in my infinite wisdom, have now convinced her otherwise. So, Franco Rosina, I now ask if a lowly person such as yourself would relieve me of Antonia's presence for a few hours each day so I might find some peace in what little time I have left?'

Franco's heart was beating so fast he feared it would leap from his chest. The lump that had returned to his throat prevented him from speaking. This was not the case with Toni. 'Just say no,' she said in a matter-of-fact way. 'Don't be such a wimp.'

Wimp, never had Franco heard the word before but from her tone did not mistake its meaning. He stood up and bowed slightly but stopped short of genuflecting. 'It would be my pleasure, Signora Fantino, whatever I can do to ease your burden.'

Bruna made a guttural sound and said, 'Sit down, you fool.'

Franco lowered himself into the chair, only then realizing Bruna did not want him towering over her. She leaned across the space separating them and said, 'Never are you to refer to my nipote as a burden, mine or yours. And if you so much as lay one finger on Antonia, or disrespect her in anyway, I will place a curse on you, one so extreme it will follow you to your grave, which is what I should have done to the evil one who led my Clarita astray.'

Of course Franco agreed to Bruna's conditions. They did not seem unreasonable at the time. 'Go now," she said. 'And take Antonia with you. A nice walk through Pont should satisfy the villagers, let them know Bruna Fantino forgives from the heart of a gentle woman.' She remained seated while Toni kissed her cheeks and Franco stood by, confident Bruna would not expect the same from him.

As soon as Franco walked into the sun-drenched day with Toni, he thought about taking her arm in his but decided not to because of Bruna's warning. 'You are so lucky,' Toni said as they distanced themselves from the Fantino house. 'The guys Fil sent around could barely speak English and didn't appeal to me so I convinced Granny that the mere thought of you made me want to toss my cookies.'

Franco stopped and opened his palms, a gesture he would frequently employ during their times together. 'Toss your cookies,' he said. 'I do not understand.'

Toni gave him a look of annoyance. 'Why does this not surprise me? You're here, aren't you? With me, aren't you? That's all you need to understand. So, where are we going?'

They started walking again and Franco asked if she'd like to see the cemetery, the graves of her relatives. He did not mention the manner in which her nonno had died. She stuck out her tongue, made a *pernacchio*, and said, 'Ugh! You have got to be kidding. Do I look like a cemetery junkie?' She stopped and pulled out a pack of cigarettes from her handbag. 'What I *am* dying for is a smoke.'

Franco told her not on the street; her nonna would not approve. Nor in a bar, not that there was anything wrong with the bars in Pont. He waited for another *pernacchio* but instead felt her breath on his face. She leaned in closer and before he had a chance to step back, she pressed her lips to his cheek, not to his lips as she'd done with Filippo at the station. 'Stop with the excuses,' she said. 'You're such a sweet guy.'

This time he did step away from her and got as far as to say, 'Your nonna—'

'Would not approve,' Toni said. 'But the old gal's not here. She put you in charge, a huge mistake on her part because I have a problem following orders, *capice?*'

'Not exactly,' he said, wiping the sweat forming on his brow. 'You are speaking too fast for me again.'

Toni laughed, showing him a mouthful of teeth better than her nonna's and many of the girls he knew. She told him not to worry since a cool guy like him would soon catch on. *Him* a cool guy, he did not want to disappoint Toni, which would've meant disappointing Bruna. About the possibility of a curse, he could not decide.

Instead of going to one of Pont's many bars, they spent an hour or so walking around the village. Along the way he introduced Toni to every villager they encountered. Without further explanation, the villagers already knew she was related to Bruna Fantino, the only daughter of her only daughter. Those who recalled Clarita Fantino asked about her, in Italian, of course, with Franco translating their questions into English. After the third translation, Toni answered for herself. '*Bene, bene,*' she said, meaning her mother was fine. 'Enough is enough,' she said after the fifth person to inquire had moved on. 'Is there someplace quiet we can go?'

Going to Franco's house was not possible since he lived with his father. She asked about Filippo's house, or as she called him, Fil. Did she have to ask? Franco did not like where this might be headed. He told her Filippo lived with his parents and they both worked. And that Fil worked at night, same as he did. 'Perfect,' she said. 'Fil should've crawled out of bed by now, and I need to give these puppies a rest.'

Puppies, he did not understand until she explained her feet were killing her. The cobblestones, they took getting used to, although in this matter Toni may've been wiser than her years. So many of older woman were hobbled by the impractical shoes they insisted on wearing.

El poked me, a pointy elbow-jab to the ribs. "Did you hear that, Margo? Franco knows what he's talking about."

I moved the half-empty glass sitting in front of El. "As do I, little sis. You have surpassed your daily intake of wine."

She waved a shaky hand in Franco's direction. "So … so … sorry for Margo's rude interruption."

"No problem," Franco said. "Perhaps my story does not interest you."

"On the contrary," I replied. "El and I are here and we want to hear."

"Good," Franco said. "It pleases me to continue."

When Toni and Franco arrived at Filippo's house, they found him standing on a ladder, cleaning the windows. He climbed down, invited them to enter, and opened a bottle of wine. Toni only wanted a little. She drank that little and asked for more because the walk had made her thirsty. She lifted her glass to Filippo and said, 'Thanks for sending all the wrong guys to meet me. Not one of them passed Granny's evil eye.'

Franco asked if it was the eye Bruna might use to put a curse on him. 'Not to worry,' she said. 'Granny wouldn't hurt a fly, let along the son of … what is your father's name, I keep forgetting.'

Forget his father's name, Franco did not think so. Still he played along. 'Stefano, Stefano Rosina. Your mother never talked about him?'

Toni made a face, as if deep in thought. 'Not that I recall,' she said. 'I really should meet this Stefano. You can make it happen, can't you?' He started to bring up her nonna again but Toni silenced him with a press of two fingers, to his lips not hers, just the opposite of what Bruna had done earlier. 'Shh, do not make me repeat myself,' she said.

Two days passed before he called on Toni again, one day too many according to Bruna Fantino, who claimed she could not tolerate Antonia's unreasonable demands much longer. What those demands were, Bruna did not say. Instead, she grabbed her broom and swept the two of them out the door along with a trace of dust.

Franco apologized to Toni as they walked down the road. 'I did not realize your nonna expected me to entertain you every day.'

Toni stopped. 'You have a problem with the entertaining? Just say the word and I'll find a new friend, one who won't mind being seen with me.'

He said he would be honored to take her anywhere, as long as her nonna approved. Toni responded by punching him in the arm. In a playful way, by then they were growing more comfortable with each other. 'How many times must I tell you," she said with a shake of her finger. 'Forget about Granny. Now, on to more important things—do you have a car?'

Franco told her his father allowed him to use his macchina. 'Terrific,' she said. 'Then take me to meet this guy my mother never talks about. And if he lets you borrow his car, take me down a road I've never been down before.' He explained the complications of her request, how the village crones would be watching their every move and report back to Bruna Fantino. 'As if I care,' she said. 'If you won't take me, I'll find my own way there. So, what's it gonna be, Franco?'

Disappointing Toni was not an option so Franco walked her to Filippo's house, along the way explaining that the macchina they had used at the train station belonged to Filippo's pappa, not his. As things turned out, it was Filippo's pappa who met them at the door, Filippo's pappa who invited them inside. When Franco introduced Toni to the legendary Lucca Sasso, she hesitated before offering her hand to shake. Lucca took her hand in his, also hesitating before he kissed it, a gesture which surprised both Toni and Franco.

Lucca had married late, a man now in his seventies but powerfully built. His eyes wandered over Toni's face, stopped at her eyes when he asked, 'Your mamma, she is good?'

Toni removed her hand from his. 'Is good, yes, but she works too damn hard.'

Lucca's eyes closed for a moment. 'As did Clarita's pappa, her mamma too,' he said. 'If Clarita desires a long life, she must take the time to play even harder.'

'My mother makes her own rules,' Toni said. 'She doesn't listen to me or anyone else.'

He smiled. 'Clarita never listened. Tell her Lucca Sasso sends his love.'

Franco explained that Toni would like to meet Stefano Rosina since she'd not heard of him before coming to Pont. 'Humph,' Lucca said. 'Get in the macchina. I take you now.'

With a lift of her brow Toni said, 'I suppose this means you're not afraid of Granny, my nonna.'

Lucca grunted as only he could. 'Me afraid of Bruna Fantino? Is more like the other way around, and don't you forget it. *Andiamo*, let's go.'

On the drive to the house Franco shared with his pappa, an uncomfortable silence filled Lucca's macchina, the only sounds coming from Lucca grumbling as he shifted into gear, grumbling when he circled up and down the hills, or grumbling when he slowed down for pedestrians. More drama Franco did not need and wherever Lucca went, he always brought drama with him.

By the time Lucca pulled into the driveway, Franco had decided not to invite him inside. Too late, Lucca had already turned off the ignition and opened his car door before Toni and Franco had opened theirs.

Stefano Rosina met them at the door, first hugging his godfather Lucca and then hugging Franco harder, even though they'd gone through this same routine earlier in the day when Franco left. Although they'd not discussed Clarita's daughter before, Franco knew Stefano must've heard about him escorting her around Pont. When he introduced Toni, Stefano shook the hand she offered but did not kiss it as Lucca had done. He did, however, take more time with her face, starting with the pouty lips and from there the refined nose, his blue eyes peering into the depths of hers, as if trying to capture the very essence of her soul. The connection unraveled when Lucca expelled a weird snort through his nose, giving Toni an excuse to turn her head.

Stefano gestured for everyone to sit at the table. Toni declined the wine he offered, an insult Franco did not think she understood. But that did not stop Stefano from filling a glass for Franco and Lucca and one for himself. Lucca took the bottle and poured one for Toni. At that point Stefano asked if she knew about him and her mamma.

Toni took a sip of wine and wrinkled her nose before answering. 'Only what I've been told since coming here, and not from Granny … Nonna Bruna. She does not allow your name to be spoken in her house.'

Stefano and Lucca grunted as one although only Stefano spoke. 'But she does allow you to see the son of Stefano Rosina.'

'Granny thinks I hate Franco,' Toni said. Then Stefano asked her what she thought of Franco. Toni glanced in his direction, the look on her face revealing *niente* ... nothing. The few words she spoke reeked with indifference. 'He's okay.'

'Okay?' Stefano narrowed his eyes and raised his voice. 'No son of Stefano Rosina is just okay.'

Toni's eyes never left his when she said, 'Oh really? Well, let me put it this way and in no uncertain terms. I, Toni Riva, will not be making the same mistake with the okay son of Stefano Rosina that my mom made with his less-than-okay daddy.'

'What happened between Clarita and me was no mistake,' Stefano said.

Toni leaned across the table to where Stefano sat. 'Excuse me, I beg to differ and am happy to do so. It's a good thing my mom left Italy, a good thing she went to America. Otherwise, she wouldn't have met my father and I wouldn't be having this conversation with you now.'

The expression on Stefano's face did not change although Franco noticed a slight tremor on one hand accompany his next words. 'Your pappa is a good man?'

Toni leaned back and relaxed the anger in her face. '*Was* a good man, a banker or so I've been told. He died before I was born.'

Stefano lifted his brow in a way Franco knew all too well. Already he regretted bringing Toni to meet his pappa. 'I know what you're thinking,' she said. 'Don't say it or I'm leaving.'

'Is not for me to question,' Stefano said. 'My wife died ten years ago, leaving me to raise Franco on my own. Not one day goes by that I do not think of her, or of Clarita Fantino.'

'Hmm, that does seem rather odd,' Toni said. 'My mother never talks about Stefano Rosina.'

'But she does think about me, of that I have no doubt.'

Toni shrugged. 'I wouldn't know since I'm not a mind reader.'

Having downed more than his share of wine, Lucca Sasso seized the moment as only he could. Spit flew from his mouth when he spoke. 'Nor do I read minds, little girl, but I knew Clarita and Stefano back then, when they were younger than you are now but not as spoiled as you. In fact, not at all spoiled. They had seen death up close and the devastation of war. Si, they were passionate and foolish and made regrettable mistakes, but no one goes through what they did without being left with wounds never meant to heal.'

Toni hesitated before speaking her next words. 'For the record I am *not* spoiled. But I am tough, which comes from living with a mother who's even tougher.'

Stefano responded by pouring more wine, and Toni lifted her glass to him before drinking its contents. After listening to the clock ticking for a few minutes, Franco pushed his chair back, hoping Toni would do the same but she had not finished with his pappa. 'So, about this great romance you and my mother supposedly had, I'd like to hear more.'

Stefano shook his head. 'I got nothing more to say. Franco already told you what I told him.'

'Which amounted to a big, fat zero,' Toni fired back.

Not wanting the discussion to turn any uglier, Franco suggested they leave before her nonna started to worry. Toni checked her watch and said they hadn't been gone long enough. Still, he persisted. 'But if your nonna finds out where you've been, I do not think she will allow me to see you again.'

'Franco, my friend, you are so naïve,' Toni said with a laugh. 'Don't you get it? I'm here because Granny wanted me to meet the man who destroyed her family.'

Naturally, Stefano had to defend himself. 'What happened long ago I leave to history and when I meet God on Judgment Day," he said. 'You seem happy with the way things turned out, but I do not think you should take up any more of my son's time.'

Toni's eyes flashed. She ran her tongue over lips drawn into a thin line. 'Just tell me this,' she said through gritted teeth, 'which one did you kill: that boy or my grandfather? Or did you kill both of them?'

It was not the first time Stefano had been asked these questions. He clenched one angry hand into a tight fist and slammed it onto the table, causing the bottle to topple over and spill what little wine remained. 'Neither Tommi Arnetti or Vito Fantino died by my hand,' he said. 'This I swear on my mamma's grave. You should go now, Antonia Riva. Tell

Bruna Fantino what I told you. And tell Clarita that Stefano Rosina sends his love, now and forever.'

Franco sighed. "So there you have my story. After the meeting ended in such anger, Toni and I did not speak of Stefano Rosina again. Nor did I speak to Pappa about Toni Riva. Although I ignored his comment about not seeing Toni again, I did not allow her to enter my heart. Nor did we kiss in any way other than as friends.

"On the day Toni left for America, I accompanied her to the train station, this time with Lucca Sasso behaving in a sane manner behind the wheel of his automobile. Standing on the platform, Toni and I parted as friends, both wiser than when we first met.

"As for Lucca, whatever parting words he whispered in Toni's ear, I did not hear, but to this day I can still picture the tears Lucca's words brought to her eyes."

21
HOUSE TOUR

"Oh, Franco," I said, wiping away a few of my own tears. "Thank you for sharing those recollections of our mother."

"And of her grandmother," El said. "Our mom certainly has changed over the years."

"As have I," Franco said. "But never will I forget our summer together. Aside from losing her husband—I'm sorry, Pappa told me—has life been good for Toni?"

"You're looking at her greatest achievements," I said.

"Si, you have your mother's … humor and Elena has her—"

"Intellect," El said before I could.

"And both of you, her beauty."

"Stefano Rosina thinks otherwise," I said.

"Pappa did not know Toni as I did, an unfortunate situation I regret to this day. Is there anything else you would like to know?"

"One thing for sure," El said. "Where the Fantino family lived."

"Might as well go for broke," I chimed in. "If at all possible, we'd like to walk through their house and the stable. Really get a feel for what the place was like when Nonnie Clarita lived there with her parents, and later when our mother came to visit."

"Is not a problem," Franco said. "In fact, a pleasure. We are sitting in what once was the house of your nonna and her parents."

"What? No way." The irritation in my voice came through loud and clear, one I made no effort to hide.

"Why didn't you mention this before now?" El asked, more like demanded.

Franco's cheeks turned red. His shoulders fell into a droop. "Mi dispiace, it was not my intention to mislead either of you. Nor, would I have let you leave without revealing the history of my home."

Naturally, I backpedaled with a sincere apology.

To which El added, "Please forgive us, Franco. Our coming to Pont has evolved into an emotional rollercoaster, one we didn't expect."

"Rollercoaster, this word I understand but not in the context of which you speak. No apologies, please, just allow me to continue."

"So … never mind. Please explain how you acquired the Fantino property."

"With pleasure," Franco said with obvious relief. "After Bruna Fantino died, Clarita expressed no interest in returning to Pont so she put her parents' property for sale. For an amount most villagers would not have paid, which is why Clarita finally sold it to me at a lower price, after much negotiating back and forth. In the end I think we were both satisfied with what I paid. From money my pappa lent me and I have since repaid.

"While looking for the right girl to marry, I added indoor plumbing to the bathrooms, one on each floor. I found love and then renovated the kitchen and lounge, whatever it took to please my new bride. Years later after she left this world and our daughter moved to Torino, I renovated *la cucina* again." He paused before continuing with a grin, "This time to please myself. The rest of the house has not changed for many years, or so the neighbors have told me. Not since before the war when your nonna lived here. Do you have time to see it now?"

"By all means," I said. "Please show us everything."

"Even what once was the stable?"

"Especially the stable," El said. "Isn't that where Nonnie's father died under such horrible circumstances?"

"Si, and you still wish to see it?"

"More than ever," she said. "Please, lead the way."

El and I followed Franco up one flight of narrow marble stairs. "Watch the last step," he said, "is easy to trip over." He opened one door to the ceramic-tiled bathroom, its main feature a large tub with jets. "For my sore muscles," he said with a stretch of his arms. "Do you have this in America?"

"Both sore muscles and jet tubs," I said, "but no jet tub at home."

"The two of you live together?" he asked.

"No way," El said with a laugh. "I would have to kill Margo before she killed me."

"You make a joke, si? Although I have known of brothers who hated each other enough to kill. But not your nonna's pappa, if that's what you're thinking. To my knowledge, Vito Fantino had no brothers, at least none buried around here."

We followed Franco to the next room, its door already open. "Where I sleep, usually alone unless I get lonely," he said. "Then I invite someone to spend the night. Is the same for you?"

Since he was looking at me, I said, "Why, Franco, I do believe you're flirting."

He answered with the red face I'd seen before. "It was not my intention, Margo. Nor do I think it would be appropriate under the circumstances."

"Under what circumstances?" I asked but got no answer.

"Dear God, not another May-December," I heard El mumble under a breath from which she quickly recovered, and then asked. "So, where did Clarita sleep?"

A few more steps brought us to her room. El and I went inside. We walked around, fingertips touching the plastered walls as if hoping to glean something from Nonnie's past.

"This furniture came with the house," Franco explained from his position in the hall. "But the mattress we bought new when our daughter was a little girl. Is only right, si?"

"Absolutely," I said. "Every girl needs to start out with her very own mattress. Mine get such a workout, I buy new every five years."

"Margo!"

"Only kidding, El. Look, I made Franco blush." Again, how sweet, a confirmation of the long-ago friendship between Franco and Mom, who obviously wasn't sweet when he knew her then. Nor would she be considered sweet in today's world. On the other hand, *sweet* didn't exactly describe me either. While Franco shifted from one foot to the other, I ran my hand across the oak dresser, gazed into the beveled mirror, and thought about the Clarita from long ago, looking into the same mirror, while El from today looked out the window, probably thinking the same thing.

"Was anything left behind that might interest us?" El asked.

"A box of photographs," Franco said. "Some letters tied with a ribbon, a few pieces of jewelry. Memories I did not feel right about examining or throwing away or giving to Pappa—out of respect for my mamma and the life they shared. But for the daughters of Toni Riva, I would be happy to pass on what rightfully belongs to the Fantino family."

"You would?" I surprised Franco with a kiss to his cheek that made him blush again. "How positively, excruciatingly wonderful and most generous of you to make this gesture on behalf of El and me. Oh, and for our mother Toni and her mother Clarita."

"Please, Margo. Not so fast. I do not understand a word you said."

"She means *yes*," El said. "We will take the photographs and the letters and the jewelry. And anything else we can carry with us. But first, may we see the stable?"

"But of course. Please to follow."

The stable still contained its original floor, two centuries of soil patted, smoothed, and worn down from constant use to create a surface as durable as some modern flooring. Damp, yes, but damp was to be expected. Damp gave the floor character. It spoke of generations past. The foundation walls were made of the same stone used in the exterior of the main house, and around the perimeter of those walls, a ledge deep enough to sit on with room to spare. We walked every inch of the stable, with El stretching her neck or bending over as if searching for a particular item, which finally occurred to me what she wanted to see.

"Can I help you find something?" Franco asked.

"Do you have a hook for baling hay?" El asked.

"Ah, the *balla gancio*, for that I have no need. Nor do I collect tools for show or morbid curiosity."

Now El blushed but for a different reason. "Please don't relate our interest to morbid curiosity. To most people Vito Fantino may be a distant memory, a name on the cemetery wall no one visits anymore, but to Margo and me he is still our great-grandfather."

"My apologies," Franco said with a slight bow. "Having come all this way, of course you would want to make a connection with the people you never knew and how they lived. He removed a scythe hanging on the wall, placed it on the work bench, and from the drawer underneath pulled out a sharpening stone and hammer like none I'd seen before. "This came with the house," Franco said, "a tool your *bisnonno* … your great-grandfather would've used to cut hay in the field. If you like, I can demonstrate how he would've sharpened the blade."

"Perhaps another time." El put her hand on Franco's arm, a light touch but nevertheless a stretch for one who rarely initiated personal contact—that is, before the Cinque Terre portion of our Italian adventure. "Margo and I need to know the details of his death. Any chance we could see the police archives?"

"This I cannot promise; however, I will make some inquiries." Franco heaved his shoulders, no doubt wishing he could rid himself of the Savino Sisters.

I looked around the stable and noticed no trace of the obvious. "What? No cows?"

"Those I got rid of years ago," Franco said. "Ah-h, but I do have chickens, enough to give me fresh eggs every day and then some. Come, I will show you."

We walked down a few rugged steps and from there into the sunshine of a penned area. El's head bobbed to the rhythm of the forefinger she used for pointing. "I count six hens."

"Make that seven and no rooster," Franco said. "Him I ate last week after the neighbors complained about the early morning crowing."

"How early?" El asked.

Franco held up four fingers. "Four in the morning, he had to go."

"And so do we," I said. "Could we have the photos and other things? Better yet, perhaps we should come back with our car."

"Not a problem," Franco said. "I will drive you back to the hotel, along with the promised treasures."

"Before we go, is there anything else around here that might interest us?" El asked.

"Perhaps the house of Tommaso Arnetti. Is not far from here."

"By all means, please take us to the Arnetti house."

∞∞∞

I assumed my usual shotgun position and El climbed into the back seat, taking with her the box of treasures that was bigger than I'd imagined. Than El had imagined too. Already she was sneaking a peek at first one thing and then another while Franco backed out of the driveway. His home, our ancestral home, had taken on a whole new meaning for El and me. As for our host Franco, I could've planted a big fat kiss on him. However, it didn't take rocket science to sense his desire to avoid close contact with me. Oh, well, can't win them all. Or, at this rate, any in Italy other than Amadeo.

Franco turned onto the main road, turned left and left again at the next side road, passing four attached dwellings before stopping at the first of two detached houses, some distance apart and each with a stable located below. "Where Tommaso lived with his parents," Franco said.

"Do you know the people who live here now?" El asked.

"Distant relatives of the Arnetti family who make their home in Bologna," Franco said. "They use this place as a summer residence but as yet I have not seen them this year."

"I don't suppose there's a chance of our going inside," I said.

"Not without first asking. Is the same in America, si?"

"The same," El said. "Please excuse our impertinence. There's so much to see and so little time."

"Not to worry, American sisters. Tomorrow I will make a phone call and request permission."

∞∞∞

As soon as we returned to the hotel, we took the elevator up to my room. El and I made ourselves comfortable on the bed, sorting through Nonnie's box of treasured possessions. I untied the ribbon securing a dozen or so letters, and flipped through the pages of neatly written words, all signed by Stefano Rosina. Unfortunately, they were written in Italian and although I could've done a half-way decent job of translating his words, I didn't want to take the time to do so, at least not then.

"Maybe we should return these to Nonnie without knowing what they say," El said. "Somehow it doesn't seem right ... reading her letters while she's still alive."

I agreed, unusual for me where El was concerned. "Let's wait and see how much we can find out on our own. Although ... one phrase keeps repeating itself in some of the later letters. *Perdonatemi per piacere.* It means *please forgive me.*"

There were a number of black and white photos, again Nonnie would have to go through them. One copper bracelet, hand-crafted to perfection. A narrow gold band, no inscription inside.

"What the ...." El said, holding up the wrapper from a US government issue Hersey's chocolate bar. "There has to be a story behind this." She placed the wrapper back in the box, making sure nothing prevented it from staying flat. Two journals, their red covers inscribed with the name Clarita Fantino in faded gold lettering, were written in the small, perfectly formed cursive I recognized as Nonnie's. More personal than Stefano's letters, Nonnie's words still belonged to her, not her nosey granddaughters. El returned Nonnie's journals to the box.

She opened a gray photo folder, stared at its contents for a minute or so and without saying a word, passed the folder on to me. Not what I had expected but so endearing, this charcoal drawing of a young, dark-haired and dreamy-eyed couple. Side-by-side profiles of them gazing somewhere beyond the artist's rendition. A second drawing sat under the first, this of the couple kneeling face-to-face. Not a stitch of clothes on either one and wrapped in a tight embrace, they were kissing with such passion, just looking at them gave me goosebumps.

More to the point, whatever would've possessed them to pose in a manner bordering on erotica? A closer look at the lower right corner of each sketch revealed the artist's singular name—Serina.

22
CLARITA AND TOMMI

"You brought Nonnie's journals to breakfast?" El asked with a raised brow after she sat down.

"Ever tried reading foreign-language handwriting under a 40-watt light bulb at midnight?" I countered, grateful for the natural light filtering through the dining room curtains.

As if on cue, Ivanna presented El a steaming cup of cappuccino and El nodded her thanks. While Ivanna refreshed our bread basket, El moved her gaze from my blood-shot eyes to Nonnie's journals and back to my eyes. Mission accomplished; she'd made me squirm. "I know, El. We agreed to return the journals to Nonnie unread but I thought there might be some clue to those horrible deaths from her past."

"And you a paralegal. Ever heard of incriminating evidence," El said. "Don't even think about showing her words to anyone here in Pont."

Before I had a chance to respond, our morning light went dim, blocked by the figure of a man looming over us.

"Pio!" El said with a lilt in her voice. She patted the empty chair next to her. "Please, join us for coffee."

He rubbed his flat stomach, giving me a conjured-up image of six-pack abs under the tight T-shirt.

"Grazie, but already I have had the double espresso my nonna prepares for me each morning." Pio moved his gaze from El to me and back to El, far more welcoming than the disapproving one El had given me moments before. He went on to say, "I thought the two of you would enjoy a walk through the *mercato*."

"The market, of course we would," I answered for both of us. "Right, El?"

"Absolutely." What else could she say? After all, we had nothing going on until late afternoon and another phone call to Nonnie. I stood up, Nonnie's journals pressed to my chest. "Be back in a jif," I said.

Pio raised an eyebrow. "Jif? This I do not understand."

"Jif means right away," El said.

"Ah-h," Pio said, eyeing the journals or my boobs or perhaps both sets. "The books, they look like something my nonna would keep."

"Our Nonnie Clarita's journals," El said, "from long ago."

Really, El, why not tell the whole village. Talk about incriminating evidence, the need to protect Nonnie's privacy. Pio or no Pio, he wasn't owed the Savino Sisters or their nonna a damn thing. I gave El my if-looks-could-kill stare-down. And then hurried back to my room where I placed the journals back in Nonnie's box of treasures. When I returned to the dining room, Ivanna was clearing our table. On seeing me, she gestured toward the outside, where I found El and Pio waiting.

The alpine morning smacked me in the face with its bright sun and promise of the warmest day we'd yet to experience since leaving Cinque Terre. Pio led the way, sandwiched like a yummy slice of Italian marinated beef between the likes of El and me. After a short walk we wound up at the one place in Pont that El and I knew better than any other—Piazza Craveri where we'd encountered Filippo Sasso on two different occasions.

On market day the piazza presented a much different ambiance, with row after row of canopy-covered booths displaying the everyday necessities of life—pots, pans, kitchen essentials, curtains, linens, clothing, hardware, tools, and garden seeds among others. Shoes, I picked up one pair and then another, none of which lived up to my expectations. "Not all Italian shoes are created equal," I explained to El while she shuffled through those I had rejected and others I wouldn't have insulted my feet by holding in my hands.

"Humph." She handed me an okay pair of open-toed clogs. "These will have to do. I will not have you wearing my shoes one more day."

Rather than argue with her, I slipped my bare feet into her selection, wiggled my toes into place, and wound up buying them, vowing never to be seen in the damn things when we returned home.

We continued to wander among the shoppers, a mix of young mothers pushing strollers and middle-aged women lugging canvas shopping bags, along with older men and women who knew exactly what they wanted. I picked up a ravioli cutter with fluted edges, gripped the handle, and made a few motions with my wrist.

"Don't," El said, "unless it's a gift for one of your chef friends."

"I don't have any chef friends."

"My point exactly."

"Nonna Donata has a drawer full of these," Pio said. "She will be happy to give one to each of you."

"Pio, how sweet of you but no thanks," I said with an awkward smile.

After returning the cutter to its rightful place, I moved on to the clothes racks and ran my hands along the small sizes. No designer gems here, nor anything I couldn't live without. Snippets of conversations drifted in and out of my ears—a mix of standard Italian, most of which I understood, and the Piemontese dialect, some of which I'd picked up from Nonna Clarita. As had El.

"Did you hear what that woman said?" El whispered to me.

Pio overheard El and laughed. "She wants me to marry her daughter."

"And what do you want?" I asked.

"My freedom, at least for a few more years."

Pio's freedom, with Donata Abba watching his every move. Good luck with that. On the other hand, she did take care of his cooking, his cleaning, his laundry, his housing, and possibly matchmaking when she would deem the time to be right. Maybe life for the unattached Italian guy wasn't such a bad deal after all. Across and one aisle to the left I spied a familiar face and poked El. "Look, isn't that Ivanna's sister."

"Sasha," El said. "Do you know her, Pio?"

"*Si, un po,*" he said, demonstrating *how little*, a quarter of an inch space between his thumb and forefinger.

A second glance in Sasha's direction made me take a third. "Is that your nonna waving at us?"

"Ah, so it is. We must say hello or she will be offended."

Of course, mustn't offend Donata Abba. El and I followed Pio to where Donata stood and greeted her in the usual way. And would've greeted Sasha too had she not already disappeared into the crowd.

"You must visit me again," Donata said. "This evening at seven."

"Grazie," I said, "but we already have plans." Okay, that may've been a stretch but El and I would think of something.

As had Donata. "Then I will see you tomorrow at seven."

"But, Nonna," Pio said, "tomorrow evening I will be working."

"*Si,* you do not have to remind me." She turned to walk away and from over her shoulder she said, "Show *le sorelle* my favorite part of the mercato."

Whatever Nonna wanted. After following Pio to the fresh produce, El and I oohed and aahed over leeks and fennel, gigantic yellow and red peppers, tomatoes the size of softballs, some with deep ridges reminding me of miniature pumpkins. Wheels of cheese, prosciutto in small display cases, salami sold whole or by the slice, such an assortment made me want to buy what the locals were buying.

"Do either of you fish?" Pio asked.

"Only for compliments," I said with a smile.

Pio didn't get it. Nor did I expect he would. "Come," he said, grabbing El's hand. I followed behind, thinking *this had better be good.*

Our dad had been a fisherman, one who kept what he caught, and cleaned his catch before bringing it home. A nasty business I was okay watching as a kid as long as no hands-on participation was required of me. El, on the other hand, didn't mind helping out if Dad was in a hurry. He would've loved the fish-cleaning station Pio brought us to observe.

A smiling fish monger stood behind his waist-high stainless steel table containing a machine, maybe twice the size of a breadbox and also made of stainless steel. From one end he put a whole fish inside the container, pressed a button, and waited a minute or so until a bell rang. From the other end he removed the cleaned fish—minus it scales and guts. How sweet was that?

Sweeter than my mouth, for sure. It felt like cotton and my lips were parched. I couldn't decide if I needed a cold beer or a good nap. One look at El told me she must've been thinking the same thing. Pio pressed a finger to El's cheek.

"*Una birra fredda*, perhaps?" he asked. "You, too, Margo. Come, I know just the place."

You bet, around the corner from the market. A cold beer plus pizza margherita, it just didn't get any better than chunky tomatoes, stringy mozzarella cheese, and fresh basil baked over a thin dough until it turned golden brown and crusty. After that, naptime back at the hotel.

∞∞∞

That afternoon at five o'clock and not one minute sooner, I initiated the highly anticipated call to Nonnie Clarita, ten in the morning St. Louis time. El and I had already agreed not to mention the box of treasures Franco had given us the day before. Those would be our gift to her when we returned to St. Louis. Her gift to us would be explaining why she had held on to certain items and then left them behind.

"Need I remind you to stay on topic," El warned while I located the number on my phone and placed the call. "Do not give Nonnie any excuse whatsoever to let her mind wander."

"Look who's talking, Sister Almost-A-Nun who couldn't concentrate on her prayers."

With that, the ringing stopped and Nonnie answered with a brisk, "Make it snappy. I don't have all day."

"Nonnie, hi! It's me, Margo. Ellen's here too. You'll never guess where we went yesterday."

"If you have one ounce of common sense, Lake Como, and hopefully, you're still there."

"Of course not," I said. "We're still in Pont and having so much fun we may never leave."

"Your nose is growing again, Margo. I know Pont inside and out."

"Hi, Nonnie. Ellen here."

"Where else but."

"Just wanted to make sure you were paying attention," El said. "Yesterday we had lunch at Franco Rosina's house. You know, Stefano's son."

"You don't say. Who did the cooking?"

"Franco did, in the same kitchen where your mother once cooked, and maybe you."

"You're telling me something I don't already know? After all, I did sell the place to Franco."

"That's what he said, which really surprised El and me."

"What's with the surprise? Franco wanted his own place and I wanted to get rid of mine. That's how these things work, real estate 101. Whatever happened to the wife?"

"She's with the angels," I said, "and his daughter lives elsewhere."

"With the angels, huh? Next thing you'll be going to Mass again, which wouldn't be a bad idea."

With the angels, had I really said that? This place was getting to me, in ways I'd not expected. Still, I made a quick recovery. "Franco gave us the VIP tour, loved the whole scene, especially your bedroom."

"Don't even think about spending time in there with Franco. You hear me, Margo?"

"Please, give me some credit. Franco is old enough to be my father."

"As if that ever stopped you before."

El was gesturing for me to move things along so I changed the subject. "As you may recall from our conversation yesterday—"

"You called yesterday. I don't remember … just kidding. Yeah, I remember. In fact I didn't close my eyes last night, not one wink of sleep did I get. Dammit, I hope the two of you are satisfied. And don't start with that namby-pamby sorry shit or I'll hang up so fast your ears will be ringing louder than those every-hour-on-the-hour church bells you gotta be hearing from every village within ten miles."

Nonnie got that right, the part about the bells. They'd kept me awake at first and after a while became the train whistle my brain had become so accustomed to I no longer heard the racket. El lifted an imaginary glass to her lips and pretended to drink. Great. That's all we needed, Nonnie tipsy at ten in the morning.

"Okay, Nonnie, you're the boss," El said. "Margo and I are anxious to hear whatever you have to say. Now, about Tommi and Stefano and you and your pappa …."

"Yeah, yeah, sorry about blowing my top. You know how I get on an empty sleep. Or is that an empty stomach; I always get those two mixed up."

"Either one works for El and me."

"In that case the two of you had better sit down if you're not already because this involves Donata Abba too."

"She was your best friend, right?" El said, winking at me.

"Depends on who's doing the talking. Do you want her version or mine?"

"Sorry, I won't say another word."

"Okay, here goes."

∞∞∞∞∞

It was the summer of 1944. Italy had made peace with The Allies and Mussolini had been kicked out of office. A lot of good that did with Hitler occupying our country, putting us at the mercy of his soldiers, those damn *Tedeschi* with their boots on our soil and up our rear ends. They took our food. They took our land. They took control of our police and local government.

In Pont Canavese and the other villages around Pont, sympathy favored the Allies, even though men-in-the-know like my pappa never spoke openly of this. Vito Fantino, a wounded soldier unable to return to battle, would've been shot as a traitor. No questions asked; just bang, bang, you're dead—who's next. Whatever the risk, it didn't stop Pappa from drinking wine and smoking cigars with men too old or too crippled for the Italian army, men who secretly belonged to The Resistance or were aiding those who were aiding The Resistance.

As for me, at fourteen I could've passed for sixteen, the age of Stefano Rosina who could've passed for eighteen. Good thing Stefano wasn't eighteen or the army would've claimed him. Instead he did odd jobs around the village and whatever else it took to help support his widowed mamma. For months during Mass he'd been staring at me with those piercing blue eyes of his, which I found odd since we'd known each other for as long as I could recall. His special interest in me also annoyed Donata Abba who might've been jealous. Either of him or of me, this I cannot say for sure. Only that Donata kept herself in a constant snit.

One night after my fifteenth birthday I lay in bed listening to the snores of Mamma and Pappa drift from their bedroom into mine. I waited a while longer, until half past ten before tiptoeing down the steps and then outside to more stairs, all the while expecting to find one of two village boys waiting for me. Either Stefano Rosina or Tommi Arnetti, one of them had been writing me unsigned notes of a romantic nature. Harmless by today's standards—don't get me started on the crap kids say or do to each other. Anyway either Stefano or Tommi wanted to meet me, in our stable of all places … as if I was the village *puttanesca*. Okay, so maybe I exaggerate the hooker part. These notes were more sweet than nasty and at fifteen, I was more curious than sweet.

Imagine my surprise on going inside the stable. Instead of a young suitor, there at the far end sat Pappa, whose snores I'd thought had joined Mamma's for their nightly duet. A careless mistake on my part since Mamma on her own could make enough racket for two and then some. I can still see Pappa, dressed in his work clothes and sitting at our rickety green table with Lucca Sasso, a man who'd supposedly drowned a few years before while fishing in a lake so deep his body had never been recovered. Pappa's head was bent to Lucca's, almost touching as they spoke in low voices yet loud enough for my tender ears when I moved closer to them.

I overheard Lucca say they needed a courier, an insignificant person to deliver messages to other insignificant people who would deliver those messages to The Resistance. His words left no doubt in my mind. Somehow I found the courage to speak from the dark shadows. 'I am an insignificant person. Let me be your courier.'

Pappa and Lucca Sasso scrambled to their feet, knocking over the chairs and causing our animals to stir. 'Clarita!' Pappa half-yelled, half-whispered. 'Come out and show me your face.' Ever obedient, I came forward and showed him my face and that's when he slapped it. Something he'd never done before, unlike Mamma who made what she referred to as love taps a part of her daily routine. 'You little sneak,' Pappa whispered, his calloused hands squeezing my shoulders until they hurt. 'Forget you ever saw Lucca Sasso. He is a dead man and will remain so until I tell you otherwise. Now go to your room and never speak of this to anyone, especially your mamma.'

Ever defiant, I told Pappa that I really did want to help. He pressed his forgiving lips to the sting on my face. 'Shh. Not you, Clarita. If your mamma ever found out, God help us all; every man, woman, and child in Pont would soon know. And after Pont, the Tedeschi would know, the Tedeschi who have eyes and ears everywhere, even on those we would never suspect. Reprisals would follow, starting with Lucca but not limited to him. *Paesani* trying to do good for Italy would die in front of their families, their property confiscated by the Tedeschi. Your help, however sincere and well-intended, would not be worth such a risk.'

Lucca Sasso had been standing by in silence but now he spoke, telling me to listen to my pappa. 'But I hate the Tedeschi too,' I said. 'Everyone in Pont hates the Tedeschi.'

Pappa said, 'Not everyone hates the Tedeschi, a dangerous problem for those of us who do. Now go to bed.'

I lifted my chin and folded my arms across my chest. 'Not until you agree to let me help.'

Pappa lifted his hand, as if to strike me again. When he hesitated, Lucca Sasso lowered Pappa's hand with his. 'So, daughter of Vito Fantino,' Lucca said, 'you want to help. Good. Perhaps you know a brave young person. Like you but not you, one who would keep *his* mouth shut, do what *he* is told to do.'

Always a *he*, never a *she* back then. Only later did I learn Isabella Rocca's daughters had been messengers during the war and they never got caught. Had I known then, things might've been different. But I didn't know and instead said to Lucca, 'I could ask around.'

Pappa shouted in a whisper. 'No! Do you not understand? Asking around will only get us killed. Is that what you want? Me dead? Your mamma too because the woman cannot keep her mouth shut.'

Lucca moved closer to me. He stuck his face so close to mine I could smell the wine and garlic filtering through his next words. 'Give me one name, one person I can trust. Whisper his name in my ear.'

I leaned into his ear without my lips touching it, and said, 'Stefano Rosina.' Lucca remained in the same position, his only movement a single shake of the head, as if our stable walls had the eyes and ears Pappa worried about. 'You can trust Stefano,' I whispered, only then realizing by Lucca's silence that he already did. Lucca asked for another name. One other person came to mind, Tommaso Arnetti. Tommi had been delivering notes to me supposedly signed by Stefano Rosina. If Tommi had written those notes but was too shy to admit his interest in me that still would've made him a reliable messenger, just not a very brave one. On the other hand, if the notes came from Stefano, as Tommi had insisted they did, that would've made Tommi an honest person as well. I whispered his name in Lucca's ear.

Lucca stepped back and gave his approval with a single blink of the eyelids. 'Grazie, Clarita. Now obey your pappa and go back to bed. But for all our sakes, never ever repeat this conversation to anyone, capice?'

More than a few days passed before Tommi delivered another note. Instead of me reading the note while he waited or me walking away with it stuffed in my pocket, I tore this one into little pieces and let them fall to the ground like a spray of breadcrumbs for the *polli* even though our chickens would've known better than to eat anybody's words. 'No more notes,' I said. 'Tell Stefano I will meet him in the stable tonight at midnight. Or, don't tell him and meet me there yourself. The choice I leave to you.'

Oh the look on Tommi's face, so boyish and incapable of hiding his feelings, however torn they might've been. He stuttered and stammered and finally said, 'But, Clarita, you do not understand.'

Ah, but I did when I said, 'Maybe it will be you and I who see each other, maybe not.' Without saying another word, Tommi hopped on his *bicicletta,* I mean bicycle, and off he rode.

It was almost midnight when I made sure the snores drifting into my room really came from Pappa and that he was sleeping alongside Mamma. On my way through the kitchen I stopped at the honey jar and using one finger, scooped up a glob to enjoy while hurrying down the outside steps.

The stable was empty except for our animals who didn't bother to stir since they knew me as well as I knew them. While waiting near the door, I could hear my heart pounding, only to have it sink in disappointment when Tommi showed up instead of Stefano. To Tommi's credit he did insist Stefano had sent him.

I stomped my foot and said, 'Liar! You didn't tell Stefano to meet me.'

Tommi crossed his heart and swore he did, on the life of Nerone. Oh how he loved his big black dog. Nerone followed him everywhere. Even then, that quiet night in our stable, I knew Nerone would be waiting outside, however long it took to bring his young master home safely. I lit a candle, scooted onto a stone ledge supporting the wall, and patted the space next to me. 'Since you're here and I'm here, we might as well talk for a while.'

Tommi said he'd like to sit with me but he was worried what Stefano would think. As if I cared since Stefano had not showed up. I gave Tommi the choice of joining me or going home. He scooted next to me, leaned back and bent one leg to his chin, letting his foot rest on the ledge. The candlelight flickered on a face prettier than mine. His eyelashes were longer than mine too. He begged me not to blame Stefano for not coming because he had important work to do.

My mind wandered back to the night with Pappa and Lucca Sasso. 'What about you, Tommi?' I asked.

He tapped a row of slender fingers to his chest. 'Me? I am nothing more than an insignificant person. But that does not stop me from doing this.' To my surprise he leaned over and kissed me. 'You have nice lips,' he murmured, his lips a few inches from mine. 'They taste like honey.' He kissed me again. Only then did I feel the brush of downy hair on his upper lip. Oh, the sweetness of that moment, the innocence of it, never to be repeated. Before I could catch my breath, he planted a third kiss, this time pushing what honey remained on my lips into my mouth. The boldness of this shocked me as much as it must have shocked Tommi, but the simplicity of it also stirred my curiosity and his. I allowed him to continue. Allowed him to touch me with the tips of those slender fingers. Allowed those fingers to feel the beat of my heart, but only my heart. I did not have the courage to let him explore any further.

I told him maybe he should leave, hoping he would stay. He asked if I was going to tell Stefano. 'Tell him what? Tell him you tasted my lips before he did? Stefano Rosina doesn't own me.'

Tommi kissed me again. 'Good,' he said, 'because if Stefano ever found out, he would be very angry—with me more so than you.'

This time I kissed Tommi. 'Like I said, Stefano doesn't own me. Nobody owns me.'

Tommi opened his hands with a shrug. 'With me and Stefano it is different and too complicated to explain. *Buonanotte*, Clarita.'

One more kiss and Tommi was gone, but I knew he'd be back and I'd be waiting. On my return from the stable I climbed the steps with knees feeling as if they belonged to someone else. I should've stopped in the kitchen to rinse Tommi and the honey from my mouth but I wanted their taste to last a while longer. My knees were still shaking when I crawled into bed. But I slept. I slept like never before.

After that, whenever Tommi approached me with a note from Stefano, I'd tell him to drop it by my house around midnight. Our version of post office evolved around Tommi and me in the stable. There sat Stefano's note waiting to be read while Tommi and I kissed a lot, and petted a little—innocent stuff, it never went any further although in time who can say what might've happened if ... if only ... how many times have I said those words over the years ... if only I hadn't told my *stupido* so-called friend about Tommi and me.

Donata Abba and I were walking home from our sewing lessons with the nuns when I told her. She nearly peed in her pants. 'You let Tommaso Arnetti kiss you, ooh,' she said. 'The things I heard about that ... that *finocchio* you would not believe.' *Finocchio*, humph, as if she even knew what the word meant. Trust me, Tommaso Arnetti did not march to the beat of a different drummer. Tommi knew how to treat a girl, how to make her feel special.

Donata had not yet acquired *the feeling*. She did, however, have this annoying little-girl habit of kicking up rocks with every step she took, a habit I pretended to ignore because good friends were hard to come by in a village the size of Pont. I also ignored her comment about Tommi because I'd seen more of him than she ever would.

She asked what his kiss felt like. *His kiss*, as if I'd only tasted one. Sweeter than honey I told her, to which her eyes grew wide and she licked her lips. I could've said more but didn't think she'd understand. Especially when she asked why Tommi and I kept meeting in the stable so late at night. What a knuckle head she was. Me, too, when I explained about

Tommi delivering notes from Stefano Rosina.

The look that crossed Donata's face could've soured milk in a cow's udder. 'Stefano Rosina sent you love notes,' she said. 'Ugh, how disgusting. I wouldn't let Stefano anywhere near me.'

I asked Donata if she knew something I didn't know. 'Not really ... well, maybe,' she said. 'But don't you dare tell anyone what I'm about to tell you.' We stopped at the fork in the road separating the rest of her way home from mine. Although not a soul stood within earshot of us, Donata lowered her voice, something the loudmouth rarely did. 'Do not think of Stefano as the boy we once knew. He is not a boy anymore. He comes and goes at all hours. Sometimes he stays away for days at a time. Stefano is heading for trouble if he's not already there.'

I asked how she knew so much about Stefano. Donata pressed one forefinger to her temple. 'Look inside your head, Clarita. You've been upstairs in my bedroom. From there I can see his house.'

What stupidity, I could not help but laugh. 'Only if you hang out the window and stre-e-tch your neck like a giraffe.' I stretched my own neck, to rid myself of the pain in it Donata was causing.

Donata bristled like the silly goose she was. 'I know what I saw, day and night, any time.'

I came back with, 'Maybe Stefano goes hunting in the mountains.'

When we started walking again, I didn't have to hear the wheels in Donata's empty head to know they were turning. 'Maybe Stefano goes hunting for girls in the village,' she said. 'Or, maybe Stefano spends his time helping the damn Tedeschi. My mamma knows everything and she says Pont has spies everywhere.'

I should've ended the discussion but instead added more kindling to the fire. 'Stefano Rosina and the Tedeschi, no way,' I said. 'He works for the ... the ... never mind.'

Donata sucked in her breath and released hot air with her next words. 'You mean the *partigiani* ... The Resistance?'

I shook my head, so hard my brain almost rattled. 'No, no, no. Those words did not come from my mouth.'

Donata wagged a finger in my face and said, 'They didn't have to,

Clarita. What about the rifle Stefano carries on his shoulder and knows how to shoot?'

As if she didn't already know that every boy learned this before becoming a man. 'Even I know how to shoot a rifle,' I said. 'Pappa taught me. Last winter I shot my first two rabbits. Mamma served them with the best polenta I've ever eaten.'

Okay so maybe I'd lied about the polenta being the best but Donata had it coming. She kicked another rock and said, 'This is the first I'm hearing about the rabbits. You used to tell me everything.'

What could I say? Even though I only had six months on Donata, the girl could not keep up with me. For God's sake, she was still playing with her doll collection. Then a strange look came across her face, as if a light bulb went off in her thick head. 'What about Tommi Arnetti,' Donata said. 'Tommi keeps to himself, except when he's doing bad things with you—kissing and God knows what else. He could be talking to the Germans.'

I told her no way, that Tommi knew better. Donata stopped, hands cupped to her chunky hips. 'Says who, Clarita?'

I rammed my hands against her flatter-than-pancakes chest and pushed. She fell to the ground like a discarded rag doll. 'Says me, Donata, and do not forget who told you.' I walked away and did not turn around even though her pathetic crying followed my every step. What a silly squabble, it dampened our friendship and set into play an irreversible course that would change my life forever after.

Just like that the line went dead. "Nonnie, hello, hello," I yelled. "Are you there?" Damn, my phone had run out of juice. So much for the premium plan. "Hurry, El. Call Nonnie back on your phone before she loses that special place in her brain."

23
CLARITA AND STEFANO

El to the rescue. While I set my phone to recharge, she used hers to get Nonnie back on the line. To our thumbs-up relief, Nonnie sounded primed and ready to continue her story.

Two days later on my walk-alone from helping the nuns, I heard a soft whistle erupt from the shadows separating the *panetteria*, I mean the bakery, from the *formaggio* shop that carried Mamma's cheeses. There stood Stefano Rosina, motioning me to come closer. I glanced around, making sure no one was watching, then stepped into the walkway, and asked, 'What, no Tommaso Arnetti?'

Stefano told me to forget about Tommi, that ugly stories were being spread about Tommi and me. My heart leapt, more for Stefano's reaction to Tommi than for myself. Still, I stayed calm. 'What kind of stories? I don't understand.'

Stefano sent a wad of spit through his teeth and it landed on the ground, a tough-guy habit he'd recently picked up that didn't make him look tough. 'Forget about the stories,' he said. 'Whoever spread them has promised to stop. Besides, only a couple of people know—me and … and, never mind.'

Of course Stefano meant Donata. As for Tommi, I figured as long as the rumors didn't bother Stefano, Tommi could take care of himself. Big mistake—God forgive me. But what did I know then, not a damn thing.

Stefano held out a folded note. 'This I will do myself.'

Did I take his latest words into my hand, no. Instead I said, 'Whatever you've got to tell me, just tell me. No more notes, no more delivery boys.'

A hint of pink crept into his cheeks. Those cheeks could've used a razor, making me wonder how often he shaved and if his mamma had taught him, what with his pappa being dead for some years. He shifted from one foot to the other before asking if he could see me that night. 'You're seeing me now,' I said. 'Besides, my parents would not approve.'

Stefano seemed disturbed by this and wrinkled his brow when he asked, 'Why, what's wrong with me?'

I shrugged. 'Nothing, I guess, even though Donata thinks otherwise.' Bringing up her name was like rubbing manure in Stefano's face, given the look on it. I stepped back, only to have him close in on me. He braced one hand against the stone wall, pinning a few strands of my unruly hair. He showed me a side of him I'd not seen before when he spoke through clenched teeth. 'That prissy busybody, who cares what Donata thinks.'

I told him I didn't care but my parents would, if what Donata said about him and the village girls was true. He told me to forget about the village girls. 'Only if you forget about Tommi and me,' I said. 'Anyway, my parents think I'm too young.'

Stefano gave this some thought. 'Too young for what? It's not like we'd be doing anything wrong.' He stuck a cigarette between his teeth and lit it with the single strike of a match. When I asked when he started smoking, puffs of smoke came with his next words. 'Since you refused to answer my notes.'

Donata had been right about one thing. Stefano had moved up to the next stage of his life, a stage too advanced for mine. I should've walked away, left him with that cigarette dangling from the corner of his mouth. Instead I allowed those blue eyes of his to caress mine in a way I did not think possible. I opened the door further with an innocent tease. 'So-o, you want to come to my house at eight o'clock, sit around the table with my parents, maybe look at old photographs. We have this big box—'

Stefano shook his head. 'No, no ... I mean the stable, just you and me, after your parents are asleep. Just to talk, you understand, like we're doing now. The two of us sitting down, maybe next to each other. Or not. You trust me, don't you? I could bring some wine, better yet, *cioccolata*.'

Cioccolata, dear God. The very thought of chocolate made my mouth water. Between the war and feeding not only our Italian soldiers but the Tedeschi too, we'd been without sugar for so long I'd almost forgotten how good it tasted. Our sweets amounted to the honey Pappa harvested from his bee hives, as did many of the villagers from theirs.

Stefano held up two fingers. 'Two cioccolata bars,' he said, 'one for you, the other for me. Mine I will split with you.'

Even then I was no dummy. 'And what must I do in return?'

His next words came with a grin, his first since I stepped into the walkway. 'Just show up at midnight, that's all.' I asked about the cioccolata, just to make sure he'd bring it. He dropped his cigarette to the ground, crushed the ember with a twist of his work boot. 'Stefano Rosina only makes promises he can keep. You'd better go now, Clarita. We don't want to make your mamma angry.'

At me, not Stefano, I thought. No way would I have told Mamma about this new Stefano Rosina, no longer the little boy she'd known all his life. Nor would I have told her about Tommi or any other boy interested in me.

Again, curiosity dogged me into the evening and later into my bed. After making sure both of my parents were asleep, I went outside and down the steps. Stefano was waiting at the stable door. Unlike Tommi, he seemed surprised to see me dressed in nothing more than a shawl wrapped around my nightgown, one that covered more of me than a skirt and blouse, except I had nothing on underneath. I tightened my grip on the shawl and asked the most important question, 'You brought the cioccolata?'

He patted the pocket of his vest and whispered, 'Shh.'

The tone of my whisper matched his. 'Show me.'

He said, 'Not here, we should go where no one will see us.'

Or smell any trace of cigarettes after we'd gone, so I insisted on no smoking since Pappa preferred his tobacco in a pipe.

Stefano already knew his way around our stable, having been there many times with friends of my pappa. Manly stuff not meant to include me or Mamma. He opened the door and followed me inside. After I put a match to the candle, we sat on the ledge of the stone wall, just as I'd done with Tommi. As promised, Stefano produced the two chocolate bars. He passed one to me, watched in silence as I ripped off the wrapper. I stuffed the damn thing in my mouth, square by square non-stop, relishing each bite and not caring how greedy or unladylike I must've looked.

When I finished the first bar, he offered me the second. Without saying a word I broke off half of it and continued making a fool of myself. When he offered me the last half, I shook my head, maybe too hard for those chocolate squares that got stuck on their way down to my stomach. Next thing I knew the chocolate turned into an out-of-control volcano threatening to erupt, just as Vesuvius had erupted a few months before in the Gulf of Napoli. Good thing God had given me enough sense to turn my head before the gusher shot from my mouth and onto my nightgown. Good thing Stefano did not witness the worst of my humiliation although I did hear him gasp in disgust. Or, maybe concern. 'Mi dispiace,' I said in a half-whisper, half-screech, giving the cows every reason to stir.

Hand over my mouth, I hopped off my perch, grabbed the candy wrappers, and headed for the door with Stefano scrambling at my heels. 'Tomorrow,' he said. 'Can I come back tomorrow night? No, wait a minute, not tomorrow, the next night.'

Even though my throat was burning, I managed to say, 'If you insist but please, no more cioccolata.'

This new Stefano Rosina did not impress me. Always talking about himself doing this and himself wanting to do that but not really saying much of anything. Still, I agreed to meet him again and again and again. One thing was for sure. The ordinary boy had grown into a damn good-looking young man, like none I'd seen in my little corner of the world. He'd grown some muscles too, from shoveling manure and pitching hay and herding cows up and down those infernal foothills.

It took some weeks of sneaking into the stable before we got around to less about him and more about me. While I grumbled about my day of making cheese with Mamma, he moved one hand to my hair, twisting his fingers through unruly curls the damp night air had made even worse. Out of control, just like me, Mamma used to say. The more Stefano twisted, the less I grumbled. My talk went from complete sentences to phrases making no sense. After a few moments of no talking or twisting, he asked if I'd ever been kissed. Recalling the lingering sweetness of Tommi Arnetti, I gave him a seesaw answer. 'Maybe yes, maybe no. What about you?'

He cleared his throat and said, 'The same.' His next words strained with an awkwardness unlike the new Stefano. '*Permesso* to kiss you now?'

I did not look at him when I gave my answer. 'One time, no more.'

Nor did he look at me when he asked, 'And if you enjoy the one time?'

I told him I didn't think it likely but he should go ahead and try. I leaned back, shut my eyes, and waited as he closed in on me. What started with Stefano's lips caressing my cheek moved to my trembling lips and a push of his tongue into my mouth, just as Tommi had done, but minus the sweet taste of honey since I hadn't stuck my finger in the jar after Tommi's first kiss. *Mamma mia*, forget the honey. I thought my head was going to explode, what with my heart thumping so fast my ears couldn't keep up.

Silence again from Nonnie's end, El's phone must've died. She shook her head, pointing to the active bars.

"Hello, Nonnie. It's me, El. Are you still there?"

"Yeah, Margo doesn't worry me. She can hold her own. But I'm thinking the next part of my story might be too racy for you, what with me being your nonna and you … you still, you know … a virgin. Not that there's anything wrong with waiting for the right match. No matter how long it takes."

"El got herself matched in Cinque Terre," I said. "Unfortunately, things didn't work out."

"Margo!" El sputtered.

"Matched, you say? Would that be … you know, when two become as one?"

"You got it, Nonnie. El crossed over."

If looks could kill, I would've been dead. "What next, Margo?" El said. "An announcement on Face Book?"

"Not to worry, Ellen, you can trust me not to tell your mom," Nonnie said. "Or anybody else. Those words will have to come from your mouth."

"Thanks, Nonnie," El said. She wiped a tear from one eye, making me feel like the shitty sister we both knew I'd been.

"Same goes for you, Tattletale Margo. Promise you'll keep your lip buttoned about Ellen."

"Cross my heart, Nonnie."

"No fingers crossed behind your back."

"None whatsoever, now please continue."

"Okay, here goes."

My first kiss from Tommi may've been the sweetest but those of Stefano Rosina went beyond sweet, more like slipping back into the Dark Ages. You know, how it must've been when people were so uncouth they didn't bother to bathe, not even once a week, or remove food rotting between their teeth or comb out the lice living in their hair. And yet they became one and made babies and had more sex and more babies, many who never took their first breath, and still those people kept doing what came naturally.

What happened in the stable next happened so fast I could not find the guilt within my conscience to push Stefano away. Or at the very least, tell him to stop. Or, maybe the guilt was waiting for me all along but I chose to ignore it. We were still on the ledge but now I was laying on my back and Stefano had climbed on top of me. I felt his hand wrestling with my nightgown and after some maneuvering, he figured things out and pushed into me, slowly at first, and then charging ahead like a bull. Tears spilled from my eyes, a combination of fear and relief but minus the shame I should've felt but did not. We were clinging to each other so tightly I could not figure out where he ended and I began.

I'd experienced my first taste of sex, crossed the line from which there'd be no returning. I never wanted the feeling to end, never wanted to know life without that boy. Which is how I still thought of Stefano Rosina because I wasn't ready to think of myself as a woman, even though my body told me otherwise. After that first night with Stefano, my every day started and ended with thoughts of him, my every hour anticipating our next time together, how we would make love in ways I could not have imagined on my own. But nothing lasts forever, especially first love because the first of anything only lasts for a brief moment in time. That's what makes it so special.

One night Stefano had me backed against the wall, his naked body warming mine, the few hairs on his chest tickling the space between my breasts. Without warning, the stable door creaked open, allowing a strip of moonlight to join the small candle flickering on the floor near us. Talk about bad timing. We stopped, not moving so much as a single muscle, our two bodies shivering as one, Stefano's heart pumping wildly against my breast, my heart doing the same against his chest. He pressed his finger to my lips as we listened to the low voices coming from the stable doorway.

Lucca Sasso stuck his head inside and with narrowed eyes made a quick sweep from right to left until they landed on Stefano and me. The expression on Lucca's face never changed when he said, 'Mother of God, it stinks worse than a *cesso* in here.' He meant shithouse.

I could hear Pappa speak from his position behind Lucca. 'Must be the cows and their damn farts. Better we should sit outside.'

Lucca raised his voice louder than needed, I think for our benefit. 'Better yet, around back,' he said, 'that bench under the chestnut tree.' When Pappa asked what was wrong with the bench closer to the stable, Lucca said, 'Not a damn thing but my legs need a good stretch as do yours. *Andiamo, Amico mio.*'

The door closed with a reverse creak and I felt Stefano's body relax against mine. 'Lucca saw us but he said nothing,' Stefano whispered, his lips so close they tickled my ear. 'The man has been my savior more than once. I owe him my life.'

Not me and not my life, I thought, but was too shook up to argue the point. We slid down from our perch, gathered our clothes, and started to dress. I lifted my arms and let my gown slip over my head. After the gown fell into place, I stood like a barefoot statue, watching Stefano tuck his shirt into the waistband of his trousers. In a way I'd almost wished Pappa had caught us. Had we not been allowed to marry, I would have run away with Stefano Rosina. Into the woods, into the mountains, into France or Switzerland, I didn't care. As long as we could've been together.

He leaned his rear end against the wall, stooping over as he pulled on his work boots. As soon as he finished tying the laces, he took me into his arms, kissing me hard but not long enough. Never were his kisses long enough but this one was definitely shorter.

After the night of almost getting caught, my obsession over Stefano continued, if anything it grew more intense. I could think of nothing but Stefano Rosina. I wanted to taste his skin again, smell his newly shampooed hair, and feel his tongue exploring every inch of me. The next time we met, I sensed a difference in Stefano. He didn't have much to say and seemed distracted during our lovemaking, which stopped at the worst possible moment when a noise from outside disturbed the animals. Even though we weren't aware of anyone entering the stable, Stefano pulled away from me. He dressed in a hurry, planted a quick kiss on my lips, and left without making a sound.

Pappa found me minutes later at the entrance to the stable door. He held up the lantern, showing me a face more relieved than angry. 'Clarita! What are you doing down here at this hour and in your nightgown?'

I kissed his cheek, and lied with a straight face. 'Forgive me, Pappa. I thought I'd lost my favorite bracelet, the one you made from copper. Then I remembered leaving it on the ledge while cleaning out the stalls so I came down to get it.'

Slowly, he shook his head. 'In the middle of the night, Clarita? What were you thinking?'

I showed Pappa the bracelet dangling from my wrist, where it had been all the while Stefano made love to me. 'What was I thinking? How much I loved the bracelet and you for making it.' Oh the shame of my lie, even though the bracelet was my favorite. Pappa got teary-eyed. I kissed his cheek again and he kissed mine. But had it been Mamma, she would've slapped my cheek. The other one too. And maybe that's what I wanted, to feel the sting of my deceit.

As for Stefano Rosina, that night of the disturbed animals brought our stable meetings to an abrupt end. No note, no lingering kiss or shitload of tears, nothing—*niente*. So maybe Lucca Sasso or some other *partigiani* needed Stefano more than Stefano needed me. So maybe he was protecting me just as I would've protected him. These things happen during wartime, peacetime too. So maybe there was more to what happened, lots more, but nothing I care to discuss at this time, not after so many years of trying my damnedest to forget.

What the hell. Stefano Rosina may've owned me for a brief moment in time but not forever. Nothing lasts forever.

24
MIKE SOMETHING

"Hel-lo out there," Nonnie said, adding her familiar whistle that brought me back to the moment. "Are you two still on the other end or should I hang up?"

"Wow, Nonnie," Margo said. "Count El and me as positively speechless."

Margo speechless, highly unlikely. My convent years had taught me the art of communicating in silence, which didn't translate well when using cellphones. I wiped the single tear trickling down my cheek, my second during our conversation with Nonnie, neither tear related to the other. Or perhaps they were more than I first thought.

"Lesson learned the hard way," Nonnie said. "Nobody was going to own me. Humph! Boy oh boy, did I ever get that wrong. We all wind up answering to somebody—our parents, our lovers and mates; then our children, and eventually their children. Right, Margo? Right, Ellen?"

"Come on, Nonnie," Margo said. "That's not fair. Since when do you answer to El and me?"

"Ain't that what I'm doing right now?"

I nudged Margo, gave her my knock-it-off look, and said, "So, Nonnie, what happened next? Tell us more about Tommi, the way he died. How your father died too."

"Don't get mad but I gotta go," Nonnie said. "I mean really go. Nature is calling and if I don't answer, there'll be a big mess for me to clean up before your mom gets home. And you know how she likes nice and orderly."

"Sure, Nonnie." Nice and orderly was somewhat of an understatement but I didn't want to go there. "Shall we call back in say … thirty minutes?"

"Not today, Ellen. All these forgotten memories are scrambling my head and wearing out my voice. What's more, I got things to do. Goodbye for now, both of you."

As soon as the line went dead, I asked Margo if she believed everything Nonnie had said.

"Has the old gal ever lied to us before?" Margo came back at me, answering my question with another question.

Not wanting to answer her question or mine with another question, I gave some thought to my response. "Nonnie lie? Not exactly, although never have I known her to be so open about her private life. And what a private life she must've had. I cannot imagine Nonnie ever being a teenager, let alone a teenager having sex with another teenager."

"Come on, El. Better with another teenager than some guy who knew better. Call it the romance of first love. Just listening to Nonnie brought back memories of my first time."

"Not that again. I've heard you rehash the pick-up truck scene so often I feel like the proverbial fly on Arnie Eveready's dashboard."

"*Ford* dashboard. You make it sound so … so *tawdry*."

"Your word, not mine, literally. The one word you never fail to use when reliving your *first* in such detail."

"Okay, forget about Arnie and me," Margo said. "Let's talk about your one and only teenage romance. Had it gone on much longer, you could've lost your virginity years ago instead of a few weeks ago."

"*Could've* but didn't, thanks to the good sense I had back then, which amounts to more than you have now."

"I'm going to ignore that because … well, because it borders on the irrelevant." Never one to miss an opportunity to hassle me, Margo stuck one finger in her cheek and pondered her next dig. "Hmm, now what was his name?"

"I don't recall."

"You were how old?"

"Almost fifteen. He just turned 16."

"Almost fifteen is still fourteen. More like fourteen and a half if memory serves me well." Margo snapped her fingers. "M ... M ... Mike ... it just hit me, Mike Something or Other. Weird, you forgetting a guy who hung around the house for almost a year."

"The porch, Mom said no boys inside when she wasn't home."

"That's right, Mike and his entourage of how many like-minded boys: two, three, four?"

"Something like that. Not that it matters now."

"Wasn't he Indian ... Native American?"

"Half Cherokee, half-Irish; give it a rest, Margo."

"Yeah, if Mom only knew. Remember that Fourth of July when she and Dad took Nonnie to visit her Southern Illinois friends, leaving you and me on our own since we were too cool to go with them. Mike came by in his beat-up truck, along with a guy way too grubby and a girl too cute to be dating the grub. Before I could give my blessing, you hopped in the truck, and off the four of you went."

I winced internally at the memory. "It's not like I needed your blessing."

"Er, right. Except you did say you were going to the riverfront fair. You know, catch the air show, munch on hot dogs, listen to the Beach Boys or whoever was playing that year, stay for the fireworks. Next thing I know, you were back home again, alone and slamming the door to our bedroom."

"Drop it, Margo. In no way do I wish to discuss the matter any further."

"Now you know how Nonnie must've felt."

"As if you didn't extract your ounce of flesh from her."

"Guilty as charged," Margo said. "But Nonnie already knows most of my secrets. Your secrets have been sequestered in your brain for too many years."

Too many years, Margo got that right. She'd backed me in a corner, using Nonnie's teenage confession as an excuse for me to spill mine. Not that mine in any way compared to Nonnie's. Still, knowing Margo as only I did, Margo the Rottweiler wanting a bone on which to chew, I decided to acquiesce with a painful tidbit. "One time, Margo, that's all I'm giving you."

She responded with a triumphant grin. "Shall we go down to the bar for some wine?"

"No, dammit. I'm perfectly capable of revealing a ridiculous incident in my past without resorting to an alcoholic crutch."

"But, El, you must admit, a glass of wine tends to loosen the tongue."

"Precisely, which confirms why I prefer recalling this incident without the aid of fermented grapes. So, shut up and listen while I'm still in the mood. There's not much to tell, really.

Mike finally got his driver's license, after driving illegally for a year. The girl was named Sally, a friend of Mike's older brother's girlfriend. The grub, as you so aptly called him, turned out to be Mike's cousin, Yancy. Nineteen, with stringy yellow hair and pond scum coating his crooked teeth. He showed me a picture of his wife and baby back in Tennessee, as if I cared.

When we got to the fair, Mike paired off with Sally and passed me on to Yancy, like some comic book he'd finished reading and decided to share. Talk about the teenage break-up from hell. Without saying a word, I walked away from the three of them and took the next bus home. So there, are you satisfied, Margo?"

"What a jerk," she said with a cluck of her tongue, an expression she rarely used, nor did I, unlike our mother who made clucking part of her daily vocabulary. "It doesn't take a rocket scientist to figure out this dumper-dumpee scenario. Since Mike could drive legally, he decided you were too young for him. Sally, on the other hand, was a different bird, older and good friends with the girlfriend of Mike's brother. With you out of the picture, the four of them could double-date and go places not suitable for the much younger you."

"That's what one of the guys who hung out with Mike told me." Talk about the proverbial light bulb, on reconsidering Margo's words, I felt like such a dunce head. "Wait a minute, Margo, you already knew about Mike dumping me, didn't you."

"Not your side of the dump so don't go spastic on me."

"So much for secrets. I must've been the laughing stock of the neighborhood."

"The neighbors loved you. Okay, they *liked* you way more than me, which speaks to your character. As for our immediate family, this much I do know: After Mike got his license, Mom was worried sick he'd take your relationship to the next level, push you into having sex with him. So Dad made him an offer he couldn't refuse. Not *The Godfather* kind but basically he told Mike to get lost, that if he ever laid so much as one finger on you ... well, you know.

First time I'm hearing your version of the dump though—just wish you would've confided in me back then. After all, that's what big sisters are for. Just thank your lucky stars Mike showed his true side, dumping you in a way so cruel it made you hate him forever after. Good grief, I hope that jerk wasn't your reason for wanting to become a nun."

"Give me some credit. Sure, it was a humiliating experience but I got over it by erasing Mike, like chalk from a blackboard. The religious vocation came much later. I truly believed I had a calling."

Margo patted my hand, a sisterly gesture meant to take the place of words. Knowing her, any further words of comfort would come later, with me not in the mood to hear them. "Enough about your past," Margo said, stretching her arms overhead. "How shall we spend our evening, perhaps another visit with Nonnie's one-time best friend, you think?"

"Let's wait until tomorrow. Arriving in time for a light supper would be rather awkward, don't *you* think?"

"Hmm, without an invitation, I suppose you're right," Margo said. "Unless I misread the hotel chalkboard, today's special is *agnolotti* in cream sauce."

"*Agnolotti*, never heard of it."

"Sure you have, but in St. Louis those yummies filled with cheese or meat are better known as ravioli."

Memo to Self:

1. *Erase Mike again, shouldn't take but a minute or two.*
2. *Be more sensitive to Stefano Rosina.*
3. *Don't give up on the rest of Nonnie's story.*
4. *Tell Margo only what I want her to know.*

25
OUCH!

Having already indulged myself with a relaxing afternoon nap, followed by generous portions of agnolotti and tiramisu, I had no intentions of calling it an early night and said as much to El while we sipped our after-dinner drinks. Sambuca with three coffee beans for me; Frangelico for her.

Our server Ivanna overheard my comment and evidently understood it well enough to rub her belly with one hand and let two fingers do the walking with her other. El had been struggling with her sleepy eyelids but finally agreed to a walk-about. As soon as we got outside, she glanced at my feet, nodding with satisfaction on seeing the okay clogs I'd purchased earlier in the day.

"And where are we walking to?" she asked as we stood side-by-side in front of the hotel.

"Well, Piazza Craveri would be a possibility, if only we hadn't spent several hours there at the market."

"The cemetery?" El asked. She glanced upwards to where dark clouds were taking over the setting sun. "On second thought, no."

"No to what? The cemetery after dark or the possibility of a downpour?"

"Both," she said, flipping a sweater over her shoulders. "I wouldn't mind strolling down a few narrow streets but ..."

"Stefano did warn us about the Boogie Man after dark."

"Mustn't tempt fate," El said. "Remember what happened to you in that dark alleyway in Monterosso?"

"Wouldn't be here today if you hadn't come to my rescue." I slung one arm over her shoulder and gave a squeeze. The temperature felt twenty degrees cooler than earlier that day and the warmth of El's sweater made me wish I'd brought mine. "Grazie, little sis."

She patted my hand, her silent *prego* to my *grazie*. "What about San Constanza? It's near the piazza."

"At this hour? The doors are probably locked."

"We won't know unless we try."

I shrugged a *whatever*, and we headed in the direction of the church, passing a number of villagers along the way. Not one of them spoke although a few did nod. Having Pio or Amadeo with us would've made a difference but not enough to ruin the evening we'd been dealt. As for the church doors being locked, of course they were, although I did refrain from saying, *"Told you so."*

As we came down the church stairs, El sniffed the air and said she smelled rain. By the time we reached the piazza, a few sprinkles were gathering momentum. We hurried across the piazza to the perimeter of buildings and while continuing our trek back to the hotel, the skies opened up and pelted us with a steady stream of rain. When we arrived at the hotel, our clothes were soaked, our hair limp and dripping. I took off the okay clogs and shook water from them before making my less-than-grand entrance.

Ivanna stopped us in the foyer and rubbed an imaginary towel over her head and body before she hurried away to locate some real towels for us. As if I wanted to stand there, waiting for the Ukrainian to put me back in order. Forget the towels, El and I got our old-fashioned keys from the hotel clerk, hopped in the elevator, and punched our floor number. As soon as we came to the doors of our respective rooms, I said a single word to El, "Tomorrow."

The big sister in me waited for El to open and close her door before I jiggled the key in my lock. It took some jiggling before key and lock came to a mutual agreement. I stepped inside and encountered what can only be described as plowing into a concrete wall, face-first before falling down so a steamroller could pass over my sorry body, leaving an imprint in its wake.

How long I was sprawled out on the floor, I have no idea. When I finally came to, I crawled to the bed, clutched the mattress, and pulled myself into a standing position. My nose itched like crazy so I lifted an incredibly sore arm to scratch it. What the hell—something felt wet and sticky. I switched on the light and even with its 40-watt bulb, could plainly see the wet and sticky translated to blood covering my fingers. My nose, my nose. Damn, it hurt like hell. What about El? Somehow I got myself to her door and pounded on it. And pounded, until my knuckles turned raw and I slumped to the hallway floor.

∞∞∞

"Signorina ... Signorina Savino," I heard a voice calling from somewhere in the depths of my brain.

"Margo, Margo ... I know you're there." El's voice, followed by a light tap to my cheek. I forced one eyelid open and looked into her tear-stained face and runny nose. El's nose; what about mine? Instinctively, I sent one hand to the throbbing appendage. "Ouch. Quick, El, call a doctor. I think it's broken."

"Signorina, I am a doctor." Again the voice I first heard, that of a man. Gently, ever so gently, his fingers probed my poor nose. "Lucky you," the doctor said. "No break, just bruised. You had a bad fall."

"More like an assault," I said. "Please help me to the bed."

"You are in bed," El said. "I found you outside my door. The hotel clerk called the doctor. It's two in the morning."

"No broken bones," the doctor said. "I already checked. Vital signs are within normal but you will be sore for a few days."

"For the record, I did not fall. Someone, something—a steamroller, I think—was in my room and ran over me on the way out."

"Sleep now, signorina. When morning comes, I suggest you take an inventory of your possessions; and if anything is missing, ask the hotel clerk to contact the police on your behalf. In the meantime take these painkillers and you will sleep soundly."

I did, and only awoke to daylight and El shaking my shoulder. "How did you get in?" I asked. "Did the key work all right?"

She stretched her arms overhead and yawned. "Never left. I slept at the foot of your bed."

"No way, you did that for me?"

"Got the aching muscles to prove it," El said. "Not that I'm complaining."

"I think I'm going to cry a shitload of tears."

"No, you're not. You always say that but never do. So, tell me what happened last night."

"There's not much to tell. I walked in. Slam, bam, thank you, ma'am. I crawled to your door and banged and banged. You were what, praying?"

"As you well know, it's part of my nightly routine." She pressed the tip of her thumb to my forehead and made a quick sign of the cross.

"Thanks, I needed that."

"Me too," El said, blessing herself. "We should look around, see if anything's missing. I've already checked your purse—passport and credit cards still there, about two hundred euros."

"Good. What about my Jimmy Choos?"

"Where you left them, next to the bed."

"Nonnie's treasures?"

She gestured to the dresser. "Right there. I didn't think to look inside. As if anyone would've cared."

"Use your imagination, El." I conjured up an image of the nude couple in charcoal while El took three quick steps to the dresser, opened the box, and inspected its contents.

"Where'd you put Nonnie's journals?" she asked.

"They should be where I left them, on top of everything else."

"Well, they're *not*."

26
DONATA'S STORY

Margo spent most of the day in bed, dozing off and on while I did the same from my room, although I did check on her every hour or so. By late afternoon I'd curled up at the foot of her bed when a rattle at the door sent Margo into an upright position and my heart to pounding. I hurried to the door, relieved to see Ivanna, hands shaking as she balanced soup and hot tea for two on the serving tray. After setting it on the dresser, she waited for Margo to nod a thank you, and then backed out of the room. Neither of us touched the tray.

When the church bells had tolled five times, I threw back the bed covers and said, "Shower time, you'll feel better." Having searched Margo's luggage for the closest thing to a robe, I settled on a fishnet beach cover-up. Far from perfect but it would have to do. I walked her down to the shared bathroom, relieved we didn't encounter any other hotel guests. Hopefully, that would be the case on our return trip. Although, knowing Margo, modesty had never been an issue in the past and often created an excuse for making new and sometimes bizarre friends. While she got undressed, I turned on the shower and when the water was as warm as it would ever get, I shoved her inside.

After a minute or so of wailing and cursing, she started singing a painful rendition of Adele's "First Love." When the song ended on a merciful low note, she called out, "No way are we ruining a perfectly good evening. Meet me in the lobby at seven."

Margo at seven in the evening looked terrific in a backless dress and lightweight wrap covering her shoulders. Thanks to the magic of properly applied make-up, the damage to her nose appeared minimal, especially to anyone who might've been meeting her for the first time. She did, however, seem a bit unsteady on her feet.

"Don't bother checking the menu," she said in a voice sounding like pinched nostrils. "We're not eating here."

"Are you okay?" I asked.

"Of course. Twenty minutes of yoga combined with two aspirins did wonders for me."

"What about the pain pills?"

"Those too. Did you contact the police?"

"Er ... not yet. I thought it would be better coming from you."

"Good, we'll worry about that tomorrow."

"And this evening?"

"To Donata's, we don't want to disappoint her."

∞∞∞

I sat next to Margo at the table of Donata Abba Bartolini, watching as Donata opened a bottle of dessert wine displaying a hand-written label. After filling three small goblets and passing two of them, she opened a tin of almond biscotti and insisted we help ourselves. Not bad, in fact, better than any I'd eaten back home. The wine surprised me in a good way, sweet without being cloying. In the event Donata offered a second glass, which seemed likely, I'd already decided to push my goblet in her direction. But at that particular moment an awkward pause had filled the room, its only sound emanating from a ticking clock and the crunch, crunch, crunch of twice-baked cookies being devoured. Except for Margo, who preferred an initial dunk of biscotto in her wine, a habit she picked up from Nonnie and one I abhorred. As did our mother. Only Nonnie's hand never shook and Margo's had been for a few minutes.

Shaky hand aside, Margo took charge and with a clearing of her throat, broke the silence. "We had a long talk with Nonnie Clarita yesterday."

Donata paused in the middle of her next bite and returned the half-eaten biscotto to her plate. "What did she say about me?"

"She might've mentioned a quarrel from long ago," I said.

"Is that all?"

"Well, something about the quarrel ending your friendship," Margo added with a slight smile.

"Not from my end because I am a forgiving person. Ask anyone in Pont and they will tell you that Donata Abba does not hold grudges, at least not for long and never forever. Unlike some people I know. After Clarita moved to America, we wrote letters to each other although mine were always longer than hers. Or maybe I wrote the letters and Clarita never wrote back. Or, if she did ... I don't recall. Clarita's daughter—your mamma—did stop by once or twice that summer she spent with her nonna, Bruna Fantino. Once for sure, with Franco Rosina—I think he cared for her more than she did him."

"What can you tell us about our mother?" Margo asked.

"Too American for Pont," Donata said. "And more than a handful for Bruna, which is all I got to say and even that's too much."

Margo snickered, prompting a scowl from Donata. Not wanting our time with her to end prematurely, I asked, "What about Bruna?"

"No worse than most parents during the war, trying to protect their sons and daughters from each other and, of course, from the Tedeschi."

Donata got up in one fluid motion, reminding me of the same agility Nonnie Clarita possessed. She left the room and within minutes returned with the same box of photographs from our first visit. "I think maybe there's a picture." She shuffled through a series of black and white photos, mumbling in Italian about one and then another. A few she held up to the light, others brought a tear or two to her eyes. One photo she spit on, then wiped it clean with the edge of her blouse. Success at last, she flipped a photo over and checked out the hand-written description. "Si, here they are, Bruna and Vito Fantino in 1942, after he had been injured in the war."

Donata placed the photo in Margo's outstretched palm and I moved closer for a better view. There in a doorway trimmed with rough-hewn stones stood our great-grandparents, neither of them smiling and Vito leaning on an elaborately carved cane. A dark mustache covered his upper lip. He wore a workman's cap, white shirt, and dark trousers held up with suspenders. Bruna stood straight with an unyielding back, proud breasts complementing a slender waist. She wore a print dress, black stockings and t-strap pumps. Margo tapped one manicured fingernail on the shoes. "Kind of classy, don't you think?"

"Si, for the 1920s," Donata said with a snort. "But not fifteen years later when our soldiers needed Italy's leather for their boots." She pushed another photo across the table. "One more of Bruna and Vito, this time with my parents. They were friends; sometimes good, sometimes not so good."

The two couples were seated in a courtyard, around a table holding an earthenware jug and four short glasses filled with wine. Donata reached over and pointed to the first couple. A cigarette dangled from the man's mouth. The woman was prettier than Bruna. "My pappa, Giuseppe Abba; my mamma, Olga. They both died too young, making me an orphan before I became a bride. That's when I moved into this house." She made a broad gesture, taking in the entire room. "The family home of my new husband, because it was closer to *il centro* than the house of my dead parents."

"How sad," I said. "I mean about your parents."

Donata lifted her shoulders in resignation. "Such are the ways of life. Losing my parents and later my husband was difficult but nothing could compare to losing my daughter. No parent should ever have to bury a child, whatever the age. Good thing I have Pio and Pio has me. Someday he will need to find a nice girl—a nice *Italian* girl."

Not a problem, I thought, nudging Margo's foot with mine.

"About Bruna and Vito," Margo said.

"Forget about them, at least for now," Donata said. "You should be asking about their daughter Clarita."

"Well, sure," Margo said with the crooked smile I knew so well. "We'd love to hear more about our nonnie. Do tell us."

∞∞∞∞∞

To repeat what I said before, there was a time long ago when Clarita Fantino and I were the best of friends. But then she discovered the temptation of grown-up boys before I did; and due to an unfortunate misunderstanding or two, life was never the same between us. Although I tried to make amends with Clarita, she pretended to forgive me but her actions told me otherwise. Such is life—her loss more so than mine. Same goes for Stefano Rosina and what went on between him and Clarita. Between me and them too, thoughtless words never to be taken back, thoughtless deeds with consequences that turned deadly.

As for the stupidity of my girlish feelings toward Stefano Rosina, who behaved too old for his actual years, I could not decide if I liked him or if I hated him or if I feared him. How he felt about me amounted to no more than a hound dog's awareness of a sparrow perched on the limb of a chestnut tree. Ah, but the sparrow within me had been watching this hound dog's every move, an unhealthy curiosity I would later regret.

Stefano and his widowed mamma lived across the road from me and my parents. Although my mamma respected his, they did not visit back and forth as neighbors often do. Whereas I spent my free time learning all I could about my surroundings, good or bad, a habit I have nurtured to this day.

Late one night while fingering the beads of my rosary, I heard a single bark from our dog Max. Fearing a retaliation raid by the Tedeschi who'd recently lost two of their own in Ivrea, I went to the window and was surprised to see Stefano Rosina giving Max a hunk of meat. While Max chewed on what could've fed a family of four, Stefano hurried down the road. Where he went or what time he came back I did not know; but for the next two weeks whenever evening turned to night, he would leave and not return for hours, sometimes waiting until the sun began to rise.

My curiosity kept gnawing at me until one night I crawled out of my window and followed Stefano into the dark. Imagine my surprise when he stopped at the house of Clarita Fantino. She was waiting outside and together they went into the stable. I waited five minutes before following them inside, my one hand bracing that tired old door to keep it from creaking. Clarita and Stefano did not see me but I saw them, way more than I ever expected to see. Both naked and acting no better than barnyard animals. Stefano I could almost excuse, given the nature of men and boys, but Clarita—how could she have lowered herself to what I then imagined a common whore.

I wanted to make Stefano and Clarita stop but lacked the courage to embarrass either of them or myself. Instead, I backed out the door and straight into a bucket of fermenting manure. The manure bucket clattered into a second bucket. Such a commotion the animals made, after sleeping through the obscenity of what I'd just witnessed. Upstairs in the Fantino house one light went on and then another. I took off running and did not stop until I got home. That night I lay in bed with a pounding heart, thinking about Clarita more than Stefano, but also about a boy named Tommi who had also kissed Clarita, at least that's what she had told me. What more she'd done with Tommi I did not know.

The next day after our sewing lessons, I confronted Clarita with what I'd seen the night before. I expected tears and denial but Clarita took advantage of my naivety. 'You followed Stefano into our stable,' she said. 'Why would you do such a thing?'

How could I explain my insatiable curiosity, the jealousy I could not admit to myself, let alone Clarita? Instead, I lowered my eyelashes and offered a flimsy explanation. 'I thought Stefano might've been spying for the Tedeschi. Can you blame me for worrying?'

Clarita moved closer to me. Never had I seen her so angry when she said, 'Worry about yourself, Donata, and forget about any girl you may've seen with Stefano because that girl was not this girl.'

I'd felt the sting of Clarita's anger in the past. This time I locked my eyes with hers. 'I know what I saw. You really should move that bucket of manure before someone else steps into it.'

Clarita stepped back and said, 'That racket you created brought Pappa downstairs with his rifle. Good thing you were no longer around or he might have put a hole through you. By accident, of course.'

If only Clarita hadn't lied to me, her best friend. I thought about this for several days before deciding what needed to be done. On Saturday after Pappa left to take our cows up the hill, I told Mamma what I'd seen in the Fantino stable. Well, not quite everything. In my version the stable was so dark I could not make out the boy's face, only that Clarita had shamed herself and her family.

Mamma whipped me for sneaking out, which came as no surprise. Then she grabbed my arm and pulled me down the road. As soon as we arrived at the Fantino house, she made me repeat my story to Bruna because that's what good friends are supposed to do—report the transgressions of each other's children before they find out through a not-so-good friend. Or three.

To my everlasting shame I was there when Clarita walked into the kitchen. I cried when Bruna pounced on Clarita and started whipping her with a broomstick. Bruna demanded to know the boy's name but Clarita wouldn't tell her. In fact, Clarita said nothing. So, Bruna whipped her again and again until she crumpled to the floor like a pile of dirty laundry.

I threw myself over Clarita and yelled. 'Basta! I lied. There was no boy, only Clarita smoking a cigarette in the stable. Please forgive me, all of you.'

Mamma grabbed the stick from Bruna and whipped me while I lay on top of Clarita. Soon we were all crying, which was how Vito Fantino found us when he came limping in. He asked what was going on, in a voice more concerned than angry. Since no one spoke up, he turned and left, shaking his cane at the air while mumbling about the full moon turning otherwise normal females into half-crazed bitches. His words shocked me because never had I heard Vito speak this way before.

After that horrible day Clarita wanted nothing more to do with me. Whenever I walked past Stefano's house, he turned his back to me. On the last day of our sewing class Clarita, who was the best student, told Sister Marta she would not be returning in September. Clarita's pappa must have suspected there was more to her decision because he went around the village asking about this boy and that boy, without bringing up Clarita's name. Getting no satisfaction, he asked me if Clarita had been sweet on any boy. I might've mentioned Tommaso Arnetti but this I cannot say for sure. It's been so long ago and my memory is not as good as it once was. Or maybe I told my mamma about Tommi being a messenger for the partigiani. God only knows who she told.

Then Tommi died a horrible death and after Tommi, his mamma from a broken heart. And after Tommi's mamma, his pappa. And Clarita's pappa. The whole village of Pont talked about nothing else. Were the Tedeschi involved? Some villagers thought this did not seem likely since the Tedeschi preferred the fear and humiliation of public punishments to discourage further rebellion. The same goes for the Italian Comandante Avino, who tried to maintain order without interference from the Tedeschi, or the Piemontesi or God forbid, The Resistance who hated the comandante as much as they did the Tedeschi.

As for the local partigiani, having already killed the wrong man two years before, they were not likely to repeat such stupidity. In times of war the young and old, men or women, all do stupid acts without first considering the consequences. Was Vito responsible for Tommi's death? Was the killing of Vito an act of retribution? And what about Tommi's pappa? So many questions, so few answers, more like none.

After Vito died, Bruna Fantino did not set foot in the village for months. Nor did Clarita. Several times my mamma and I went to their house, knocked on the door, only to leave when no one opened it. Then one night while I lay in bed saying my rosary, a rock sailed through the open window. Attached to the rock was an unsigned note, a warning that someday I would pay for the pain I'd brought to others. Little did I know then how my pain would eventually exceed any Clarita might have been feeling.

Si, I have paid for the stupidity of my sins. And then some.

∞∞∞

After we left Donata's house, Margo walked with steadier feet than she had earlier. Her pain pills had worn off, only to be replaced by feathers ruffled and words flying out of her mouth. "Did you see the way Donata wiggled out of the Tommi tragedy? Blaming her poor memory, humph! No wonder Nonnie wanted nothing more to do with her. As for Nonnie and Stefano, a teenage romance is one thing, but one so convoluted it avalanched into a series of unresolved tragedies I'm not buying."

"Excuse me? As I recall from our recent conversation, you said people were no different back then than they are today."

"But this isn't just anybody," Margo said. "We're talking about our no-nonsense nonnie."

"All right, I get it. We really do need to call her back so she can finish her story from yesterday."

"She told us to wait until tomorrow," Margo said, "because she had things to do today."

"Tomorrow was yesterday. You lost a day."

"Oh, yeah, I keep forgetting."

"What? Stop, do not take one more step." I backed Margo against the nearest building and pressed my hand to her forehead, as if I actually knew what I was doing "Tell me you don't have another concussion."

"Another concussion? Oh, you mean like the one from that car crash in Monterosso?" She thought a minute. "No, I'm fine, really. And do not suggest bed rest. The last thing I want is ten more hours of sleep."

"You're sure?"

"Enough, El. Or I will fake a concussion and ruin what little time we have left in Italy."

Yes, Margo had returned to her old self. I checked my cell phone. "Now seems as good a time as any to call Nonnie since Mom won't be home for a while."

This time Margo stopped. She gave me a shitty grin. "Why, El, do I detect a bit of contrariness from you, of all people."

"A big reason for my leaving the religious life."

"Brava!" she said with a single clap of her hands. "Someday you must tell me the whole story."

"Someday but not this day." Nor any day in the near future. I'd already shared one secret about … a boy from long ago. "We really do need to call Nonnie."

"Let's wait another day or so," Margo said. "Until I get my head back on straight."

27
AMADEO ON LUCCA

I woke up the next day with piss and vinegar running through my veins, always a welcomed feeling. Desperate times called for proactive measures, I told myself, at least in my Type-A world, which explained my reason for pressuring El to contact Amadeo Sasso.

"What am I missing here?" El asked with a look of annoyance. "Why me and why Amadeo?"

"Well, for starters, unless there's an emergency, or an unfulfilled need, I do not initiate phone calls to members of the opposite sex. They call me."

"And why do I want to speak to Amadeo?"

"El, El, were you not listening to Nonnie? Amadeo's Grandpa Lucca came to the stable the night Tommi's dad murdered Nonnie's dad."

"Lucca Sasso has been dead for years."

"True, but perhaps Lucca shared the details of the infamous stable night with Amadeo."

"So I'm stuck with calling Amadeo since you don't happen to have an unfulfilled need."

I squeezed El's lips between the fingers of my left hand and tapped her cheek with my right hand. "Not at the moment, thanks to my ... buddy toy."

El dislodged my fingers with a twist of hers. "Ugh! That's way more information than I need to know."

"Don't knock what you haven't tried. If you like, I'll order a buddy for your birthday." El responded by blowing me a raspberry, so junior high and unworthy of her former vocation. "Enough, little sis," I told her. "Now make the phone call."

"What about Pio?" she asked.

"No Pio. Amadeo doesn't need an interpreter and you don't need a distractor. Besides, we don't want another set of ears inhibiting Amadeo from revealing any juicy tidbits. What's more, for the record I do not have a thing for Pio."

∞∞∞

Mission accomplished, at least Phase One, the phone call to Amadeo. With a bit of coaxing from me, El explained that Nonnie Clarita had finally opened up to us and now we wanted to clarify a few things from the perspective of the late Lucca Sasso, as to what he might've told his son or his grandson. Since Amadeo had some free time, he agreed to meet us at Piazza Craveri. El was already wearing her sensible sandals with cushioned soles so before leaving the hotel, I switched from the Jimmy Choos to my cutest pair of flats.

We took our sweet time strolling to the piazza only to find Amadeo had beaten us to the bench. There he sat, one leg bent, his ankle resting on the opposite knee. On seeing El and me, he straightened out his leg and stood up. After the usual greetings the three of us sat down and I got right to the point.

"Uh, we've been on the telephone with Nonnie Clarita ... I mean Clarita Fantino, as she's known around here and we ... El and me ... we were wondering ... uh."

"If my nonno, Lucca Sasso, ever talked to me about the deaths of Vito Fantino and Cosimo Arnetti, sì?"

I poked El. "Told you so."

"Before I tell you about that night, I should mention whatever bad blood there may've been between Stefano Rosina and Tommi Arnetti, my nonno made sure it was resolved before ... before he went any further."

"You mean before Lucca recruited Tommi as a partigiani messenger."

"Si. I apologize for not making this clear the other day when I told you about Tommi and Clarita."

"You didn't want to bring it up in front of Pio, right?"

Amadeo hesitated before answering. "This is … true. Pio may be my good friend and cousin but Lucca Sasso was my nonno, *il patriarca della famiglia*, the patriarch of our family." Amadeo patted his heart. "These things he swore me to secrecy, I only tell you now with the permission of my pappa."

"Talk about apologies," El said. "Please accept ours for not asking about your mother. How is she?"

"Doing better but the foot she must keep on a stool. Pappa did not feel right about leaving her."

"Please give both of them our regards," I said.

To which Amadeo responded by leaning over and kissing me. Not your friendly peck on the cheek but an unexpected locking of the lips that curled my toes and opened the pores of my still tender nose until he pulled away, breaking the suction. A moment so delicious I could've taken a bite out of him had we been anywhere but this public bench in the heart of Pont Canavese.

"Grazie, Margo," he said, assuming his former position. "I will tell both my parents."

"Be sure to include me," El said, fanning her flushed face with one hand. "By the way, has Filippo ever mentioned our mother Toni?"

"But of course," he said with a laugh. "But never in front of Mamma. She keeps Pappa on … how you say … a tight leash. Not that he ever strays, at least to my knowledge. Now, what can I say about Lucca Sasso that the two of you do not already know?"

Between El and me, we relayed what Nonnie Clarita had told us about Lucca Sasso, starting with the first night she saw him in the stable with Vito Fantino. "Back to Tommi and Stefano," El said. "Anything else we should know?"

Amadeo thought a minute before answering. "In spite of the rift over Clarita, Tommi still looked up to Stefano and they forgave each other. This happened before Stefano trained him to be a good and loyal messenger.

Word of Tommi's death came to Stefano while he was working with The Resistance in a remote area of the Alps. That night he and Lucca Sasso took the lives of two German soldiers—for reasons other than self-defense Lucca did not explain to me. Nor did Lucca say why he and Stefano were sent back to Pont soon after, only that it was part of their regular routine.

"First Tommi, then Tommi's mamma, Cosimo Arnetti made himself sick with grief. He sought help from Isabella Rocco who had connections with the local Italian military. Isabella convinced *Comandante* Avino to secure an extension on Cosimo's military leave. What she agreed to in return, only God knows since both Isabella and the comandante left this world some years ago. Cosimo should have been satisfied with what Isabella did for him, a chance to recover and perhaps never return to the front. Instead he started asking questions, too many questions, and making too many threats. Whatever allegiance he may have felt toward The Resistance soon turned into an unreasonable demand for justice with no thought of the deadly consequences.

"Cosimo paid a visit to the one person who knew everything going on in Pont, Donata Abba's mamma. Olga Abba told Cosimo that Donata had told Vito that Tommi had been meeting Clarita. From this, Cosimo surmised it must've been Vito who reported Tommi to the Tedeschi. Ridiculous, si, but also dangerous since Cosimo knew many of the local partigiani and planned to turn over their names to Comandante Avino. Cosimo had to be stopped before he blew the entire operation."

"So, who killed Cosimo?" I asked, unsure I wanted to hear the answer.

Amadeo hesitated before he spoke. "War forces good man to do bad things, to commit unspeakable crimes. But when good men stand by and do nothing, this becomes an even worse crime. To answer your question, I do not know if Lucca Sasso killed Cosimo Arnetti. Or how many other men he may have killed. As for Stefano Rosina, you will have to ask him."

"Stefano couldn't been more than seventeen or eighteen," El said.

"And Tommi had just turned sixteen," Amadeo said.

"Both of them too young," El mused, "although you did say Stefano and Lucca killed two German soldiers."

"In self-defense according to my nonno."

"Who never lied," I said.

"Believe what you choose to believe. Revenge is not always sweet but in wartime, often comforting."

I asked Amadeo if he could think of anything else that might interest us. He mentioned the former police station, no longer in use as it had been during the war. As with every landmark in Pont, the building was only a few minutes away so we hoofed it, making my tootsies zing in appreciation for the switch to flats.

The two-story building occupied one corner of a side street and had been converted to administrative offices. On the lower level an old wooden door facing the side street invited us to enter. Amadeo turned the knob, pushed the door open, and ushered El and me into a dark, foreboding area. He made sure the door stayed open, allowing the sunny day to illuminate walls made of old brick, as was the floor, its intricate design sloping toward a center drain.

"Where the suspects were held," Amadeo explained. "Among others, Stefano Rosina."

"For what crime?" El asked.

"The killing of Vito Fantino. But with no evidence and no witnesses the *polizia* released him after a few days."

"What about Cosimo Arnetti?" I asked. "Any suspects in his death?"

"Ruled a suicide, a father gone crazy grieving for his dead son."

"And Lucca Sasso?"

"At the time presumed dead."

"Oh, yeah, the man who went fishing and never came back," I said. "Are there any police records to confirm all of this?"

"Perhaps at the headquarters in Cuorgnè," Amadeo said. "I can take you on my scooter. Unfortunately, as you already know, there is only room for two people."

"Not a problem," El said. "We'll take our car."

What a knucklehead, my little sis. Some things went over the top of her sweet head. "Are you sure, El? You're looking awfully tired. Perhaps a nap before our next meal."

"Me take a nap," El said. "You were the one who was assaulted."

"Assaulted? Margo, why did you not say something before now?"

Between El's straight-forward account and my more descriptive one, we gave Amadeo a blow-by-blow of the assault, ending with Nonnie's stolen journals. He kissed the tip of my nose, a gesture almost as appealing as his earlier kiss. "You have not reported this to the police yet?" he asked.

"To what purpose," I said. "The doctor wanted me to believe I'd stumbled over my two left feet."

"It's Nonnie's journals we want returned," El said.

"Well, those and an apology from whoever ran over me." I touched my nose, my ribs, my forearms. Maybe Amadeo would take the hint and touch them later.

"I will make some inquiries," he said.

"Do *not* involve the police," I said. "There may be incriminating evidence we wouldn't want the police to see."

"You've read the journals?" Amadeo asked.

"Not exactly. We planned to return them to Nonnie Clarita."

"As it should be," Amadeo said. "Do you still wish to visit the police in Cuorgnè?"

I locked eyes with El, hoping she'd get my message. Alone time between Amadeo and me didn't seem unreasonable, considering the recent lip-lock he'd planted on my neglected mouth.

"No problem," she said. "I'll figure out something to occupy my time."

She stomped away. Well, not exactly stomped but headed toward the hotel while I waited for Amadeo to return with his Vespa.

∞∞∞∞∞

It didn't take long before Amadeo and I were astride the scooter, cruising through the streets of Pont on our way to the main highway. I leaned into his muscular back, skirt hiked above my knees, legs flanking his narrow hips. As we crossed the Soana, I stretched my neck for a better view of the rushing water tumbling over assorted rocks, from white and pale blue pebbles to large boulders settled in for generations if not centuries. Out on the highway the wind played with my hair, blowing it into a tangled mess until we slowed down for the roundabout at Cuorgnè. Once again we crossed the Soana, its raging waters every bit as foreboding as they'd been in Pont. At the main piazza in Cuorgnè, Amadeo turned onto one side street and then another before he parked the Vespa in an open lot.

We walked less than a block to the police station, a modern two-story building with a security fence surrounding the landscaped property. When we reached the main gate, Amadeo announced his name into the intercom. The lock clicked open and we went inside. A short sidewalk brought us to a flight of stairs. Before we reached the top tread, the door opened and a policeman came out to the landing. He held out his hand to Amadeo, pulling him up the last step. After they exchanged greetings, Amadeo introduced me to the comandante, Captain Bernardo Sasso. No way, another Sasso. I raised my brow.

"Si," Amadeo said with a laugh. "The head of police here in Cuorgnè happens to be my cousin."

"And a nipote to Lucca Sasso," I said under my breath.

Amadeo responded with a slight grin.

The comandante all but clicked the heels of his polished-to-a-sheen black shoes. Although the temperature hovered in the low nineties, not one bead of perspiration dotted his forehead. Not one wrinkle marred his crisp blue uniform nor that of the second policeman who joined us on the landing. The creases on their trousers were razor-sharp, defying the slightest interruption of a clean line. Both men could've passed for actors in an Italian flick. Damn, if only El could've been standing beside me.

"Please to come in," Captain Sasso said in broken English, reminding me of my first meeting with Amadeo, who later spoke English much better than my Italian.

We entered the building, getting as far as a foyer leading to more stairs we had yet to climb. While we stood in the foyer, Captain Sasso and Amadeo carried on a lengthy, animated conversation. One I might've understood had the two men slowed down, so I explained this to Amadeo with hopes of being included.

"Would do no good," Amadeo said. "My cousin prefers to communicate through me. No offense, Margo, but Bernardo … Captain Sasso … does not want his words misunderstood."

"What's to misunderstand? I haven't discussed anything with him yet."

"But I have, which for now is all that matters. Now please to follow me. The captain has given us permission to review information regarding the deaths of Cosimo Arnetti and Vito Fantino. As yet none of this has been transferred to microfilm so we must research the old-fashioned way, which may be the more convenient. Also, I am told to expect some newspaper articles as well."

"Did you happen to mention my relationship to the Fantino family?" I asked.

"Was not necessary. The captain already knew."

Up the stairs and down a long hallway brought us to the archives. Within minutes, the captain's sidekick brought out the case files for Cosimo Arnetti and Vito Fantino. Also, those of Tommaso Arnetti, a nice plus I'd already planned to request or demand—as if playing the ugly Americana would've gotten me anywhere other than back on the street.

Good thing I had Amadeo. Good thing for Amadeo too. We'd barely made a dent in the files when I imagined him slipping one hand under my skirt. Ever so slowly, his fingers would travel up my leg, inch by inch as if testing my will, seeing how far I'd let him go. All the way seemed reasonable. There is a certain something about Italian men, whatever their age. They send out these unmistakable vibes that actually deliver what they promise. *Carisma*, the Italians would say; their enunciation much sexier than the American version. Perhaps it's in the Italian genes. Or maybe the water. My imaginary charismatic connection ended with a soft knock on the door, the captain's aide asking if we needed anything. To which Amadeo told him we were fine.

"What's up?" I asked. "For the cousin of the captain, you're getting more than a fair share of respect."

"I would do the same for Bernardo or his men."

"You're talking in circles, Amadeo."

"Sorry, did I not tell you before? I too work in law enforcement, as a detective in Torino. And like you, I too am on holiday."

Amadeo a detective, no way would I have guessed. "You gave up precious hours of free time to help me—how sweet." I planted a kiss on Amadeo similar to the one he'd given me in the piazza, only to have him pull back.

"Not here, Margo. Would not be right. Now where were we?"

Back to researching decades-old information, looking for clues as to who killed whom and why. Clues either ignored or buried too deep for anyone to challenge. Together we poured over one report after another with Amadeo translating and explaining with more patience than I ever possessed, and with me wishing I'd included El in this part of our investigation. Jeez, color me selfish, hoping for a bit of *rapporto sessuale*, not knowing Amadeo was too much an officer and a cousin to compromise the trust given him.

He looked over the yellowed newspaper clippings and then passed them to me, including front page photos of Cosimo Arnetti and Vito Fantino in their army uniforms. I pulled out my phone and snapped photos of the photos. None of Tommaso Arnetti, I suppose due to the questionable nature of his death and out of respect for the grieving family. As for the articles, they were faded and blurred. Still, I snapped away to satisfy myself more than anything else.

After we'd gone over the numerous reports, Amadeo took one final pass through the files before closing them. "Shouldn't there be photographs of the crime scenes?" I asked.

"Si, but these I do not think you want to see."

"In case you haven't noticed, I am a big girl … er, grown-up."

"This I know but—"

"The photos, please." I held out my hand.

Amadeo opened the files, removed the death scene photos, and gave them to me. He'd been right, or in this case wrong about one thing. I, Margo Savino, was not a big girl, not grown-up enough to prepare myself for the remains of a teenage boy with his neck bruised and stretched, his eyes bulging. Nor of the boy's father, face disfigured with open lacerations and water-logged from the Soana. Or of his body sprawled over a boulder in the Soana, its waters rushing by with no regard to the grisly scene. And certainly not that of my great-grandfather, a dark stain of blood having crept from Vito Fantino's work shirt to the suspenders holding up his trousers and the upper portion of those trousers, stained at the crotch where he'd soiled himself.

"Where's the hook?" I asked in my big girl voice.

Amadeo glanced through the report again. "Already removed when the police arrived. Perhaps in an effort to save his life. A wound like that, I think he was already dead."

My hand was shaking when I picked up the phone and started clicking, adding the death scene photos to the rest of my afternoon collection. As for El, how would I ever explain to her what she'd missed that afternoon, all because of a stupid need to be fulfilled that failed miserably and was still unfulfilled.

I felt the light touch of Amadeo's fingertips on my arm and jerked away. "Do not think about the past too hard," he said.

"Easy for you to say. You didn't know any of the deceased."

"Nor did you, Margo."

"But your nonno will always be remembered as a hero. My great-grandfather, my bisnonno, still has a question mark surrounding his death. As do the others. Three deaths never resolved.

"But they were, Margo. Perhaps not as they would've been in today's world but in the time of war, the lack of answers, better yet, the decision not to pursue answers was in itself the most logical of answers."

28
NIGHT OF THE STABLE

Who's that knocking at my door? Why Margo, of course, all red-faced and regurgitating a string of apologies for not having included me in the afternoon research. I allowed her to enter, having learned the art of gracious humility during my convent days. We plopped down on the narrow bed, our best option for perusing the photos of photos she'd taken at the police station. Before we got started, I just had to make one comment. "So, I guess this makes us even."

Margo twisted her mouth as if to stimulate her sluggish brain cells. "Explain yourself, El. I excel in many things but mindreading has never been high on the list."

"You know, dumping me this afternoon makes up for the awkward mishap with Jonathan, which, I repeat, was totally innocent on my part."

"Jonathan? You mean the guy from Iowa. He's so yesterday. But if it makes you feel better, okay, I hereby declare us even. Pinkie?"

We hooked the little fingers of our right hands, the ultimate junior high, sisterly make up. As for the photos, more disturbing than I'd imagined, these people I only knew through the memories of others and yet seemed so real to me. After several hours of pouring over Margo's handwritten notes from the police reports, we stuffed everything in the mesh laundry bag I'd just emptied, and then went for a walk instead of eating another meal. Again, not one villager stopped us and only one nodded, which I didn't mind but Margo took as a personal affront.

"We should've invited Pio and Amadeo to join us," she said. "Don't you think?"

"I think not. After a while, making small talk with near strangers, who will never amount to more, tends to wear down the brain cells."

"You didn't think so in Cinque Terre."

"Learned my lesson the hard way." And with no regrets. I still thought about *him* every day. Still remembered the touch of his warm lips and gentle fingers. The strength of his arms when he held me close. Enough. He was my yesterday. Perhaps one day we would share a new tomorrow.

∞∞∞

Back at the hotel we decided to call Nonnie again and agreed to do it from my room. Her number came up as soon as I opened my phone. "Let's take this slow and easy," I told Margo while we waited for the connection.

Right. As soon as Nonnie answered, Margo grabbed the phone out of my hand. Never mind that I'd already set the speaker so we could both hear. "Nonnie, hi-i," she said in a shrill voice vibrating through my ears.

"What now," Nonnie replied.

"Must we have a reason to call?" Margo asked.

"You know damn well you wouldn't be calling unless you wanted something. "What is it this time?"

"Hi, Nonnie, Ellen here. We just wanted to finish our conversation from … uh, two or so days ago."

"Now who's losing it, not me; that's for sure. I told you to call back tomorrow, which was yesterday or maybe the day before."

"Whatever the day, please don't be mad," Margo said. "We talked to Donata again."

"And now you want my side, right?"

"Right, because hers seems a bit … a bit—"

"Over the top, I told you to stay away from her. But would you listen to me? No-o. Shit."

"That's why we wanted to know more about you and Stefano Rosina," I said. "You know, why the romance ended so abruptly."

"Oh, yeah, the sour taste that comes after too much honey, otherwise known as Bittersweet Hell. Some memories are better left unsaid. Memories to die for, I call the worst of them. Better yet, regrets to die for."

"Are you talking about your father?" I asked.

"And Tommi," Margo added.

"One story cannot be told without the other," Nonnie said. "Both so long ago yet almost like yesterday."

"Please, no more games," Margo said. "Just tell us what happened and we won't bother you again."

"What Margo means is we won't bother you until we get home."

"Yeah, yeah, you don't have to spell it out for me."

"L-o-v-e, that's the only word that matters," Margo said. "We love you."

"Enough with the bullshit, you two. What I am about to tell you, I've never told anybody else. By anybody I mean my mamma—God rest her soul, however flawed it may have been. Nor have I told your mom because she's … well, need I say more. You know how she can be about the sins of others. Practiced perfection is such a heavy burden for unyielding shoulders, right?"

∞∞∞∞

Anyway, like I said before, I gave Tommi's name to Lucca Sasso. After that Tommi stopped coming around so I figured he was delivering messages for the partigiani and had been ordered not to tell me or anybody else. Then I got mixed up with Stefano in ways I never imagined and forgot about Tommi. That is, until he supposedly hanged himself although no one in the village believed Tommi capable of such an act. Neither did I. Nor did I think he was confused about his side of the fence. Not after the way he kissed me, which would've made any number of girls blush with thoughts of what was yet to come.

Since Mamma had been monitoring my monthly visitor, I pretended to bleed on schedule. I even sipped chamomile tea to soothe make-believe cramps. After the second month passed with no sign of my visitor, desperation controlled my every thought and action in ways exceeding my desire for Stefano. I laughed when I didn't feel like it, never daring to shed a single tear. I ate even though the thought of food made my stomach turn summersaults. When I used the outhouse, I always locked the door before silently puking my guts into the fly-infested hole. Talk about stink, that's one crappy memory of Italy I don't regret leaving behind.

Then, one horrible day who should darken our doorstep but blabbermouth Donata and her nosy mamma. Donata's mamma made her repeat certain accusation she'd made against me, about seeing me in the stable making out with a sex-crazed boy. Mamma pounced on me, demanding to know what boy had stolen my virginity. For not revealing his name, I got a beating unbefitting any young girl, pregnant or not. Donata was so upset she wound up taking back her story, and for lying she got a beating too. From her mamma not mine. Little did either mamma know how true Donata's lie had been, but my mamma would soon find out.

As for Stefano, I really needed to talk with him about Tommi's death and this new life growing inside me. But when Stefano didn't show his face for weeks, I wrote a note and asked Donata to give it to him. Okay, not exactly asked, more like threatened to cut out her tongue if she didn't deliver it. Or if she read one word of the note or showed it to another living soul. That night with so many things on my mind, I forgot to listen for Pappa's snoring before I hurried down to the stable. Ever so quietly I crept inside and hid in the shadows, my heart racing with thoughts of seeing Stefano, of him holding me and making love to me, if nothing else, with his words and his lips.

Instead of Stefano, who do I see but Pappa and Cosimo Arnetti, Tommi's pappa. Good Lord, such an argument those two were having. Pappa denying he had anything to do with recruiting Tommi as a partigiani messenger, Cosimo crying and accusing Pappa of betraying Tommi, of causing his death and later that of Tommi's grieving mother.

Cosimo went nose to nose with Papa, spit flying in all directions when he talked about the Tedeschi banging on his door one night. 'They'd followed my Tommi home,' Cosimo said, 'and were holding him in the stable. They ordered my wife to stay put and took me to Tommi. My boy was shaking so hard I wanted to cry, but for him I put on a courageous face. I told the Tedeschi about me being a loyal soldier on leave from the army. The Tedeschi said this was not about me. They'd heard a rumor about Tommi delivering messages for The Resistance and demanded the names of local partigiani, names Tommi insisted he didn't have because he'd never communicated with anyone directly and only delivered messages to obscure locations late at night. My boy a messenger, I could not believe such a thing. Do you know he was barely sixteen?'

Pappa nodded and Cosimo went on. 'Do you know what the Tedeschi did to my boy? They put a noose around his neck, stood him on a box, and threatened to hang him in front of me. I begged them to let me take Tommi's place. They demanded names. I should've given them yours, Vito. I should've given them Lucca's. He was supposed to be dead. Instead I kept my mouth shut. What happened next no pappa should ever witness. One of the soldiers kicked the box away and the others forced me to watch my boy choke to death.'

Dear God, how I wish I could've taken back those nights in the stable, starting with Tommi, and later the night when I gave his name to Lucca Sasso. And all of the nights thereafter, every damn one of them, but especially that night Cosimo argued with Pappa. If only I had stepped out of the shadows like I did with Lucca Sasso. If only I had shown my face for Pappa to slap, Cosimo would've left every bit as angry as when he came and Pappa would've gone back to where he belonged beside Mamma.

Like a dummy, I stood by in silence, watching Pappa pour wine from his jug. Cosimo took the peace offering and threw it in Pappa's face. He punched Pappa in the nose and the eye and his shoulder. Each time Pappa staggered but did not lose the footing of his one good leg. As Cosimo reared back to strike the fourth blow, Pappa bent down and grabbed Cosimo by the balls, causing him to double over. 'Basta,' Pappa said, 'Be proud of your son. He gave his life for Italy.'

While Cosimo was catching his breath and I was catching mine, Pappa found a rag and used it to wipe the blood from his face. Big mistake, he should not have turned his back because it gave Cosimo an excuse to lift that damn baling hook off the wall. Cosimo spoke in a calm voice when he said, 'Forgive me, Vito.'

When Pappa turned to answer him, Cosimo raised his arm and plunged the hook into Pappa's chest. Blood spurted into Cosimo's face and eyes. He stumbled around like a blind bull before falling to his knees. While Cosimo cried like a baby, I ran to Pappa, held him to my heart, and seconds later felt the Angel of Death suck the life from him. Ever so gently, I let Pappa slip from my arms onto the ground. Then I stood up, went to his work bench and grabbed the first tool I saw, the hammer he used for sharpening his scythe. Cosimo was still crying and hadn't moved from his knees, making it easy for me to whack the hammer over his head. Again and again until he slumped forward without making another sound. The animals did more than stir; they created a small raucous, especially the goats banging against their stall, which would've infuriated Mamma had she been there. As if I cared about her damn milk and cheese.

Then Stefano showed up—too late to save Pappa, not that I blamed him for the horrific crime Cosimo had committed. Or the one I'd committed. What happened next continued as a blur of my worst nightmare. Stefano didn't say a word when he pulled me away from Cosimo, I tried to scream but nothing came out of my mouth. Next thing I knew, I was sitting on the same ledge where Stefano and I had made love.

Tears filled my eyes but not enough to stop me from seeing Stefano's right arm wrapped around Cosimo's waist, his left hand holding the arm Cosimo had draped over his shoulder. Legs that moments before held Cosimo erect now wobbled worse than a marionette's. Foam had spilled from his mouth and ran down his chin. Blood smeared the rest of his face, a mix from the holes I'd pounded in his skull and the gash he'd put in Pappa's heart. To my horror yet weird sense of honor came the realization that I had killed Cosimo Arnetti, just as he had killed Vito Fantino, my pappa whose blood had spread across the stable floor, turning the ground into a muddy pool.

The only voice I heard belonged to Lucca Sasso, the soldier in him issuing orders to Stefano. After Stefano left with Cosimo, Lucca walked over to my shadowy corner and kissed the tears running down my cheeks. 'Never tell anyone what happened here,' he said, 'especially your mamma. Promise me, Clarita.' Lucca took the forefinger of my right hand and crossed my heart with it. All I could manage was a simple nod but I knew what he meant. If that blood-filled night ever got back to the Tedeschi, freedom fighters like Lucca Sasso and Stefano would be among the first to die, just as Tommi had died.

Lucca carefully cleaned Cosimo's blood from the hammer before returning it to Pappa's workbench. The jug of wine and spilled glasses he did not disturb but he did take with him a fresh jug of wine from Pappa's plentiful stock. Alone at last, I tried to clean the blood dripping down my legs, the blood covering my feet but when the horror of it became too much for me, I sank to my knees and crawled over to where Pappa lay. I showed him my face, hoping against hope he would slap it one more time. But when he didn't, I turned out the light in my head and put myself in God's hands.

After all these years I still can't escape the reality of my nightmare. I lay awake, trying to relive the night of Pappa and Cosimo, or trying to forget it, I'm not for sure which. So maybe this is God's never-ending justice, His way of protecting me from the truth I've always been too much of a coward to face."

The sound of Nonnie choking back a sob came through loud and clear. I couldn't recall a time when I'd seen or, in this case, heard her cry. Margo was shedding a few tears too. For all her cynical bravado, she occasionally indulged her softer side. "Oh, Nonnie, we're so sorry," she said, "both of us."

Nonnie blew her nose, in a less-than-delicate manner. "Yeah, yeah, it all happened a lifetime ago. And then some."

"About the baby ...." I began, to which Margo kicked me in the shin and yet Nonnie continued.

Mamma found me lying in a pool of my blood mixed with Pappa's. And that of the baby who was no more. After cleaning up the mess I'd made, she managed to get me upstairs and then ran for help, although no amount of help could have brought Pappa back from the dead. Or Cosimo Arnetti, who had no one left to weep for him. No wife or mother should have to go through what Mamma went through that night and those dreadful days thereafter.

Sure, life goes on but it was never the same between Mamma and me. For one thing, Mamma never hit me again. Stefano I could've hit. He just *had* to tell her how crazy in love we were. How stupid was that? Did he really think she'd let him come around, court me in a proper way after all the misery the two of us had caused. Hell, no; but that didn't stop him from climbing into my room one night, crawling into my bed and making love to me. And after that, in his stable, the woodlands, or one of many caves used for storing cheese. Nor did it stop us from spending time together in Ceresole Reale when Mamma went away for a funeral—why she left me behind I'll never know, except to watch over her precious cows and goats. After Ceresole, Stefano and I continued to meet whenever we could. Talk about obsession—I'm not sure whose was worse, Stefano's or mine.

Whenever I brought up Cosimo to Stefano, he'd change the subject with a kiss and then some ... you know, nookie. Not that I ever objected. I needed him as much as he needed me. I needed him to help me forget the night of bloodletting, the guilt we shared—mine more so than his since he'd only covered up the murder I'd committed, a sin Don Luigi had absolved me from but one I'd not absolved myself from. As much as I hate admitting it, Stefano owned me, body and soul. His possession became my obsession, my obsession his possession. Neither of which I could control. Nor could he. After a while I needed him to hate me more than he'd ever loved me.

So I was the one who ended it. Or tried to, eventually refusing to see or speak to him for well over a year, yet always aware of his eyes following me whenever I walked down the street or kneeled in church. Or went to the village dances that resumed after the war. Him, always with a girl on his arm, trying to show me he didn't care when all the while I knew he did.

I sensed fatigue creeping into Nonnie's voice but pressed on with, "Stefano mentioned the dinner on your eighteenth birthday."

"Ah, the dinner in which Stefano insisted Mamma tried to poison him. Boy, did he ever get that wrong. It wasn't Mamma. It was yours truly, me."

Our Nonnie, no way. And yet, what did Margo or I know about her then. I let her continue.

The poison wasn't meant to kill Stefano, just make him sick. A potion I bought from this gypsy named Serina, who specialized in such matters. Before turning gypsy, she lived high in the foothills above Pont. Imagine that—running away from a much older husband and two babies, only to return every now and then to watch from a distance without letting them see her.

Anyway, after looking into my eyes, the windows of what she called my damaged soul, Serina offered to cast an evil eye on the source of my pain. Some gypsy she was, I had no one to blame for the pain except myself. But even if I had blamed Stefano, Serina would've vetoed giving him the *malocchio*, I mean evil eye. The woman had her own eye on Stefano. Even then, at eighteen he could've charmed the tiny heart-shaped tattoo off that breast she loved showing off. Me, he had under his spell as much as I had him under mine. I sometimes wonder if Serina had cast a spell on me instead since I couldn't stop thinking about the night I'd hammered Cosimo Arnetti, how Stefano had walked out with Cosimo, and how Cosimo's body later turned up in the Soana.

More than anything, what I really needed was to get away. Not only from Stefano but from Donata, from the whole village, but most of all, from Mamma, who wanted me gone as much as I wanted to go. She enlisted her good friend Isabella Rocca to arrange my passage to America, which meant traveling with an older couple who acted as my chaperones. Before leaving, I saw Serina one last time. She whipped out a handful of amulets and insisted I buy them, protection on my journey to a new life. From all the regrets, for what I'd done in the name of first love, you know what I mean?"

Our nonnie, a hysterical sixteen-year-old who killed a man every bit as hysterical, who'd just killed her father, who'd only been trying to do the right thing for Italy—dear God, never had I expected to hear a gut-wrenching confession such as this. Nor had Margo, judging from the look on her face that must've mirrored mine. And Nonnie's first love—far more tragic than the silly humiliation of my youth. Or, the heartache of first love I'd experienced before arriving in Pont.

I'd been mesmerized by Nonnie's story, so wrapped up in her words I didn't want to let go when Margo broke the spell with a clearing of her throat to say, "Speaking of Donata, she thinks someone put a curse on her, I mean back then."

Nonnie made a disgruntled noise. "Not me, I had better things to do with my time, Besides, I don't believe in curses."

"Then why buy the amulets," I said. "Actually, one of them sort of worked for me during my recent stay in Cinque Terre."

"Good for you, Ellen. So maybe they did help me since I haven't felt cursed in many a year. Now if you and Margo have had your fill of my memories, I'll say goodbye for now."

"But Nonnie," Margo said with an annoying whine. "We have more questions."

"Save them for another day. I got things to do and places to go."

29
FRANCO AND STEFANO

Margo and I were in the hotel dining room, indulging our morning with second cups of cappuccino when Franco stopped by. He accepted our invitation to sit and from there stammered out an apology more disappointing than Margo's from the day before. The Arnetti family had denied our request to enter the house where Tommaso had lived with his parents, Cosimo and Aida Arnetti.

Margo stuck out her lower lip, made a quick recovery, and then asked, "Did the family give a reason?"

Franco shrugged. "Not one I care to repeat. Word gets around. The *due pronipoti*, the great-granddaughters of Vito Fantino are not welcome on the Arnetti property, no matter how sincere their interest, or how long ago the tragedy occurred, or what role their bisnonno played in it. I should not have suggested the possibility of a walk through the house. Again, I apologize."

"No need for apologies," I said. "Anything else you could suggest to aid in our research?"

"Well, Pappa has agreed to speak with you again. That is, if you are interested. At my house would be most convenient."

"How very generous of you and Stefano." Margo blew Franco a kiss from her fingertips, making him blush again.

He got up and with a slight bow he said, "I will wait outside until you are ready to leave."

"*Perfetto,*" Margo said, circling her thumb and forefinger. "It'll only take a minute for El and me to freshen up."

And to make sure we came prepared.

Franco didn't have much to say on our sun-drenched walk, giving me some quiet time to gather my own thoughts, which kept drifting back to all the things Nonnie had told us. Knowing Margo, she would've been thinking of Nonnie too. Also our mom, the sassy teenage version Franco had revealed to us in great detail. The lack of conversation combined with our brisk pace made the walk seem shorter than the time before. Plus the anticipation, I suppose, to again see Stefano Rosina, perhaps as Nonnie had once seen him, and the house that had belonged to our family and now to Franco.

We arrived to find Stefano sitting outside, hunched over the patio table and looking older than when Margo and I first met him, as if bogged down by more burdens than he was capable of carrying. Or perhaps those burdens resurrected from the past, only Stefano knew. And God.

On seeing us, the expression on Stefano's face changed, taking away an excess of years. He stood and we exchanged reserved greetings before joining him at the table where four glasses and a jug awaited our arrival. My dry mouth started to water in anticipation of the wine I'd come to expect wherever Margo and I were welcomed.

This morning the church bells of San Costanzo had just finished their tenth ring, only to be followed by another ten from a nearby village, and beyond that set, a series from two more villages. Long enough for one round of vino to pass over our lips. Stefano lifted the jug to invite a second pouring, but Margo refused with a show of her palm.

"Grazie, but no," she said. "Not one more drop until Elena and I get the answers we came for."

Thanks for nothing, Margo. Ever heard of subtle diplomacy, honey attracting more ants than salt would, vino loosening the tongue? I, for one, could've used a refill of what Stefano had poured for himself and Franco. Oh well, there'd always be another round, as sure as the bells would ring again at eleven o'clock and every hour thereafter. During her refusal of more wine Margo had referred to me as Elena, her *kumbya* for connecting us with them, however long it would take for Stefano to fill in whatever gaps Nonnie Clarita had chosen to omit. Only one way to find out—I reached into my purse and pulled out several wrapped items from the treasures Nonnie had left behind, those the thief had overlooked or decided not to take.

Stefano glanced from one item to the other before unwrapping the larger package. He opened the folder and briefly stared at its contents before removing the two charcoal drawings from his past. The expression on his face did not change as he ran one fingertip over the youthful images of Stefano Rosina and Clarita Fantino, as if to recapture a precious moment in time. Just as he'd done with the up-to-date photo of Nonnie we'd shown him days before at Donata's house.

I gave him time to reminisce internally before asking, "Do you remember the day?"

"As if it were yesterday. Clarita and I were so young, too young." He passed the drawings on to Franco. "If only I'd waited a few more years."

"Careful, Pappa," Franco said while viewing the images from several angles. "If only you had waited, I wouldn't be here now."

"*Perdonami*, my son."

"What is there to forgive?"

Stefano leaned over, clasped Franco's face between his hands, and planted a quick kiss on the mouth. "I did not mean to disrespect my love for you or the memory of your mamma. She was a good woman."

"But not the love of your life, si?"

Stefano put his hand to his heart. "To say otherwise would be a lie and I've had more than my share of lies. Some memories I carry serve a purpose other than sentimentality. Always they lurk, a constant reminder of the … sins of my youth."

"If you mean a heated romance before marriage, those sins would barely cause a ripple in today's world," Margo said. "Other than the tender age of you and Nonnie Clarita back then."

"Youth does not excuse some of what happened," Stefano said.

Margo was fishing, of course. And this time not for the usual compliments.

Stefano refilled his glass and quickly emptied it while I unwrapped the second package. Holding the single item between my thumb and forefinger,

I showed it to him. "Margo and I were wondering about this."

Stefano inhaled a gulp of air, reminding me of a drowning man who'd managed to resurface, perhaps for the last time. He took the gold band and let it rest in the palm of his left hand. From there he slipped the band onto the first knuckle of his little finger and pushed as far as it would go onto the second knuckle. "Clarita's," he said, straightening out his fingers for a different perspective. "Mine, I still have."

"That is so-o sweet," Margo said. "You were planning to marry … perhaps elope?"

"Your nonna did not tell you? I thought she would have by now. Clarita and I got married in Ceresole."

Three jaws fell open to a knee-jerk reaction. Margo grabbed the jug, hand shaking while she poured from glass to glass, half of which spilled onto the table.

"In church by a priest?" I asked.

Stefano shook his head. "No church, no priest. The friend of a friend married us."

"Pappa! Does this make you a bigamist and me a *bastardo*?"

"And by friend do you mean Serina the gypsy?" I asked. "Does that even count?"

"Our marriage counted in the eyes of God. But not in Italy even though the person who married us said otherwise. In Pont when I later attempted to register our marriage to make it legal, I learned the bride had to be at least eighteen to marry without permission. I should've told Clarita but to my everlasting regret, I did not."

"Which may be one of many reasons as to why she poisoned you," Margo said.

"No, no. You misunderstand," Stefano said, shaking his head. "It was Clarita's mamma who tried to kill me."

"That's not what Nonnie told us yesterday," I said.

"Go on," Stefano said with a snap of his fingers. While I repeated Nonnie's version of the poisoning, Stefano aged before my eyes, making me wish I hadn't been so matter-of-fact about a life-altering event, even though it had happened long ago. He buried his face in calloused hands, his body shaking with silent sobs saying more than any words could have.

"So sorry, Margo and Elena," Franco said. "Perhaps I should walk you back to the hotel." He pushed back his chair and started to get up but Stefano lifted his head and stopped him.

"No need to leave," Stefano said. "Clarita's granddaughters want the rest of my story and I will finish what I started."

I poured the next round. Good thing we'd started with a full jug.

∞∞∞

Whatever the *partigiani* needed from me, I did not refuse, even if it meant leaving my mamma with all the work for days, sometimes weeks, at a time. This was the case when I returned home one day in late spring, after three weeks in the Alps helping The Resistance. Within hours of my return Donata handed me a note from Clarita. She needed to see me, if possible that very night.

I was on my way there when Lucca Sasso came by in a borrowed macchina and told me to get in. 'There might be trouble at Vito Fantino's house,' Lucca said. 'Not Clarita, if that's what you're thinking. I mean Cosimo Arnetti. The man has gone *pazzo* with dangerous talk.' Lucca meant crazy in the head.

The night was overcast with the threat of rain looming and behind those clouds a full moon waited for lightening to strike. Or disaster. Maybe both, but what did I know then. Never had I seen Lucca in such turmoil. He banged his fist on the wheel. His voice choked when he said, 'This is my fault. I recruited Tommi.' To argue with Lucca would've challenged his authority but Tommi was as much my fault as Lucca's. I taught Tommi the importance of being a loyal messenger, one who would die before betraying our partigiani.

Unfortunately, we arrived at the stable too late to save Vito but not too late to see my beautiful but hysterical Clarita pounding Cosimo's head with a hammer. So much blood—I did not realize some of it came from Clarita when I carried her to our special place on the ledge.

Tears ran down Lucca's cheeks as he made the sign of the cross over Vito. Then he said we had no time to waste and motioned to where Cosimo lay, the man not moving so much as his little finger. After Lucca lifted Cosimo onto my shoulder, I half-carried, half-walked him to the door.

'Should we tell Bruna?' I whispered, not wanting to leave Clarita alone.

Lucca bopped me on the side of my head, and said, 'With her mouth? Not if you want to live long enough to see next week. Now hurry to the macchina while I make sure we leave nothing behind that would damage our cause.'

As I walked Cosimo into the night, sheets of unforgiving rain assaulted both of us and brought Cosimo out of his stupor. Thunder rumbled as lightning lit up the foothills. One bolt shot across the sky, followed by another, reminding me of The Resistance fighting from days before when I got lost and was forced to kill a Tedeschi soldier before he killed me. A second Tedeschi would've ended my life had it not been for Lucca ending his. I owed Lucca my life, in more ways than one, and loved him like the pappa who died when I was too young to remember him.

Another bolt of lightning lit up the sky and seconds later a tree snapped. The ground around the Fantino trough turned muddy but not once did I lose my footing or my grip on Cosimo who could not make his feet work. But that didn't stop his mouth from babbling about people having to pay for the death of his only son.

Since Lucca had parked the car in a wooded area, I stayed away from the road to make sure no one would see Cosimo and me. As if any other fool would've been stupid enough to venture out in a storm such as this. By the time we reached the car, our clothes were soaked and Cosimo couldn't stop shaking.

I propped him against the nearest tree, held my arm against his chest, and spoke from the heart. 'Listen to me, Signore Arnetti. You must stop talking about the Tedeschi or The Resistance or the partigiani. I beg of you, promise Lucca you will stop before it's too late.' Cosimo answered by spitting in my face.

When Lucca arrived, Cosimo started railing again about Tommi, how he was going to report the Tedeschi and anyone else responsible for his son's death, meaning the partigiani. Lucca said nothing to Cosimo. To me he nodded but once. Together we shoved Cosimo in the back seat. Lucca followed him inside, along with a jug of wine I recognized from Vito's stable. 'To the bridge,' Lucca said, handing the car keys to me. I knew he meant over the Soana. After two years with the partigiani I knew what happened to people who could not keep their mouths shut. But this was Tommi's pappa, a man I'd known my entire life. If he went to the *polizia*, it meant more people would die.

From the rearview mirror I watched Lucca squeeze Cosimo's mouth until it opened. He poured Vito's wine down Cosimo's throat until it overflowed and spilled onto his wet clothes. Cosimo sputtered and cursed and talked about justice. After that he started singing, then crying, and soon snoring.

As we approached Pont, I could barely make out the village and figured the storm must've knocked out the electrical power. Here and there a light flickered, no doubt from oil lamps or candles. I turned off the headlights without Lucca telling me and continued driving until we were halfway across the bridge and Lucca told me to stop.

I left the motor running, hurried onto the bridge, and helped Lucca pull Cosimo from the back seat. At that moment the only sound in the night came from the river below, white caps rushing with a fury like none I'd heard before, rolling down the Soana I knew was there but could not see. When Cosimo realized where he was, he tried to hobble away but I threw myself on his back. We skidded on the slippery bridge and Cosimo went down yelling. That's when Lucca banged Cosimo's head on the deck. Again and again, whatever it took to silence Cosimo and still he kept yelling.

Lucca and I pulled Cosimo to his feet and walked him to the bridge railing. We bent him over that railing, lifted his feet, and sent him into the raging water. Splash was the last sound I heard from Cosimo. If only he'd listened to me and kept his mouth shut. But who was I, an insignificant nobody.

Stefano looked at Franco. Then to Margo and at me, both of us with our jaws dropped for the second time in less than an hour. Make that three, Franco's too. "So now, American sisters and Franco my son, you know what I've never told another soul before today. Not even Clarita, although she must've suspected after Cosimo's body was discovered the next day, sprawled on rocks beyond the village of Cuorgnè."

"To this day Nonnie thinks she killed Cosimo," I said, not hesitating to show my annoyance. "You should've told her what happened on the bridge."

"And she should've told me what she was thinking," he snapped back. "When you speak of this to Clarita, tell her I love her as much today as the last time we saw each other. Tell her I ask her forgiveness for what I did to her, just as I have forgiven her for what she did to me."

"For poisoning you?" Margo asked, clearly as annoyed as I was.

"No, although it pains me to learn Clarita would've done such a thing. I speak of another deception, far more cruel."

∞∞∞

Franco wouldn't hear of our leaving until he fed us his interpretation of a light meal—an antipasto consisting of salami, prosciutto, thinly sliced beef, fresh mozzarella cheese, shaved Grana Padano, figs, blood-red oranges, and bruschetta cut on the diagonal and rubbed with garlic and olive oil. Despite Stefano's shocking yet heart-tugging disclosure, neither he nor Franco had lost their appetites. Nor had Margo and I, although the outdoor atmosphere could hardly be described as festive. Of course, we needed more wine to wash everything down, followed by amaretto cookies, and espresso followed by cordials of Limoncello.

"To aid in the digestion," Franco said as he poured a second round.

There is something about food, the way it brings people together, hopefully in harmony, if only for a brief time before the reality of knowing when enough is finally enough. Our enough was Margo nudging my foot with hers. We pushed back our chairs and stood up. As did Franco and Stefano. We exchanged kisses and hugs. We snapped photos: one each of Stefano, Stefano and Franco, Stefano with Margo and me, Franco with Margo and me.

"El and I can find our way back," Margo said after the photo op. "We most definitely need the walk."

"How many days before you leave?" Stefano asked.

"One or two," I said. "Maybe three. We're not sure."

"Then we will not meet again. Or perhaps we will, after you speak to Clarita again."

Of course we'd speak to Nonnie, if for no other reason than to ease her conscience. All those years of guilt, believing she'd killed the man Stefano had actually killed. Lucca Sasso too. Now I understood why Amadeo had told Margo that some mysteries were better left unsolved.

Margo must've understood too. Another round of hugs prompted her to say, "Come to St. Louis, both of you."

"I do not think it possible," Stefano said, his last words before walking toward the house.

"Your pappa needs you now more than ever," I told Franco.

"Grazie, both of you. Pappa and I will sit together, get drunk together, and tomorrow we will never again speak of that night from long ago. Perhaps after talking with your nonna, it will be the same for you and her."

29
IVANNA AND SASHA

I made no promises to Franco. Nor did Margo. I did, however, expect Stefano's confession would monopolize the conversation during our walk back to the hotel. Or that we'd strategize our next phone call to Nonnie. Instead, we engaged in sisterly chitchat, enough to get us to the hotel bar where we each ordered an Italian soda along with four precious ice cubes instead of the standard two. Italian soda, not my first choice in Italy but we'd consumed more than our fair share of wine for one day.

Margo took one sip of soda, smacked her lips, and said, "Not bad, but not Diet Coke. I might be getting homesick. Next time let's try another bar."

"I thought you liked the ambiance of this one."

"Need I remind you of my recent assault?"

"Sorry, I did forget." Margo's nose had returned to normal, as had her voice; but the emotional factor, the anger and vulnerability, would not be so easily dismissed. It was the second assault she'd endured in a matter of weeks. Her first happened in Monterosso, the kidnapping she described as a payback from hell, one ending with a car crash she'd barely survived. I put my hand over hers, and said, "Really, I am sorry."

I glanced up to see a familiar face appear in the mirror behind the bar and turned to acknowledge Ivanna.

"*Scusami, signorini,*" she said, clearing her throat. "Please to follow."

We did, to the dining room, deserted at mid-afternoon except for Amadeo and Pio who were standing beside a corner table. After the usual exchange of greetings the four of us sat down, leaving Ivanna shifting from one foot to the other.

"Nothing for El or me," Margo said, tapping her throat. "We are positively filled to the gills."

"She means—"

"Si, I understand the term," Amadeo said. "We did not come here to eat or to drink. Pio has something to tell both of you."

Only then did I notice the strained look on Pio's face, how it matched Ivanna's. She took one step back.

"What the fuck," Margo said under her breath. "Not you, Pio."

"Mi dispiace," Pio said, hanging his head.

"Sorry my ass." Margo stood up, leaned across the table and with two fingers, lifted Pio's chin. "You bastard," she said, smacking him across the face. "How does it feel? Maybe I should break your nose like you almost broke mine." She reared back, this time with her fist, only to be stopped from a second assault when Amadeo got up and grabbed her arm.

"Margo, please." Ever so gently he pushed her back into the chair and then sat in his. "Let Pio explain."

"What about Ivanna?" I asked while Margo calculated her next move, hopefully one less violent. "Sasha too, do they need to hear this?"

From the hallway came the sound of water splashing from a bucket. Ivanna called out a few non-Italian words that must've translated to *get your ass in here*, which is what Sasha did. She stood beside Ivanna, both of them trembling and making me wonder if they were truly afraid or merely adept at acting afraid. Amadeo gestured an okay for Pio to have his say, most of which I'd figured out in the past few minutes but should have sooner. Shame on me for such stupidity.

Pio wiped one hand over the sweat beads dotting his brow and directed his comments to me. "I should not have told my nonna that I'd seen Margo holding Clarita Fantino's journals. Nonna just wanted to look inside, to see what Clarita Fantino might've said about her, to see if Clarita had put a curse on her. Or had arranged for someone else to curse her. You have to understand, my nonna has lost too many people before their time. Not a day passes without her grieving for my mamma, her husband and parents."

"So you hid in my room and assaulted me," Margo said. "I should have you arrested."

Whatever Ivanna said to Sasha brought both of them to their knees. "Sorry, sorry," Ivanna said with hands folded. "Sorry, sorry," Sasha repeated. She glanced at Ivanna's folded hands and copied the gesture.

"An inside job, of course," I said.

"Do not blame the sisters," Pio said. "I asked Ivanna to do this. Not for me, for my nonna."

"Jeez, a woman Ivanna didn't even know or barely knew," Margo said. "Never mind about *our* nonna, *her* right to privacy."

"So, this is what I'm picturing. Margo and I return early from a walk that Ivanna suggested we make. We're soaked from a surprise rainstorm and Ivanna wants us to wait while she gets some towels. Instead, we decide to dry off in our rooms."

"And on entering my room," Margo said, "Sasha runs me over. Thanks for nothing, Sasha," A sob erupted from one of the sisters but Margo wasn't through with them. "Quit your sniveling, both of you."

"It comes from the heart," Amadeo said. "The sisters are here on work visas. A criminal offense such as this would send them back to Ukraine. Not a good place to be in today's political unrest."

"Pio, did you pay them?" I asked.

"Si, but not that much."

"How much?"

"One hundred euros," he said in a low voice. "The money came from my nonna. She only wanted the journals for a day or so, long enough to look inside before Sasha put them back."

"Get the money," Amadeo said to the sisters. "Now."

Ivanna pulled out an envelope from her apron pocket. Handing it to Amadeo, she said, "We no leave money in room. Too risky."

"Count it," Amadeo said, passing the envelope to Margo.

She opened the envelope and ran her fingers over the contents. "One hundred," she said. "But what about the journals?"

Pio reached under the table and produced both journals. One journal went to Margo, the other to me. "Clarita Fantino's words are safe with the two of you. After what happened last night, I ... I was not sure about passing them on to my nonna."

"Make sure no pages have been ripped out," Amadeo said. "Or damaged in any way."

Margo and I moved to a neighboring table where we spent more than a few minutes inspecting each page, mumbling to each other until we agreed the books were intact. When we looked up from our task, the Ukrainian sisters were gone."

"I sent them away," Amadeo said. "But if you wish to press charges, I will take you to the police station."

Margo raised one eyebrow to me. We both shook our heads and thanked him for resolving an ugly situation. "About the money," she said. "We'll donate it to a good cause, one yet to be decided."

Pio shifted in the chair he still occupied, an unpleasant reminder of the deception he'd perpetrated on Margo and me, one that could've gone much worse than it already had. "How could you," I said to him. "I thought you cared about me. If nothing else, at least respected me."

He stood up, prepared to leave without the usual banter and Italian farewell. "I do care," he said. "And respect you. Margo too. Not this day but one day, I hope both of you will forgive me."

Margo and I waited for Pio to leave before we got up and said our goodbyes to Amadeo, hers lasting longer and with more emotion than mine. "Come visit me in America," she said.

"Perhaps one day," he replied. "In the meantime can I take you out tonight for one last dance?"

"Well," Margo said, lowering her lashes. "I suppose if you insist."

"Elena too, of course."

"Grazie, Amadeo, but I have other plans." What they were, I'd not yet decided but I'd think of something. If nothing else, the old standby of washing my hair.

He kissed me on the cheek and then turned to Margo. "In that case," he said with a forefinger leveled in her direction and then reversed. "You, me—just like our first night."

Talk about the perfect guy. For Margo, that is, not me.

30
JOHN RIVA

"One more phone call to Nonnie," I told Margo after Amadeo left. "That much we owe her and ourselves."

We took the elevator up to my room. No arguing over whose turn it was to call, I pulled out my phone. Nonnie answered on the first ring with her usual, "What now?"

"Are you feeling okay?" Margo asked. "You sound kind of down."

"You think life's a bitch now. Wait until you're my age. Not that I'll be around to say I told you so."

Nonnie didn't have to tell me what I already knew, the part about her not being around forever. Which explained one reason for my wanting answers while she still made sense, selfish as it may've seemed on my part. Margo's too. More importantly, I wanted to give Nonnie some peace of mind, that much she deserved after all these years. I cleared my throat and changed the subject. "We spent the morning at your old house, with Franco and Stefano."

"What now? More reminiscing about old times, I suppose."

"Stefano told us everything," Margo said. "Oh, Nonnie. Listening to him was positively heartbreaking, especially the part about—"

"Did he talk about the night Pappa died, what happened to Cosimo Arnetti?"

"You didn't kill Cosimo, Nonnie." I told her what Stefano had told us, how Cosimo was still alive when Stefano walked him out of the stable and how Cosimo met his death on the bridge.

The relief I so wanted to hear was not there when Nonnie said, "Lucca and Stefano cleaned up the mess that started with Stefano and me. God forgive us all."

Another excruciating silence, I couldn't find the words to move on to something more pleasant. Or less traumatic. Then Margo said, "Stefano told us about your wedding."

"Yeah, some wedding. Imagine my surprise when I found out the damn thing didn't take."

"We're so sorry," Margo said. "Well, not really since El and I wouldn't be having this conversation with you had things worked out differently."

"Yeah, so maybe life's not always a bitch. It depends on where you came from and where you're going and how much time you got left."

"Out with it, Nonnie," Margo said. "There's more to your story, right?"

"I thought you'd never ask."

∞∞∞

Had it not been for Isabella Rocca, God rest her saintly soul, I never would've made it to America. But did her help stop there, hell no. She also arranged for me to stay with people in Southern Illinois who had ties to Pont. You know, Mary Ann and Toni Roselli. I helped Mary Ann and Tony with their kids. Mary Ann taught me how to speak and dress like an American. She taught me how to use her modern Singer sewing machine, a big step up from the treadle machine I'd been pedaling at home. Tony taught me how to read and write like an American. He worked as a mining engineer in St. Gregory but at home Mary Ann ran the show, same as most women did in Italy.

When I was ready to spread my wings Tony got me my first real job, piece work at the local dress factory. How I hated being cooped up in ninety-degree weather with nothing more than rotating fans pushing hot air around. Sweat rolled off my face and down my legs while I sat bent over the damn industrial-strength sewing machine, all the while feeling like a machine myself. But my fingers moved faster than those of the American girls so I made my piece-work time which earned me more money. That only lasted so long until the bitch of a floor supervisor started me on a new project which took weeks before I picked up enough speed to make my piece-work time again. As soon as that happened, she put me on another job, one more complicated. After a while I felt like a caged hamster spinning its little wheel and going nowhere.

Actually I did go somewhere, out the door and down the street to Fred's Diner. I sat down at the counter and ordered coffee. No cream, no sugar, same as I take it now. After the waitress poured my coffee, this guy sitting next to me passed the sugar, which I ignored. Then he told me to try the pie.

I spoke without looking in his direction. 'Grazie, no ... I mean *thanks but no thanks.*'

He chuckled and said, 'Ah, I should've known. You're Italian.'

'Working on becoming an American.' I told him.

The waitress came by and asked if I needed anything else. 'The lady will take a piece of apple pie,' the guy said. 'It's on me, the coffee too.'

I turned to him and in my excited American, I said, 'The lady she speaks for me ... herself and I am ... she is no charity case.'

He showed me his palms. From there I saw the cufflinks on his starched shirt, the sleeves of his tailored suit. He smiled. 'Whoa, don't get so huffy. You look like somebody who could use a friend. My name is John Riva.' He stuck out a hand free of callouses, making me think of Tony Roselli when I shook it. 'My folks came over from the Piemonte village of Alba,' John Riva said, 'home of the finest red wines in all of Italy.'

He didn't release my hand right away, giving me time to notice his green eyes and curly hair. Hair the color of straw like Tommi Arnetti's had been. Tommi might've grown into a guy like John Riva if only he'd lived long enough. I told John my name and that I came from Pont Canavese. 'Never been there but I've heard of it,' he said. 'Try the pie. You'll like it.'

I did like the pie, and John. American by birth and still a bachelor at thirty, he'd been to war, helped liberate Italy of all places. With both parents dead, John and his sister ran the family business, one of two banks in town. 'I'm surprised we haven't met before,' John said. 'Our bank started out catering to immigrants, now we serve their children and grandchildren.'

As soon as I mentioned the Roselli family, John recognized them as customers. 'And what about you?' he asked.

I stuttered and stammered before confessing I hadn't gotten around to opening an account.

He checked his watch. 'We can do that now if you like. Ten dollars is all you need.'

Ten dollars I could've managed from under my mattress but my dreams went beyond a sawbuck or two. So I said, 'Hmm, what I really need is a loan to start my own business—dressmaking and alterations. Two hundred dollars would get me a sewing machine and supplies plus rent for a downtown location. If you really want to help ….."

Not only did John lend me the startup money, he found me a storefront, in a building he owned. The space came with a small apartment in the rear, an added blessing since I didn't have a car and the Roselli farm was located in the boonies, too far from downtown for me to walk. Not in Italy but this was America and more than anything I wanted to be American. At twenty-three and my own boss I now worked harder than I'd worked at the dress factory but I made more money and people respected me. Within six months I proudly paid off the loan.

I'd been dating John about a year when he asked me to marry him. I said I needed time to think about it. He told me to take all the time I needed. 'There's one more thing and it's really bad,' I said, dreading my next words. 'Before I came to America, a half-crazed soldier ruined me for any other man. I'm not a virgin, John. So, if you don't want me, I'm okay with just being friends.'

John silenced me by pressing one finger to my mouth. He took my hand, kissed the insides of my wrists, sending tingles down my leg. Something I hadn't felt since Stefano, but without the magic of first love. 'Damn those Krauts,' he said. 'But not you, Clarita. No matter what, I love you just the way you are and I will always love you.'

So maybe I'd stretched the truth more than a little. Stefano Rosina had been more than half-crazed, more like totally crazy in love with me, just as I'd been with him. As for John mistaking my partigiano warrior for a German, I didn't bother setting him straight. But I did let him put his hand here and there. I would've let him do more had he not set me straight by saying, 'As much as I want you now, I respect you even more. Let's wait until our wedding night.'

Fine by me. No doubt his sister too. Three years younger than John,

Anna Riva viewed me as a rival for his attention. Weird, I know, but I stayed on my half of John—the personal side—and let Anna have John's business side.

The next time John asked me to marry him, I didn't hesitate to say yes. Our bans had been announced in church one time, not that anyone in St. Gregory had reason to object to the upcoming wedding. Two more announcements and after that we'd make it official, a wedding befitting the most eligible bachelor in St. Gregory. Anna had put herself in charge of the wedding arrangements, which suited me fine since my days were spent with the sewing business even though John suggested I give it up. He insisted we invite Mamma to the wedding so I wrote the letter, knowing she'd never cross the ocean on my account or for any other reason.

John was attending a banking conference in Chicago when who should walk into my shop but a stranger in his early fifties. Handsome with dark hair and wearing a tailor-made suit every bit as stylish as John's. One look told me he was Italian. He gave his name as Pete Montagna, one I figured had been Americanized. 'I come from the Piemonte Region,' he said with a polished accent. 'The village makes no difference. I've not been back in years. In any case, I come today in friendship and not as a customer.'

Not as a customer, that part relieved me since my limited tailoring skills couldn't match the fine clothes this Pete Montagna wore. I poured two cups of espresso from the pot I'd just made and we sat down. He refused the cream I offered but stirred three sugar cubes into his little cup. 'Just like my pappa used to take it, Mr. Montagna,' I said. 'Perhaps you knew Vito Fantino.'

His eyes didn't leave mine as he kept stirring sugar already dissolved. 'I only knew Vito Fantino through others. Please accept my belated sympathy. And call me Pete.'

From Pietro to Pete, I couldn't help but think of Isabella Rocca. In Pont people talked of Pietro Rocca who went to America and never came back. That Pietro left behind his wife and two children plus a questionable third belonging to none other than his godfather's wife, Serina, before she ran off with the gypsies. This American Pete appeared to be a man of wealth, one who would not have welcomed questions about his past. After finishing his espresso in a single gulp, he pushed the cup aside, and said, 'One of your pappa's friends happens to be an old friend of mine. Because of Lucca Sasso, I am here to see you.'

The connection took longer to register than it should have. Wanting to forget has a way of playing games with the brain. 'Lucca Sasso, I don't understand. I ain't … haven't seen Lucca since … forever and a day. What could he possibly want with me?"

Pete leaned back and spoke in a slow manner, as if wanting me to absorb his every word. 'Lucca has traveled all the way from Italy. He came to St. Louis as a hero, to receive a commendation for his work with The Resistance during the war. More to the point, he brought with him a young partigiano who insists on meeting with Clarita Fantino. This man, Stefano Rosina, do you know him?'

Know him. On hearing Stefano's name I choked on a swallow of coffee. Pete got up and patted my back. While drying my coffee tears with a monogrammed handkerchief, he said, 'My driver is waiting outside. He will take both of us to St. Louis, that is, if you agree. Otherwise, I will make the trip alone and deliver the disappointing news to my old friend and his colleague.'

Stefano, dear God, never did I expect to see him again. And certainly not in St. Louis, alone and away from disapproving eyes and wagging tongues. Once again, curiosity started to get the best of me but I was older now and certainly wiser. 'It ain't that easy,' I told this Pete Montagna. 'I did know Stefano Rosina from another time but I'm a different person now.'

Pete shrugged, an as-if-I-care gesture that spoke volumes and so like the men of Pont Canavese I'd willed myself to forget. 'Stefano Rosina is different too, or so I've heard,' Pete said while checking the gold watch he'd pulled from his pocket. 'I'd like to stay and talk about the rewards of America—or the regrets of love lost—but time wasted is money wasted.' He returned the watch to his vest pocket, its gold chain dangling as a reminder of the wealth Pete must've possessed. 'So, Clarita Fantino, are you giving the grown-up Stefano a second chance? Or, are you staying behind with no regrets?'

Regrets, those I knew firsthand. And everybody deserved a second chance, even me. I packed my suitcase and made a few phone calls, telling customers and friends I was going out of town and wouldn't return for a week or so. I also called Mary Ann Roselli, who didn't seem surprised to learn I'd be shopping in St. Louis for wedding items and sewing supplies. A phone call to John Riva didn't enter my mind until Pete Montagna brought it up. When I asked how he knew about John, Pete handed me the phone and ordered me to call him. So I did; and lied through my teeth, giving John the same story I'd given to Mary Ann.

As soon as I parked myself in the back seat of Pete's car, I told him I needed to stop at the bank to withdraw money for St. Louis. 'Not to worry,' he said. 'Everything's been taken care of.' He pulled out an envelope from the inner pocket of his suitcoat and handed it to me. 'This should cover any incidentals.' Inside I found five twenty dollar bills. His only response to my thanks was a simple nod of the head.

On the drive to St. Louis with Pete sitting beside me, I soon discovered him to be a man of few words. We did, however, share a bottle of Italian wine rivaling that of Mary Ann's pappa and her uncle. 'My friends make their own wine,' I said. 'Like me, they came from Pont too. Ever heard of Carlo Baggio and his brother Jake, who used to be Giacomo?' Pete thought a minute, or maybe he pretended to. 'Not that I recall,' he said. 'It's been so long.'

I paused, unwilling to let him off so easy. 'But you have been to Pont, si? Maybe you knew Isabella Rocca. The woman is a saint. She helped bring me over.'

He sighed, showing his annoyance. 'Good for you and her. But not for Stefano, or so I've heard. None of which concerns me since I do this today as a favor to Lucca Sasso. Now if you'll excuse me, I must take a rest since my work day has already begun and doesn't end until late at night.'

I dared to ask what he'd be doing. 'Taking care of business,' he said. 'Should you need to take care of yours along the way, tell my driver and he will stop.' Pete stuck the almost empty bottle of wine and his glass into the car's convenient holders. He slid down in the seat, and closed his eyes, leaving me to mull over this whole St. Louis thing. Which finally made me think of John Riva. I'd been to St. Louis with him several times to see the latest movies and eat at the best restaurants. We always stayed at the Mayfair Hotel on Eighth Street, always in separate rooms, actually three rooms since Anna insisted on tagging along to avoid any hint of scandal, not that John would've stepped out of line.

After all, I'm talking about the fifties, the age of public decency, and nice girls didn't do what I would soon be doing. With the person I'd once married when he was eighteen to my sixteen, from my end too young to make it legal. So many memories of our time together, too many to live down. Before leaving Italy, I'd poisoned Stefano, left him to battle the painful aftereffects, hoping he would learn to hate me more than he ever loved me.

And now I couldn't wait to see him again, to lay in his arms and feel his lips on mine. To make a new start in America, away from Southern Illinois where no one would know either of us.

"Damn! Hold on you two. Somebody's at the door."

"But Nonnie," Margo and I said together. Of course she didn't answer us. We'd heard her phone clunk against a hard service. Minutes later she came back on the line.

"Sorry, kiddos. Gotta go. If you want the rest of my story, call back later."

"How much later?" Margo asked.

"Two hours, make that three. But don't count on me being here."

31
HEROES

Margo and I returned to the cemetery, this time locating a ladder that we carried to the resting place of Vito and Bruna Fantino. We took turns standing on the ladder, snapping close-ups and pressing our fingertips to porcelain images of the great-grandparents we now knew through the memories and stories of others—Filippo Sasso and his son Amadeo, Stefano Rosina and his son Franco, Donata Abba Bartolini and her grandson Pio. And, of course, our Nonnie Clarita. Our mom's personal memories would have to wait until our return to St. Louis.

We waited three hours before going back to my hotel room and calling Nonnie. She answered on the first ring. "What took you so long? I've been waiting by the phone for the past hour."

Margo jumped in with, "But you said—"

"Never mind what I said. Now where was I?"

"In a car with a rich guy named Pete Montagna, on the way to St. Louis where Stefano Rosina was supposedly waiting."

"Right, Margo. You get an A. Remind me to give it to you when you get back."

"Your story, Nonnie. Get on with it."

"Right, my story. I'm getting there."

As we crossed the Mississippi into St. Louis, I leaned forward to catch the river scene below, barges hauling coal that probably came from Southern Illinois mines. Pete Montagna stirred. He sat up and straightened his tie. No wedding ring but he did wear a diamond-studded pinkie ring, making me wonder what he did in his spare time, or if he had any.

On Twelfth Street we stopped in front of the Hotel Jefferson. The bellman opened my door and helped me out while the driver removed my suitcase from the trunk. Pete got out, tipped the bellman, and moved to the front passenger seat. 'You're not coming with me?' I asked.

Pete blinked once. 'No need to, your friends are waiting inside.'

I asked if he knew this for sure, again with a heart beating so fast I thought it would explode. Pete smiled for the first time, and said, 'As sure as the Soana flows through Pont and I got business back in Illinois. Now go, Clarita Fantino.'

I walked into the hotel lobby, glanced around for a familiar face and saw Lucca Sasso, dressed in a sport coat and heading toward me. But where was Stefano? I held back my tears and glanced around the lobby. Still no sign of him. Lucca gave me a polite hug and kissed my cheeks. 'First you must register,' he said in Italian. 'Then we go to your room.'

After registering, Lucca and I followed the bellman. 'What a kind man, this Pete Montagna,' I said, again in Italian as we stepped into the elevator. 'He came to my place, made all these arrangements, and is paying for my room.'

A confused look passed over Lucca's face. 'Pete Montagna, never heard of him.'

I was confused too, and said, 'Well, Pete certainly heard of you. He told me you were an old friend. I think he may have known Isabella Rocca but he wouldn't admit it.'

A slight smile crossed Lucca's lips. 'Oh, *that* Pete. Never mind.'

My hotel room at The Jefferson was nicer than any I'd had at the Mayfair, thanks to Pete Montagna. Lucca's tip matched Pete's earlier tip to the same bellman, making him whistle and me think that Pete might've given Lucca spending money too. After the bellman left, Lucca placed his hands on my shoulders, just as my pappa used to do.

Lucca spoke from the heart, again reminding me of Pappa. 'Make the most of this, Clarita. St. Louis is our last stop before returning to Italy. Your mamma does not know I am here in America, let alone St. Louis. Or that I brought Stefano with me. He and I are sharing a room although I do not expect to see much of him in the next few days, except for the special Soldiers Memorial events. What the two of you do in-between does not concern me. I only ask that you not hurt him again. If this does not work out, let him be the one to end it.'

I nodded again and again to Lucca's words, not always absorbing them, just as I'd done over the years with Pappa. Lucca left, shaking his head yet smiling. Within minutes I heard a light tap on the door and opened it.

Such a scene Stefano Rosina and I made in the entryway, both of us hugging and crying and kissing as if God had shone his light on us, better yet, forgiven us for the worst of our many transgressions. Our greeting took a good five minutes before winding down. Only then did we step away from each other and catch our breath.

The years had taken Stefano from emerging manhood to its full-blown version. He wore his hair longer than the closely trimmed style of most American men. His face had lost its boyish charm, replaced by lines too edgy for his twenty-six years. His jacket and khaki trousers were not as pricey as John Riva's but they did a better job of showing off his muscular frame that could've rivaled any American athlete. He looked at me with love in his eyes, bringing a fresh set of tears to mine, something I had yet to experience with John Riva.

Stefano was unbuckling his belt when a knock came to the door. I opened it to Lucca. He stepped inside and reminded Stefano about the Soldier's Memorial dinner honoring The Resistance. 'Seven o'clock this evening,' Lucca said, tapping Stefano's cheek in a fatherly way. 'That's why you're here in America.'

Stefano sighed. '*Si, si, molte grazie* for including me.'

After Lucca told him to thank their benefactor and Clarita's, he added, 'Now make love to your woman as you've never done before.'

As soon as the door closed behind Lucca, Stefano and I could wait no longer. We tore off our clothes while still in the entryway. He took me where we stood, making me cry out with every thrust as if trying to wipe out memories of those war years and that deadly night in the stable. Later in bed, I took the lead, using every technique we'd learned together. After our second round, Stefano traced his finger up and down my body and asked,

'Did you miss me as much as I missed you?'

The whole truth would've been too painful so I fudged a little. 'I did not allow myself to think of you, let alone miss you. It hurt too much.'

The phone rang. Lucca reminding Stefano he had thirty minutes to meet him in the lobby. Time enough for a third, if we hurried, but duty still called and Stefano still answered. After he left to get ready in the room he and Lucca shared, I drifted off to a deep sleep. Never had I slept so soundly, without the usual nightmares haunting me.

Hours later Stefano was knocking at my door, bringing with him a bottle of wine, one we never got around to opening. I did not think it possible to make love all night long but Stefano made a believer of me. First with our bodies, other times with our words.'

The next morning we were spooning on our sides, Stefano's lips slowly moving from my ear to my neck and shoulder as he spoke. 'Come back with me, Clarita. This time we will have a proper church wedding, Everyone in Pont will help us celebrate.'

I turned onto my back, and asked a question that reflected the new me, 'Where will we live?'

Stefano shrugged in the Italian way. 'For now, with my mamma, but only until we get our own place. I have a job at the ceramics factory in Castellamonte. We could live there if you like, after Mamma passes. As for your mamma, Bruna will be so happy to see you, eventually she will accept me too.'

My mamma, his mamma, his factory job, the life in Pont I'd left behind. 'Forgive my hesitation,' I said, 'but all this is happening so fast I can't think straight. The past year I'd been living on my own in St. Gregory, building my own business and making a decent amount of money.'

He didn't ask about my business or St. Gregory. 'Money, is that what this is about? I cannot give you America, the big cars, the fancy restaurants. But I can give you what no other man can.' With that he flipped me over, taking me in the most primitive of ways, making me forget about everything except him and the moment I never wanted to end. But nothing lasts forever and some things weren't meant to.

Later, I was thinking about coffee when there came a knock on the door. Not Lucca but Room Service with breakfast I'd ordered the night before on Pete's nickel, more like dollars. Stefano went into the bathroom while I watched the waiter set up our American breakfast—orange juice, fried eggs, sausages, toast, big cups of coffee since neither espresso nor cappuccino was on the menu. After the waiter left, Stefano came out in his briefs, that beautiful body I loved to touch as much as I loved him touching mine. Twice he walked around the breakfast setup, all the while grumbling. 'Italians don't eat eggs for breakfast, humph. What, no espresso, humph. Never have I seen orange juice this color. It's supposed to be red.' He stepped out of his briefs, took my hand, and pulled me up. 'Forget about the food. Let's go back to bed. We have time before I meet with Lucca.'

I reminded him that The Soldiers Memorial ceremony wasn't until the next day. He kissed my neck and lingered there. 'Si, this is true but Lucca wants me to meet one of the organizers today. I just found out last night.'

He undid my robe and let it fall to the carpet. He lifted my gown over my head and led me to the rumpled bed. We kissed like the teenagers we'd once been; but instead of going any further, Stefano propped himself up on one elbow. He held my chin with his fingers, my eyes with his, willing me not to turn away as he spoke. 'After your mamma poisoned me, the thought of holding you was the only thing keeping me alive. When Donata told me Bruna had sent you to America … America of all places … my heart ached so bad, I begged God to let me die.'

I started to speak but he silenced me with his lips on mine. Then he spoke again. 'Why did you let your mamma do it, Clarita? You could've run away. To France, to Switzerland, both a few hours by bus or car. Lucca would've helped. That much he owed me. And more.'

I moved away from his grip and sat up, so as not to give him the upper hand. 'Let me tell you how it was for me after Cosimo and Pappa died. Every time I looked at you, every time you touched me, I thought about them. And when I thought about them, I thought about Tommi. If it hadn't been for me and that loudmouth Donata, Tommi would not have died. If it hadn't been for you and me, Pappa and Cosimo would not have died. I stood by and said nothing about the Tedeschi killing Tommi, betraying my pappa's good name in order to save yours and Lucca's and God only knows who else. You wanted to die if God wouldn't let you have me. Well, I wanted to die if God didn't let me get away from you.'

The blood drained from Stefano's face. I waited for him to slap mine, which would've been a first for him except it never happened. Instead, he said, 'Lucca tells me you're getting married, to a banker with lots of money. Is this true?'

Unable to look at him, I turned my head. 'Why didn't you come after me right away? Instead you wait until now, weeks before my wedding.'

Stefano grabbed my chin, again forcing me to look into his eyes. Never had I seen such pain mixed with anger. 'America is a big country,' he said. 'I didn't know where you were until Isabella Rocca's daughter told me last year. Nor did I have enough money to make the trip once I found out. Had it not been for Lucca, I wouldn't be here now.'

He pushed me back onto the bed, flung one leg over me, and climbed on board. This time we didn't make love; we had sex. Big difference. I knew it; Stefano knew it. When he was finished, I knew we were finished. He rolled off me, got dressed, and left without saying another word. He should've crawled back into bed but pride wouldn't let him. I should've called out to him but pride wouldn't let me.

After twenty-four hours had passed with me not seeing or hearing from Stefano, I checked out of the Jefferson, went to Union Station, and caught the next train back to St. Gregory. Oh how I wanted Stefano to come after me, to forgive me for the words I'd spoken in truth but now regretted. And if he had come and if he had forgiven, I would've contacted Pete Montagna and asked him to help Stefano move to America, maybe even give him a job. One that would've paid enough for Stefano to have his own gold watch. Not hanging from a chain but wrapped around his wrist. We could've moved wherever Pete Montagna wanted us to move. What the hell, Stefano's mamma could've lived with us—under *our* roof, not hers.

But Stefano didn't come after me; John Riva did. And brought with him from Chicago an engagement gift—a gold wristwatch with diamond numbers, one that would've taken years for me to buy on my own. And decades for Stefano to buy for me, although I gladly would've given up any watch for a lifetime with Stefano Rosina.

Some things weren't meant to be. And other things too unrealistic to ever believe possible. Thank God for John Riva, for him loving me more than I could ever have loved him. Three weeks later I married John, already knowing I was pregnant with Stefano's baby. Served Stefano right, walking out on me the way he did.

Of course, when I told John we'd made a baby on our honeymoon, he was surprised and ecstatic. As was Anna. Poor John—God rest his soul. He died in an auto accident, five months before the baby took its first breath; and to my relief, Anna lost interest in both me and the baby. Fortunately, John's insurance provided a nice settlement, enough for me to start again, this time closer to St. Louis. I wrote a letter to Mamma giving her my new address and when I heard back from her, it was to tell me Stefano had married and was going to be a pappa."

Margo and I shared the last tissue between us. After she wiped tears from her eyes, I blew my nose into the dry side. "I am positively in shock," she said with a sniff. "If only we'd known Stefano Rosina ... was ... is our grandpa, our nonno. Which makes Franco our uncle. Don't worry, Nonnie, I behaved myself around him."

Nonnie responded with a snort.

Think fast I told myself before she decides to hang up and leaves us hanging. The best I could come up with was simple and straightforward. "Is there anything else you need to tell us?"

"Other than a report on my latest B.M., I don't think so."

"There is one thing you left out," I said, having recovered from the shock of it all. "Does Mom know?"

"Lucca told her at the train station when she was leaving Pont. It was the first thing out of her mouth when she saw me at the airport. To my knowledge she never got back to Stefano or Franco. I think out of loyalty to me."

"And what about Stefano?" Margo asked. "Do you think he knows about Mom, which naturally would include El and me?"

"The man's no dummy. He's probably figured it out by now."

"Stefano didn't think either of us looked like Mom," Margo said.

"So maybe the two of you take after your dad's side or mine from way back—a little of this, a little of that. Or maybe Stefano saw something from his family but didn't let on. How should I know?"

I cleared my throat and apologized. "Oops, I almost forgot. When we last spoke to Stefano, he said he forgave you for deceiving him."

"So he did know. I never meant to hurt him."

"He also asked that you forgive him," I said.

225

"I guess for marrying Franco's mom, not that I blame him."

"You should go back," Margo said, again with a sniff, "while there's still time to make amends. Maybe start with a phone call and go from there. He's really quite nice. Better yet, he stands tall and walks straight. Not once did we hear him fart. Right, El?"

"Er … right. It's not like you'd *have* to … you know, go to bed with him, that is, unless you really wanted to revisit your … uh, romantic past and he did too."

"Stop it, both of you. You're killing me. Some things were never meant to be. Or better left alone. Besides, it's time the two of you came home. Your mom hasn't been around whenever you called for good reason. She's got herself mixed up in a heap of trouble."

"Our mom," Margo and I said as one. "You've got to be kidding."

"Would I kid about a thing like murder? Come on, by now you ought to know me better than that."

Memo to Self:

1. *Stop by Stefano's before we leave.*
2. *Tell Stefano we know he's our nonno.*
3. *Do the same for Franco, our uncle.*
4. *Get Mom straightened out and then*
5. *Return to Pont with Nonnie ASAP.*
6. *Or, bring Stefano to America.*
7. *Please, God, while there's still time.*

ABOUT THE AUTHOR

Loretta Giacoletto divides her time between the St. Louis Metropolitan area and Missouri's Lake of the Ozarks where she writes fiction and essays for her blog Loretta on Life while her husband Dominic cruises the waters for bass and crappie. An avid traveler, Loretta has written three Italian-American sagas inspired by her frequent visits to the Piedmont region of Italy, a mystery series featuring two thirty-something sisters, a soccer mom mystery that takes place in St. Louis, and an edgy New Adult novel about a young drifter searching for the father who doesn't know he exists. She has been named a finalist in the 2015 and 2014 "Soon to be Famous Illinois Author Project" for her sagas, Family Deceptions and Chicago's Headmistress. Her short fiction has appeared in numerous publications including Literary Mama, which nominated her story "Tom" for Dzanc's 2010 Best of the Web.

Connect with Loretta Online
http://www.loretta-giacoletto.com
https://facebook.com/LorettaGiacoletto
https://twitter.com:
Loretta Giacoletto@LGiacoletto

For your added enjoyment
The opening chapters of
FAMILY DECEPTIONS

1

Pietro Rocca treasured those quiet moments on the alpine slope when he answered to no one but himself, a morning such as this that spread a blanket of solitude over the rugged terrain. He swept his long forked stick through decayed leaves, lifting and parting the undergrowth of early spring until he exposed a clump of mushrooms clinging to the base of a chestnut tree. Two more swipes uncovered the rest of the patch, sending up an earthy scent. He opened his knife and knelt to harvest the coveted delicacies when Tobi's distant barking interrupted his task. Pietro cocked his head toward the dense growth of trees and underbrush where Ugo had been kicking up rocks. *"Merda,"* he muttered, getting to his feet. Tobi didn't need to exert such effort on a fox or weasel since neither would've been foolish enough to attack the frolicking goat on his watch.

Pietro whistled; Tobi kept barking. Pietro whistled again and started walking uphill. Through the early morning haze he saw Tobi: feet grounded, body rigid, and head poised to attack. "Dammit, now what." Pietro grabbed a fallen limb and hurried toward the ruckus.

Tobi's hackles stood erect; his tail, unyielding. With lips curled and teeth bared, he was primed to defend his territory against any enemy: in this case a wild boar, the size of a young bull but with short, sturdy legs hugging the ground. As soon as the beast lowered its powerful head, Tobi lunged for the back feet. Swerving with an awkward grace, the porcine challenger raked Tobi with the curved tip of a long yellow tusk. Blood poured from Tobi's shoulder.

"Sonofabitch!" Pietro's financial investment in Tobi overruled his common sense. He jumped into the melee, delivering a solid whack to the boar's long snout. With a toss of its head, the boar sliced into Pietro's thigh, inflicting a gouge deeper than Tobi's. Pietro struck again before he fell back, reeling from the gushing wound. The boar staggered, blinked its beady eyes, and sensed fresh blood. Pietro scrambled to his feet and barely escaped the charging beast. Then Tobi leapt forward and sunk his teeth into its right ear, yanking sideways until the boar lost its footing and crashed to the earth.

As Pietro bounced away from the battle, his foot slid into a stony rut. His leg twisted with a loud snap. Pain shot from ankle to hip, so agonizing he nearly blacked out when it started back down his leg. He couldn't remember falling but felt the rocky soil cutting into his face. He heard snorting and yelping, smelled blood, and tasted the earth. Not even panic could help him up, but he did manage to roll a few meters away. For a brief moment he journeyed into the solace he treasured and when he returned, it was to the slurp, slurp of Tobi licking his face. The dog moved his velvet tongue down to the gash of warm blood on Pietro's thigh.

The leg was broken, that Pietro knew for sure. "Merda!" What stupidity, inexcusable for a farmer who'd spent his entire life mastering the foothills of the Alps. Biting his lip, he leaned on one elbow and blurted out a simple command. "Tobi, go home." The dog paused in its licking, gazed into Pietro's eyes, and then raced with the wind downhill toward a distant cluster of stone houses. The oldest had sheltered Rocca families for over three hundred years. Pietro knew Isabella would be churning butter. She seldom interrupted any chore, especially those involving her dairy products.

He sank back to the jagged earth, exhausted and cringing in pain. To his right lay the bristly-haired beast, its throat and belly ripped open to a swarm of buzzing flies. Beyond the steaming carcass, Ugo was shaking but still kicking up rocks while Vita and Fauna chewed on a patch of sparse greenery. For now the animals seemed content, but only time would tell. He sighed, uttering Isabella's name. If she even suspected his search for greener pastures and bigger mushrooms had led to the damn boar, and if all the commotion that followed had disturbed the precious milk of her livestock, there'd be hell to pay. Pietro's hell.

Meeting Isabella halfway might induce her sympathy. Pietro inched down a slope of rocky terrain that teased his aching ribs and dug into the exposed flesh of his thigh. He stopped to reconsider his strategy. Part way, he'd meet her part way instead. When the next unforgiving stone drew fresh blood, he rolled over and closed his eyes to the warm sun and chirping birds. His parents would've accepted Isabella, if only they had lived long enough to meet her. Damn the influenza for taking them in their prime. Damn the influenza for denying them the pleasure of grandchildren. Damn the influenza …

Pietro awoke to Tobi's happy barking, and his five-year old twins calling for their papa. He didn't open his eyes right away, even though he could sense Isabella's eyes boring through his. The hard ground barely acknowledged his wife of six years when she dropped to her knees. Her breath warmed his face as she issued her first order of the day. "Pietro, open your eyes."

He looked through heavy lids at the only woman he'd ever held or kissed. A triangle of paisley cloth tied behind her neck protected her dark, unruly hair from the sun. Her eyes, the color and shape of shelled almonds, registered no concern but he did catch the trace of a smile pass over her lips.

"Papa!" Riccardo and Gina shouted in unison. They knelt down, jockeying to plant wet kisses on his smooth-shaven face and to pat his stiff shoulder with their dimpled hands. What more could any man want: the unconditional love of adoring children.

Isabella sat back on her heels, waiting for an explanation before she started poking him. Pietro flipped his hand to the porcine carcass, its cavities inviting flies to deposit their eggs. "That damn *cinghiale* …"

"Could have made me a widow," Isabella said. "Bravo for Tobi, at last he proved his worth."

The cost of the pure bred had tested their willingness to compromise, one of the few times Pietro stood his ground.

"Nothing will go to waste," she said. "I'll do the butchering myself."

"Oh no, Mama," cried Gina. "Not Papa's leg."

"Silly," Riccardo said, pushing his sister aside. "Mama meant the damn cinghiale." He put his hand on Isabella's. "Don't worry, Mama. I will be your helper."

"And I'll take care of Papa," the little girl said.

After a quick examination of Pietro's injuries, Isabella got up. "I need to go back for Aldo and the cart." She leveled her forefinger at the twins. "Stay here with Papa and don't leave his side. Understand?"

Two heads of black, curly ringlets nodded. The twins snuggled next to Pietro and watched their mama grow smaller as she distanced herself from them. She'd not yet disappeared when Gina began to wiggle and squirm, then she dug her wooden shoes into the dirt.

"You need to tinkle?" Pietro asked.

"No, Papa. I need to play."

Riccardo jutted out his lower lip. "But Mama said—"

"Go on, both of you. Take Tobi and don't wander beyond those trees." Pietro scooted his back against a small boulder and reveled in the sight of his children at play. Either the pain had subsided or the joy of his twins had muffled it. In any case he willed himself not to dwell on the impending remedy.

An hour passed before he heard Riccardo call out to his mama. Pietro leaned across one elbow and squinted into the sun, trying to make out his rescue unit. In the cart next to Isabella sat his neighbor and self-proclaimed mentor, Giovanni Martino. Aldo was fighting a valiant uphill battle, straining over the additional burden of Giovanni's weight, most of which centered on his massive belly. After a few meters the mule refused to go any further. Isabella slid off the cart and walked ramrod straight, her back refusing to bend with the incline. Aldo pulled a few more meters. He stopped again, this time not continuing until Giovanni climbed down and followed Isabella. Pietro couldn't help but chuckle, an indulgence his tender ribs quickly resisted

Giovanni's six-foot frame stooped to accommodate his fifty-three years. He took off his cap and wiped a red kerchief over his brow. Wisps of graying strands crisscrossed a bullet-shaped head, flanked by elongated ears sprouting patches of wiry hair. As he approached Pietro, his face softened to display a hodgepodge of crooked, stained teeth worn with age. "Ah, Pietro, Pietro," he said, shaking his head. "For one so agile, today you moved with the grace of an old woman."

"Old woman, hell, I backed into a damn rut."

"You fell into a load of *cacca*. You're a farmer, not a goat." Giovanni used the back of his hand to clear a droplet of clear mucus hanging from his bulbous nose. Grunting, he pushed his knees to the ground, and then tore the seam of Pietro's shredded trousers. "Next time—"

"Dammit, watch the leg." Pietro sucked in warm air, released it with a moan through his clenched teeth. He closed his eyes to stifle another moan. "*Mi dispiace*," he apologized. "Because of me Isabella took you away from your work."

"Giovanni insisted," Isabella called out from the cart as she wrapped a roll of muslin strips around two lengths of tree bark padded with hay. Holding up her sturdy hands, she wiggled long, bony fingers. "These are gifted, as were my nonna's—God rest her soul. Of course, I could work alone; but with help from Giovanni ..."

"Just get the bones straight."

"Don't blame me for Mondo's limp," she said, referring to a neighbor whose leg she once set. "He got up when he should've stayed in bed."

"*Basta, basta*," Giovanni said. "Who better to trust than your wife and me, your godfather?"

"And the godfather of our children," Isabella said.

Giovanni blew her a kiss. "Remember when you were a little *rigazzo*, Pietro, that day your *nonno* broke his leg?"

Pietro winced at the memory. Papa had ordered him outside, but he still heard all the yelling when the doctor arrived and yanked the old man's brittle bones back where they belonged.

Giovanni must've remembered too. He propped a kidney-shaped vessel to Pietro's shoulder and ordered him to drink with gusto. "To lessen the pain, my friend."

Pietro turned his head and let the wine trickle down his parched throat to warm and relax the blood sending sporadic chills through his body. Closing his eyes, he took a deep breath and gulped until the pouch went dry.

Isabella called for the twins and they came running. "See those flowers, way up there." She pointed to a sweep of yellow and blue. "Take Tobi and go pick some for your papa. And don't come back until I call you."

Riccardo headed uphill toward the meadow, stopping along the way to encircle his chubby fingers around a few stray plants while Gina skipped off in pursuit of tantalizing butterflies. When they'd gone far enough not to hear Pietro's pain but still within Isabella's sight, she nodded to Giovanni.

Standing behind Pietro, he eased down, straddling his bowed legs into a vise around Pietro's upper arms. "Chomp down," Giovanni said, shoving a length of chestnut over the patient's tongue.

Pietro sunk his teeth into the wood, releasing a bitter taste that masked the lingering warmth of wine. He forced his mind to concentrate on an overhead leaf where a motionless praying mantis stalked an unsuspecting grasshopper. Isabella's hands—gifted she called them, he had his doubts—were cradling the two sections of his leg. Overhead the mantis struck, immobilizing the grasshopper. Closer to earth, gently, ever so gently, Isabella lifted and extended, lifted and extended. As she maneuvered the bones into position, the mantis slowly devoured its prey. Pietro lost interest in the mysteries of nature and squeezed his eyes shut. *Blessed Mother, how much time do those gifted hands need to remarry my separated bones. Bravo!* The marriage was blessed when Giovanni loosened his grip. Only then did Pietro sail his mouthpiece into the air and let out a pent-up A-I-E-E!

"Louder, Pietro, maybe you'll bring rain," Giovanni said, wiping his brow again. He moved to help Isabella support the leg with a padded splint. "Relax, my friend. We're almost done."

"I'll never forget this, Giovanni."

"Nor will I, but it is your wife who deserves most of the credit. Treat her like the queen she is. Kiss the hem of her skirt and from there, work your way up."

Pietro waited for his queen to look up before he offered an impromptu comment, one bound to bring regret. "Isabella knows how I feel."

With the last muslin strip tucked in place, she leaned over to brush her lips across his cheek. "You were brave," she whispered, "but the pain from a leg getting set in no way compares to that of a woman giving birth."

∞∞∞∞

Two days later and at Isabella's request *Dottore* Ernesto Zucca made the one-hour automobile trek from Pont Canavese to the Rocca home. "Your wife's skills match that of any trained nurse I've encountered," he declared after a thorough examination of Pietro's injuries. "But the extent of this ligament damage still concerns me."

"Feeding my family concerns me," Pietro replied to Ernesto Zucca's backside.

The doctor and Isabella had their heads together and were discussing Pietro's therapy as though he were in a coma. In spite of his protests Pietro wound up encased in plaster from upper thigh to lower ankle.

"Stay off that leg for at least two months," Dr. Zucca said while drying his hands with one of Isabella's immaculate linen towels.

"Easy enough for you to say," muttered Pietro from the bed he and Isabella had shared since their marriage. "My living depends on the produce markets in Pont Canavese and Cuorgnè."

"Only an idiot chooses his living over his limb, or his life." The doctor's tone softened when he turned to Isabella. "An injury such as this could still get infected. If gangrene sets in—

"It won't, Dottore. My husband will stay in bed."

"Merda," Pietro later grumbled when he and Isabella were alone. "What the hell does Ernesto Zucca know, him with his fancy suit and that Fiat 501."

"That Fiat enables him to see more patients in less time, some with broken legs and ungrateful tongues."

"You paid him?"

"With our best *tomino*."

All of Isabella's cheeses were the best. She babied the cows and goats more than their twins. Pietro turned his face to the wall. A man laid up was no better than a lame horse.

"I'll go to market," Isabella said.

"Women don't go to market alone."

"This one will."

"With everything else you have to do?"

"For now, the weather is good, the roads are safe. And it's only two days a week."

"We could send the twins to your sister."

"*Assurdità!* With four children my sister's hands are full."

"I thought she had three."

"You forget that no-good *caccata* she married."

"The twins can stay home with me."

"The twins will go to market."

"At four in the morning?"

"They'll sleep in the cart."

∞∞∞∞

On Monday the cock had not yet crowed when Isabella sat at the table, dunking the dry heel of Saturday's bread into fresh coffee. In that same all-purpose room Pietro stirred from the narrow bed Giovanni had set up, so the invalid wouldn't suffer the indignity of being confined to his bedroom.

Isabella had already loaded the cart with fresh milk and sweet butter, goat and cow cheeses, and dozens of large brown eggs. She prepared a soft pallet of warm blankets for the children still sleeping in their beds.

"Wait another thirty minutes," Pietro said. "By then Giovanni will pass by."

"Giovanni? Humph, as if I need that old goat showing me the way to Pont."

"I thought you liked him."

"I do, but not with his nose in our business. Besides, I want to be among the first to arrive." She leaned over and kissed his cheeks. "Serina offered to look in on you."

"Then leave the twins. She can help with them."

"Foist our little demons on Serina, her with a nursing baby?"

Pietro pressed her hands to his lips. "Mi dispiace, you work too hard and now this."

"And you worry too much. Now go back to sleep."

She carried the sleeping twins out the door, first Riccardo, and then Gina. The rooster—Isabella's, as were the hens since she ran the chicken house—began a cockle-doodle-do destined to continue past sunrise. Pietro didn't have to check his pocket watch to confirm the time; the damn rooster always crowed at four. Still, he stretched one arm to the bed stand and his papa's prized possession. Damn the influenza for making him an orphan before he became a man. And thank God for Giovanni who eased his pain then and ever since.

Pietro's godfather lived in the largest of eight houses sharing the same hillside with his. The Martino house, as it was now called, originated from the family of Giovanni's first wife. While Giovanni had been away fighting the Austrians, she died giving birth to their only child, a stillborn son. Had the boy lived, he would've been a few years older than Pietro's twenty-six.

Morning light filled the room while Pietro struggled with a dream about wild boars and deep ruts. He stumbled, lost his balance trying to bottom out. His leg jerked, as did his entire body, sending a surge of wake-up pain from ears to toes. He checked his watch, eight o'clock. Not that time mattered. For now, time would be measured by when Isabella left and when she returned. After relieving himself, Pietro slid the chamber pot under the bed. One hand over his rough face reminded him of the need to shave, a daily habit he seldom neglected.

"*Buongiorno*," a voice sang out with the opening door. In walked Serina Martino, with Baby Maria in her arms.

"You shouldn't have come," he said. "I don't need a nursemaid."

"Ah, but I promised Isabella." Serina set Maria down on the floor to play with her rattle. "So sorry I'm late but a hungry baby must be nourished."

She laughed, cradling her hands under heavy breasts. Serina's apron matched her eyes, the bluest Pietro had ever seen. No woman should have eyes as blue as a mountain lake washed with sun. The baby's eyes matched her mama's; the little head balder than Giovanni's.

"The bambina, who does she look like?"

Serina lifted her shoulders. "Who can say? At seven months I had but a single strand of hair." She laughed again and twisted one finger into the sienna curls piled on top of her head.

"How do you like your coffee?" She sniffed the enamel pot, shrugged, and put it on the stove to reheat. "With milk?"

"Si, but you don't have to …"

"Ah, but I must. Not a day passes without Giovanni talking about his beloved Pietro. You're the son he should've had. Does that make you my beloved stepson?"

"It makes you the wife of my good friend and godfather." He traded silly barbs with her until a whiff of foul air assaulted his nose. "What's that I smell?"

"It's your fault," she said.

After one sip of steaming milk and burnt coffee, Pietro screwed up his face. Isabella would've made a fresh brew. With food and drink Isabella never skimped.

"Too hot for your blood?" Serina asked.

"Too bitter."

He clanked the double-eared cup onto its saucer, making Baby Maria jump. She puckered her face and unleashed a splash of tears.

"Naptime," Serina sang out. She scooped up the wailer and headed to the twins' bedroom.

"You should go home. The bambina needs the comfort of her bed."

"This little angel sleeps wherever I put her."

Serina's soft lullaby grew softer until she backed out of the bedroom and closed the curtain. With a wink she circled her thumb and forefinger, then hurried to the sink and started priming the pump handle. Water gushed into the teakettle.

"What are you doing?" he asked when she put the kettle on the stove.

"Your face is growing whiskers."

He shook his head. "No, no. It can wait until Isabella returns."

"At three in the afternoon, don't be ridiculous. By then you'll have a beard and Isabella will still have her work and yours."

Pietro turned to the wall. He must've dozed off because when he shifted again, Serina was pouring hot water into an earthenware bowl. She set it on the bed stand along with his toiletries.

"Shall I hold or shave?" she asked, balancing a small mirror between her hands.

Scanning his reflected image, Pietro lowered his heavy eyebrows into a frown. Three days without sun had brought pallor to his olive complexion and emphasized an already prominent nose.

"Do not despair, Pietro," she said. "You're still the handsomest man in all of Faiallo."

Her patronizing words he didn't need.

"Maybe in the entire Canavese district," she went on. "But this I cannot say for certain since Giovanni never takes me anywhere."

Was it any wonder, Serina turned heads wherever they went. He lathered up and wielded the straightedge from side to side before finishing with the indentation in his chin. Quickly, he rinsed the remaining lather, dried his face, and ran a comb through his dark, obedient hair.

Serina's next move unnerved him as much as the perfume of her mother's milk. Until that moment only Isabella and his mama had touched the threadlike scar over his upper lip.

"The nature of man," she said, "is to inflict at least one flaw on an otherwise perfect canvas."

Pietro flinched, and lowered her hand with his.

∞∞∞

Three o'clock marked the return of Isabella and the twins. While Riccardo helped unload empty containers, Gina ran to Pietro's bedside. "Papa, Papa, everybody asked about you."

"Be careful," Isabella cautioned. "Remember Papa's leg."

"I won't let her forget it." Pietro removed Gina's elbow from his ribs as he eased over to make room for her.

"She held out a little sack of lemon drops. "Take one."

He asked for a kiss instead, and she obliged.

Riccardo pushed her aside to plant his own kiss. "We sold everything. Mama's cheese went first."

Isabella wiped her hands on her apron, leaned over, and exchanged kisses with Pietro. "Hmm, you already shaved?"

"Serina heated up some water."

"Good. She gave you something to eat?"

He shrugged. "A little cheese, a little salami."

"A little nothing, I'll make polenta and sausage for supper."

"I don't need any more aggravation. Giovanni's bambino belongs at home, so does his wife."

"It's only for a while. Don't be such a *testa dura*."

"You're calling me a hard head," he said with a laugh that coaxed a smile from her. "The day, it went well?"

"A little trouble early this morning, Flavio tried to squeeze me out."

"Sonofabitch. Did Giovanni set him straight?"

"No, I did, before Giovanni got there."

∞∞∞

On Thursday Pietro's erratic breathing vibrated through the room while Isabella finished her market preparations. He didn't hear her load the cart or add extra wood to the stove or tiptoe out with the twins. Today they headed south, to the village of Cuorgnè in the valley below. By the time Aldo had pulled the creaking load around the first hairpin curve, Isabella's rooster welcomed the new dawn and a sluggish Pietro.

He flicked his thumb to a wooden match and lit the thin, Turkish cigarette gripped between his teeth. Cranking the window over his bed, he exhaled into the crisp, mountain air. He smoked until nothing but a paper fold of tobacco remained between his thumb and forefinger. After flipping the sliver outside, he closed his eyes and drifted off. When he awoke, it was to the milky scent of Serina. She towered over him, Baby Maria in her arms.

"You shaved," she said, feigning a pout.

"Last night, before I went to bed—I mean to sleep."

Her next words spilled in lyrical syllables, each beat matching the bouncing of Maria. "Poor Pietro, destined for a long, boring spring, cooped up like a rooster tied to its perch and with no reason to crow. You need a few distractions." Maria let out an impatient whine and started rooting at her mother's breast. "All right, my little one," Serina said, unbuttoning her blouse as she walked to his children's room. "I won't be long, Pietro. A full belly helps Maria sleep."

"Feed your baby at home," he called out. "I don't need you."

Her laugh grated on his nerves. "Oh, Pietro, of course you need me."

He enjoyed fifteen minutes of peace before she hovered over him, rubbing her hands like a sly purveyor. "Now, Pietro, what would you like?"

He rolled his eyes.

"I meant to drink, silly. Those sorry bones won't mend unless they're properly nourished."

No coffee, not after Monday's. "Perhaps a little wine."

She cracked two eggs into a goblet, beating them with a fork while adding wine from the jug. Handing him the thick potion, she said, "To your health and better times."

With four gulps he emptied the contents, ran his tongue over his lip, and returned the glass. "*Grazie*, you can leave now. I'm ready for a nap." He'd not lied; the wine made him groggy.

"No, no. Sleep now and you won't tonight." She feigned another pout. "And what about Maria? She'll turn into a little demon if I wake her." Serina pulled a chair beside his bed and sat. "Please indulge me. I have a favor to ask."

"For the wife of Giovanni—"

"Not for Giovanni's wife." She made a fist and tapped her breast. "For me, Serina." Her fingers slipped between the buttons of her bodice and produced a small package wrapped with string. "Friend to friend, Pietro, a safe place to keep this?"

He hesitated, thinking of Giovanni.

"Please, don't make me beg," she said. "Giovanni is generous but every woman needs her private nest egg."

Not Isabella. She held the purse strings tight enough for both of them. He motioned to their bedroom. "Tall chest, bottom drawer, metal box."

"This must be our secret, Pietro."

"Isabella respects what belonged to my parents."

He expected Serina to leave after disposing of her package. Instead she sat again.

"I won't forget your kindness, Pietro. If ever I can repay you—"

"Mi dispiace," he said, his voice less irritable. "But I don't want to keep you any longer. You have your own work at home."

"Life holds more than work. A man like you—"

Maria's crying interrupted her mama's next words, and relieved Pietro from having to hear them. Serina got up, stretched her arms to accent an hourglass figure. "Until next time, Pietro, pleasant dreams."

∞∞∞∞∞

The next time his family went to market Pietro didn't fall back to sleep. He figured this day would be Serina's last. He'd tell her after she fixed his eggs and wine, before she made a show of feeding her baby from those breasts that bounced with her every move. Two firm raps hit the door earlier than he expected; a third pushed it open. Pietro closed his eyes and faked deep sleep through a slack mouth. He heard petticoats rustle back and forth between the pump and stove, coffee grounds hit the bottom of the kettle, crusty bread snap as it separated.

"Pietro," a voice called out. "Wake up."

He opened his eyes to a tiny woman, her back arched into a shepherd's hook. Theresa Gotti balanced a tray of coffee and bread between her spindly arms. She wore widows black, her skirt skimming the tops of clunky black oxfords. Eyes set deep in their sockets empowered a face lined with the history of eighty years.

"Zia Theresa, I did not expect you." Pietro said, according the honorary title of aunt to his beloved mama's godmother and confidante.

"Serina could not come today. She asked me to stop by."

The old woman lived two houses away, and Pietro used to play with her grandchildren when they visited from Rivarola.

"You shouldn't have—"

"For the son of Madelena Rocca—God rest her soul—I would do anything." She bent over to put the tray down. With the measured effort of a mechanical toy, she straightened up, lifted her narrow shoulders, and squeezed until her face registered the pleasure of pain. "These aching bones cry out with each task I perform, even those in the name of love. Remember when I broke my collarbone?" Raising her left arm to shoulder height, she winced. "Growing old is God's revenge."

"Hmm, the coffee is good, Zia."

"I added a little Frangelico—you look so pale. Dear Pietro, with that gamy leg prepare for the worse. No longer will you need a sniff of air to predict damp weather." She shook her head to the beat of a clicking tongue. "I pray your leg will walk straighter than my poor Mondo's. Not that I blame Isabella, you understand."

Mondo was her eldest, unmarried and with no prospects given his slow nature. Pietro patted her hand. "You are an angel, Zia."

"God chose not to bless my shriveled womb with daughters of my own. And those lazy wives of my sons ..." She rolled her eyes. "At least your Isabella respects me." She dug into her apron pocket and pulled out a dainty jewelry case. "I always meant this for your mama."

Pietro caressed the lid before he opened it. Inside, red velvet cushioned the drop earrings and matching brooch, a gold filigree of emeralds and tiny diamonds. "Mama would've cried tears of joy."

"Don't expect such emotion from Isabella. But trust my words; these jewels will make her your queen. What's more, she will regard you as her king." Zia touched her skeletal finger to his forearm. "Learn from the mistakes of others, Pietro. Pleasure delayed is pleasure denied."

∞∞∞

On Thursday Serina went straight to the bedroom with her sleeping baby.

"Poor Maria, she's teething so I gave her a touch of paregoric," she said, closing in on Pietro with that damnable scent. She asked if he missed her.

He shrugged. "Zia Theresa gave me fresh coffee."

"And what else?"

"A litany of complaints," he said with a grin.

"Ah-ha, you did miss me. Shall I fix the eggs and wine?"

"You should take your baby and go home." He waited for a snappy retort. Instead, she sniffled and rummaged in her pocket for a handkerchief. Serina pulled out the baby's bib and could've used it. But no, she grabbed the nearest kitchen towel and wiped her nose. Disrespecting Isabella's linens was akin to sneezing on an altar cloth.

"You listened to your Zia's problems. Can't you make room in that cold heart for mine?"

General aches and pains Pietro could abide, but miseries that brought women to tears embarrassed him. If Isabella experienced such miseries, which he doubted, she kept them to herself. He cleared his throat. "Perhaps you should talk with my wife."

Serina dropped to her knees, bent her head to the crook of his arm. "Forgive me for burdening you but I trust no one else. I've made certain mistakes, more than once."

"We all have, Giovanni too. But he is a forgiving man."

"He won't be after next week." She looked up, her face wet and blotched and begging for compassion. "When Giovanni returns from market, Maria and I will be gone, forever." Again she wiped her nose, this time on the bed sheet. "Please, you must help me."

"Don't talk like that. Giovanni loves you and the baby."

Sticking out her tongue, she blew a raspberry fart. "He's old and ugly and slobbers all over me until I want to throw up. Being with him feels like fornicating with my papa."

"Don't talk like that. Giovanni's your husband."

"And I am his whore. Did he tell you? I make him pay—before he touches me with those grubby paws that grope and fumble and rub me raw." She clutched Pietro's hand to her cheek. "I'm young. I need someone young, someone like you."

"But not me."

"Think of Giovanni. He lives each day for Maria and me. If we leave, he will surely die of a broken heart."

Pietro pulled his hand away. "Take your baby home."

"She'll sleep for hours."

He searched his mind for the right words. Those he pushed out sounded hollow. "I have a good marriage, one with no complications."

"And no excitement."

"Isabella would know."

"Not unless you tell her." She slipped her hand under the covers, trailing a warm finger across his rib cage and down his ribbon of hair. "I could teach you things."

Like what he wanted to ask, but that would seem like he condoned what she was about to do. "For god's sake, Serina, I can barely move."

"Pietro, Pietro. With me you won't have to move."

2

Giovanni's wife engaged Pietro in an hour of lovemaking unlike any he'd known with Isabella. When Serina's primitive cry caused Baby Maria to let out one too, the bed quit shaking and Serina stretched to disengage herself from him. Preening naked on the rug Isabella had braided with care, Serina lifted her arms to receive the first of two petticoats.

"When you look at me, what do you see?" she asked.

"The body of Venus but much warmer, in fact, it simmers." She deserved the compliment but Pietro regretted the speed of his reply. He'd experienced a similar reaction to Isabella on their wedding night, one he'd reluctantly shared with her.

"Ah-h, a lover of fine art." Serina bent over to wet his face with her lips. "You've seen the museums of *Firenze*?"

"Only those in *Torino*. Your baby, she's crying again."

"Someday, you will take me to Firenze, si?"

He shook his head. "Impossible."

"Before today, I might have agreed." She hummed a lilting tune that didn't stop until she picked up Maria. "Shall I come back on Thursday?"

"No, I don't need you."

"Pietro, Pietro. First you cheat, now you lie. Whatever would Isabella think?"

That evening Isabella prepared a supper consisting of creamy risotto, a dandelion and onion salad, and fresh bread she'd purchased from a *panetteria* in Pont.

"Can Papa eat with us?" asked Gina.

"Dr. Zucca said he must stay in bed so his leg will heal."

"We could eat with him," Riccardo said.

"No, no. Then he'd have to sleep in a pile of annoying crumbs."

Gina's eyes opened wide. "Papa?"

"Do as your mama says. Besides, I'm not hungry."

"Not hungry for risotto?" Isabella held her hand to his forehead.

"Must I be sick not to be hungry?"

"Perhaps a little wine?"

"No wine, dammit, just leave me alone."

Supper progressed as usual. First Gina spilled her milk, then Riccardo. Twice, Riccardo slid off his chair and helped their mama clean up the puddles. After restoring order, Isabella took them to the stable under their house, where they bounced a rubber ball against the stone foundation while she squeezed milk from Fauna and Vita.

Pietro was left to record market sales into the ledger, a duty he'd taken over from Isabella after the accident. He tried concentrating on the family finances. He tried listening to the music of his children. Their laughter resounded through a hole in the floor, one an ancestor had cut to capture heat generated by the livestock. Not that his bed required any additional warmth. Not after Serina.

"Bed rest becomes you," a voice roared to startle him.

Pietro's leg jerked and he yelled, "Sonofabitch!"

"Whoa, Pietro, it's me, Giovanni." A broad smile raised the older man's cheeks and stretched the peppered stubble across his lower face.

"I must have dozed off," Pietro said while trying to ignore the ricocheting pain.

"I knocked twice. Even went downstairs to visit Isabella. I told her 'Pietro cannot be sleeping. He does nothing all day,' She tells me, 'His leg heals while he sleeps.' Is this true, my friend?"

"*Pardone?*"

"Never mind, I can see you have other concerns to ponder. Look, if money's a problem, I can lend you some. No interest, of course. What's mine is yours."

Another jerk of his leg forced Pietro to hold his breath until the pain passed. "You're a good man, a good friend."

"More than a friend, Pietro. Had I not found Serina—"

"But you did."

Giovanni closed his eyes and smiled. "From out of nowhere a bolt of lightning struck. The damn thing pierced my heart, rendering me incapable of her charms. And when our baby survived her early birth, I found God again."

"What more could any man want."

"A second family, Pietro. You are the son I never held. You breathe the air he should've breathed. Now God has made up for my lonely years by blessing me with two families. Someday my Maria and your Riccardo—"

"You and Serina can still have sons."

"Perhaps, but my soldier no longer stands at attention without a helping hand. And that Serina provides. I am the *capitano* she must salute, every day."

Pietro shifted his weight, kicked the blanket with his good leg. The entire bed bounced as Giovanni slapped the corn shuck mattress with his dry, calloused hand.

"Mi dispiace, Pietro. Here I am, bragging; and there you are, disabled. Patience. Soon, you'll be dipping your stick into life's honey pot again. Unlike this old soldier, you have time on your side."

∞∞∞∞

On Saturday streaks of purple and orange had cast their spell over the mountains when neighbors arrived to encourage Pietro's recovery. After several rounds of wine, Isabella cradled a worn album of faded photographs and escorted their guests to the lower level, away from the livestock. The adults gathered at a long table flanked by wooden benches, consuming more wine and roasted chestnuts while the children played tag on the stone floor and drank tamarind syrup diluted with water.

Upstairs, Leo Arnetti propped his tooled leather boots on Pietro's bed and offered a cigarette from his tin. It would be Pietro's second that day, his own rationed at Isabella's suggestion to stay within their budget. His words accompanied the exhaled smoke of his first drag. "So, Leo, how long have you been gone?"

"Ever since you gave up your freedom." Leo grinned, his hooked nose hiding a short upper lip. "Ah-h, Pietro, America is not what we dreamed as *rigazzi*, not one street paved with gold. Still, I make good money."

"Farming?"

"Hell no." Leo pushed one hand through the persistent black hair parting on his low forehead. "I mine for copper, out West, in a wild place called Montana."

"Where cowboys and Indians fight, si?"

"Only in the moving pictures." Leo's grin revealed a gold tooth that once housed a wormhole cavity. "Sure, there are mountains, but none as high as the glorious Alps." He stretched his arms to their full span. "And ranches with cattle by the thousands, land almost as pure as the Blessed Virgin."

"Then you're going back."

"Can't afford not to ... besides, after six years on my own I feel more American than Italian, more Montanan than *Piemontese*. If only you had come with me way back when."

Pietro shredded the remnants of his cigarette into the ashtray. "That damn influenza nearly destroyed me, and the farm. If it wasn't for Giovanni—"

"That old fart, he sucked the sweet life from you. He even picked Isabella for your wife."

"Everything happened so fast."

"In America everything happens fast. Men no smarter or braver than you and me are not afraid to take chances."

"Why gamble when I got everything here."

"What have you got? Your father's house, your father's life. In America you make your own world, the one you dreamed about."

Pietro shook his head. "Easy words coming from a bachelor."

"Look, I'm not suggesting you desert Isabella and the bambini. Send for them after you get settled." With the finesse of a magician, he produced a picture postcard and wrote on the back. "Here, in case you make it to America, my address and a telephone number."

"You have your own telephone?"

"Where I board, but I'm thinking about buying the place when I go back. Buy now, invest in the future: that's my motto." He glanced at the gold timepiece pulled from the pocket of his leather-fringed vest. "Sorry, Pietro, I promised Licia I'd stop by."

"After all these years, it's still Leo and his vestal virgin."

"More like the lion and his *chiavata*. If not for me, Licia would've died intact."

"Show some respect. Licia will make a good wife."

"Not mine. She'll never leave the mama, the papa, the four *fratelli*. The whole family's got her by the *tette*."

"Come on, what do you expect? Licia is the only daughter."

"For that distinction she owes the family her life? Eternal smothering may be their way but not mine. I had to find my own way, and without the promise of an inheritance. After all, how many times can tired land be divided?" With opened palms Leo balanced two imaginary weights. "My brother or me? Me or my brother?" He shrugged. "Giorgio was firstborn."

"Me, I was fortunate to be an only child."

Leo swung his boots to the floor. "Don't be so sure, my friend. And don't forget what I said about America. Partner with me there and in a few years you'll return a rich man."

After the door closed, Pietro lit a cigarette from the tin Leo left behind. Pietro turned Leo's sepia-toned postcard over and examined a herd of majestic buffalo, another reminder of his curtailed youth, of a time when he and Leo practiced the language of America and planned their great adventure. Beyond the watchful eye of Pietro's mama, they'd lounged in the stable on piles of hay, and rolled loose tobacco into transparent paper. They smoked and talked and passed the jug. Papa knew, but let them dream. Even then, Leo had a knack for embellishing the truth.

At the party below, Pietro's neighbors were calling for more wine and trying to outdo each other with stories heard before. He pictured the scene: *Isabella filling empty glasses, reveling in her guests while the album of sweeter times circles the table. Rounds of spirited laughter swell before the emotional cleansing. After a respectful mourning, Alberto Rossini brings out his concertina. One of the men starts to clap, slow at first, and then to the beat of Alberto's lively invitation for young and old to dance. Most likely, Zia Theresa will surrender to the moment, lifting her skirts to expose the little twigs supporting her elfin frame.*

Pietro left the imagined party when the outer door rattled as it pushed open with the nudge of a familiar hip. "Shh-h, little one," Serina cooed, gently rocking to close Maria's eyes while she carried her into the twins' room. For a few blessed hours, Pietro had shoved aside thoughts of Giovanni's wife to accommodate Leo's cacca.

Serina returned, swinging her arms to free them of responsibility. "Your friend from America left?"

He directed his answer to the wall. "You should leave too."

"Poor Pietro—all alone up here with everyone down there celebrating your misery, it isn't fair. You need a party too." She lifted the covers and snuggled beside him.

"Are you crazy?" he whispered, "with Isabella and Giovanni right below us?"

"Shh," Serina cautioned with a finger to her pursed lips. Her pink tongue rolled out to the finger, depositing a dollop of saliva she trailed across his scar. "Listen, my darling, Giovanni is telling that pathetic war story, the one where he saves the bumbling lieutenant and two underlings, who in turn reward him by swearing their eternal loyalty. What a pile of cacca. When Giovanni runs out of wind, which won't be for another ten minutes, everyone must hear Bruno's tale: how Bruno, and only Bruno, captured two enemy foot soldiers. After that, Vittorio will drop his pants to show off those scrawny cheeks dotted with shrapnel. Ugh! And they haven't even gotten to the loose photographs—the ones in the box I slipped under the table to buy us more time together."

"But Isabella—"

"Works too hard, and this evening she deserves some pleasure," Serina murmured in his ear while reaching under his nightshirt. "Tsk, tsk, Pietro. Must you be so selfish?"

∞∞∞

Three weeks passed before Dr. Zucca made another house call, at which time he declared Pietro ready for crutches.

"I wanted the damn plaster off today," Pietro later told Isabella. "What the hell does Ernesto Zucca know."

"More than Pietro Rocca ... of course, you could always disregard the doctor's wisdom. Get up now and you'll spend the rest of your days straddling the road and the hillside.

"What?"

"You know, to accommodate the permanent limp you will have created. Now quit complaining. Giovanni said he'd make a pair of strong crutches."

"Giovanni, Giovanni. Him with his nose in every piss I take."

"You should thank God for such a friend, and for Serina too."

∞∞∞

That afternoon brought Serina carrying the baby, and Giovanni, the crutches. While the twins entertained Maria, Isabella and Serina eased Pietro from the bed, their shoulders supporting his sluggish weight. Pietro stood in a knee-length nightshirt, the leg thick with hair wobbling and the plastered one jutting forward to defy gravity.

"You're as pale as a baby's bottom, my friend," Giovanni said as he maneuvered a smooth chestnut limb under Pietro's arm. "You should sit in the sun, nature's great healer."

Pietro grunted. Talking took more effort than he felt like expending.

"I know," Giovanni said with a wink. "What you need the sun cannot provide. Right, Isabella?"

Pietro felt the pressure of Serina's palm against his back. "Don't be such a tease, Giovanni," she said. "Right now, Isabella has mountains of work and only two hands."

"He's right, Pietro," Isabella said. "I mean about the sun."

∞∞∞

During the next month Pietro mastered his crutches and performed simple chores outside. On market days he made coffee while Isabella loaded the wagon. "Leave the twins with me," he said one morning.

"Those little rascals make too much mischief."

"For me they'll behave."

"Si, when you can run on two good legs." She reached over to exchange kisses, her fingertips touching his cheek. At the door she paused, motioning to where he slept alone. "That bed needs to come down. It crowds the room."

Pietro felt crowded too. "Next week," he replied, ignoring Isabella's way of saying she missed their intimacy. He'd not been inside her since the accident. Juggling two women was riskier than juggling two swords. What if Isabella noticed a change? Serina had, crediting herself with improving his lovemaking techniques. He gave himself one more week before letting her go.

After he was alone, Pietro waited another forty minutes before going outside. Gripping the padded supports of his crutches, he swung his weight forward into the dark, avoiding familiar obstacles along a route he'd been navigating alone for several weeks. Giovanni's mule and cart were gone, the door to his house ajar. Pietro steadied himself and with his right crutch pushed on the door.

Wrapped in a blanket, Serina shuddered from the blast of morning air. "What took you so long?" she asked, her bare feet dancing on the stone floor.

"I can't stay."

"Then why did you come?"

"To tell you what's between us must stop."

"Someday, yes, but not this day." She opened the blanket to engulf him. Strands of her hair tickled his nose until he blew them away. If only he could blow Serina away. He closed his eyes and took in her sweetness.

"Ah-h, Pietro, your compassion feeds my heart and soul. And that shriveled up soldier's too. What more can I say? Because of you Giovanni and I have never been happier."

∞∞∞

That afternoon Dr. Zucca made an unexpected stop and removed Pietro's cast. He was clearing away the plaster when Isabella walked in with the twins. Gina ran to the bed, put her hand to her mouth, and gasped. "Papa, your leg, it looks like a prune."

Riccardo shoved her aside. He opened his mouth, but only stared.

Pietro sat up, groaned when he saw the atrophied leg. God is punishing me, he thought. "So, Isabella, ask Ernesto Zucca how he's going to fix this."

"Exercise and daily massages," the doctor replied from over his shoulder. He scribbled some instructions, handed them to Isabella. "Next week throw away the crutches."

"What about riding in the cart?" she asked.

"Of course, if you can tolerate his complaining."

After supper when Isabella was ready to milk the cows, Gina and Riccardo begged to stay upstairs. Pietro sat at the table, his leg propped on a chair and head nodding as he fought to stay awake. He dozed until he heard the teakettle rattle and felt the hot water. His stinging leg jerked to the table, and he yelled a string of profanities that sent the twins scrambling.

"Gina made me," Riccardo told Isabella when she came running.

"We tried to fix Papa's leg," Gina explained with opened palms.

Isabella carted them off, one squealer under each arm. By the time she returned from their bedtime prayers, Pietro had changed into his nightshirt and sat warming the edge of his bed.

"You can't go to sleep yet," she said. "We must exercise your leg."

Merda. He lay back and endured the agonizing routine of Isabella working his leg from hip to knee and ankle while he silently cursed her gifted hands. She massaged olive oil into his muscles, applying pressure to intensify each stroke, her way of punishing him. "Dammit, woman, not so hard."

She responded with unrelenting thumbs.

Pietro screwed up his face and gave in to her. He always did. As her fingertips slowed to a light tread, he brushed a wisp of hair from her forehead. The massage ended.

"I'm tired of sleeping alone, Pietro."

So was he. With Serina, he never fell asleep.

Later, he limped into their bedroom and found Isabella primping at the dressing table, plaiting her hair into a single braid that fell in front of her shoulder. Their eyes met in the mirror, forcing both of them to look away. After he eased into bed, she turned down the kerosene lamp, slipped under the covers, and soon rolled to his side. He was ready for her but didn't want to appear too eager. Or too polished.

"My leg aches from the damn workout."

"You want to sleep?"

"No, I want you to make me feel better."

∞∞∞

That night a loud thud disturbed Pietro's sleep. Isabella moved from his arms and lit the lamp. Their room came aglow to shadows and forms and one blank wall with a rectangle of clean plaster. Pietro leaned over the side of the bed and brought up a framed, black and white photograph. Lines of broken glass cut through two somber faces. The bride wearing a proper dress and ankle-high boots, beside her stood the groom, looking smart in the suit his godfather had insisted on buying.

"Don't get excited," Pietro said. "It's only our wedding picture."

She tore the treasure from his hands, blessed it with the sign of the cross. "If I believed those silly tales Zia Theresa weaves, this accidental occurrence would foreshadow a terrible omen."

"But you're not superstitious." Pietro waved his hand to the wall. "See for yourself. The nail came loose." He shifted under the covers and closed his eyes. "Now turn down the light and go back to sleep."

Later he awoke to a stream of daylight and Isabella nudging his ribs. "Get up," she said. "We must talk."

"After I wash and shave."

"Then hurry. The coffee's already done."

They sat down to their usual steaming latté, fresh cheese, and hard bread. Pietro thought the food tasted better, the coffee too. Perhaps the lingering sweetness of Isabella's touch had softened his edge, improved his disposition, as Ernesto Zucca liked to pontificate. Last night should've put a smile on Isabella's face. Instead she wore a thoughtful frown.

"I've been thinking," she said, stirring sugar into her coffee. "Perhaps we should consider making a new photograph."

"Maybe this fall, after the harvest."

"This Thursday would be better."

"On my first week back to market?"

"Gina and Riccardo haven't sat for a portrait since they were infants."

"Only because they can't sit still." When Isabella made up her mind, he usually backed down, more so since the accident. Today he felt like arguing. "Aha, this is about last night, isn't it? You've turned into another Zia Theresa."

"Assurdità! I've already put the money aside."

"For this I cut down on cigarettes?"

"What are a few smokes compared to a cherished memory."

"So make the appointment."

"If you insist. Of course, we'll go to Tommaso Mino."

"For him, we will wait a month."

"For me, Maso will do it on Thursday."

"For you?" "Si, for him I always save a round of cheese."

3

At dawn on Thursday Aldo pulled the Rocca cart into the main piazza in Cuorgnè, and Pietro secured a prime station on farmers' row. The area soon displayed an abundance of dairy products, fruits, vegetables, nuts, and small livestock. Stalls offering house wares, dry goods, and groceries completed the remaining rows to cover the entire square. By seven o'clock customers who crowded the narrow aisles held their money tight and gave their children free reign. Competition was spirited but cordial as vendors held up their products to entice the more discriminating.

Throughout the morning shoppers, and later vendors, stopped at the Rocca cart to welcome Pietro's return with handshakes and shoulder pats or cheek-to-cheek kisses. None left without imparting praise for Isabella's ability to take over in her husband's absence. More than once Pietro closed his eyes and thanked God for the warmth of family and friendship. He gave thanks again after he and Isabella sold all of their dairy products and most of the spring vegetables and bartered for items they didn't produce.

For the twins market day meant weaving through the rows with children no better controlled than they were. But when Isabella issued her final call, Riccardo and Gina obeyed. They stood near the cart, bouncing a red ball across the aisle until an old woman, laden with shopping bags and three caged chickens, hobbled into their game. A flash of red rolled across her path. She stumbled, her belongings scattered. The cage door flew open and amidst a flurry of feathers the squawking hens escaped. Pietro cursed himself for not moving faster than Isabella. She scooped up two hens in quick succession and returned them to their cage. Gina and Riccardo cornered the third.

"Mama, Mama!" Riccardo yelled. "We got it."

"Ouch, the damn thing bit me!"

"Watch your mouth."

"Grab the tail. Ouch, ouch."

"Quit shoving."

"Don't let it get away."

"Watch out."

"Oops."

When the owner grabbed her bird from Gina, it promptly keeled over in her hands. *"Morto, morto,"* the old woman wailed through a smattering of broken teeth.

Isabella remained calm, and with the tip of her middle finger, she revived the hen with a gentle massage to its fluttering breast.

After caging the sedated chicken, the old woman opened her arms to the heavens. "Mother of Jesus, shower your many blessings on this mother of little demons. She heals with the touch of an angel."

"It's only a chicken," Gina whispered to Riccardo.

"Shh-h! The *vecchia* might hear you and cast an evil eye."

∞∞∞∞

While church bells pealed the noonday *Angelus*, Pietro piled empty containers into the cart and Isabella carried a round of cheese across the piazza to a shop bearing the bold lettering: *Tommaso Mino, Fotografia.*

"Maso can take us at twelve-thirty, before he sits down to eat," she said on her return. "What's more, he has a room where we can change."

In less than thirty minutes the Rocca family underwent a striking transformation: Pietro in his three-year-old suit, tailor-made but inexpensive; Isabella in pale green georgette with contrasting embroidered collar; Riccardo, a belted jacket with dark socks stretching to his knickers; and Gina, rose taffeta and patent leather buckle shoes. Surrounded by a setting of velvet backdrops and ivy-covered pedestals, they allowed themselves to be readied for posterity as Tommaso Mino tilted heads, positioned hands and pinched cheeks.

At last he stepped back and surveyed the Rocca mannequins. With cupped fingers to his lips, he smacked approval, and then centered his head under the camera cloth. Clutching the shutter bulb in one hand, he spoke with reverence. "*Perfetto*. Nobody move. Nobody move. Nobody—"

Gina giggled.

"All right, everybody, again."

Riccardo turned to chastise his sister.

"Once more."

Pietro delayed another three minutes while he walked off a debilitating cramp. Then Riccardo put one finger up his nose. Gina giggled again. Pietro coughed. Gina shoved Riccardo. Riccardo shoved Gina.

The fifteen minutes Tommaso had allotted as a favor to Isabella extended to thirty. Then, forty-five. Through the curtained doorway of his living quarters drifted the aroma of garlic and anchovies simmering in olive oil. Twice, his wife called out that dinner was almost ready.

"Everybody, look at the camera."

"Wait," Pietro said, reaching in his pocket. "I almost forgot." He leaned over Isabella and pinned Zia Theresa's brooch to her shoulder. He'd brought the earrings too but decided they could wait for another occasion. The children gave up their poses to ooh and aah over the new treasure. As for Isabella, she snatched a glimpse that produced a smile worthy of the Blessed Virgin.

Using the rumpled camera cloth, Tommaso gathered mounting perspiration from his forehead. "For the last time, p-lease," he implored through a mouth no longer smiling. "I am running out of film."

"And patience," Pietro mumbled.

Isabella, regal and unflinching, raised her voice for the first time. "Nobody move. My stomach's growling louder than Maso's."

Her words restored order. The mannequins froze, and the photographer squeezed his shutter control.

"Bella, bella," he whispered.

Seconds later the Rocca family gathered their possessions and hurried to the anteroom where Tommaso waited, his sweaty hand clasping the doorknob.

"I do not waste time or money developing inferior negatives," he said, motioning the Roccas onto the cobblestone walkway. "Experience tells me that only the last shot will meet the high standards I set." He bowed as Isabella passed by. "Signora Rocca, I will have your order ready next week."

∞∞∞∞

The following Thursday Pietro traveled to Cuorgnè alone; and after the market closed, he walked over to the photography studio. Tommaso brought out the wrapped order: one reframed wedding, one large framed family, six medium-sized in gray folders—one for each twin, Isabella's parents, her two siblings, and the family album.

"I give you Tommaso Mino's best work," he said, presenting the bill. "If my work pleases you, I trust you will pay me next week."

"I'll pay you now." Pietro counted out his lire into the photographer's palm. "If your work doesn't please me, I'll return with my family next week."

A pleasing portrait, was this too much to expect? Pietro had done his part. He'd patched the wall plaster, installed a stronger hook, and tolerated the arrogant Tommaso.

As soon as Pietro walked into the house, Isabella wiped her hands and relieved him of the packages. First, she undid the wedding picture, ran her fingers over the glass, and inspected the wire holder. Her simple nod relieved his initial anxiety. Then she opened the second package, turned the frame face side up. Pietro held his breath. Please God, not another visit to the photographer. No man should have to endure such hell again.

"Maso did not fail me," Isabella said with a smile. "He has accorded us a place in history."

Indeed, Tommaso Mino had captured the pleasing image of a proud father, dignified mother, and adorable cherubs. Pietro Rocca's family had been ensured its place in history, at least on paper.

Made in the USA
Charleston, SC
29 May 2016